EXSULES FILII EVAE

(The Banished Sons of Eve)

by

Stephen Hoffman

ICENI
BOOKS

Exsules Filii Evae
(The Banished Sons of Eve)

Copyright © 2003 by R. Stephen Hoffman

Published by Iceni Books™
610 East Delano Street, Suite 104,
Tucson, Arizona 85705, U.S.A.
www.icenibooks.com

International Standard Book Number: 1-58736-162-0
Library of Congress Card Number: 2002116340

For my brothers and sisters,
Judy, Tracy, David,
Doug, Pat, Mary, and Rita,
and to the memory of Michael.

Every action has goodness, insofar as it has being; whereas it is lacking in goodness, as it is lacking in something that is due to its fullness of being; and thus it is said to be evil: for instance if it lacks the quantity determined by reason, or its due place, or something of the kind.

St. Thomas Aquinas
Summa Theologica

Though we cannot, while we feel deeply, reason shrewdly, yet I doubt if, except when we feel deeply, we can ever comprehend fully.

John Ruskin
Modern Painters, Vol. 2

AUGUST, 1986

1

Adrian Underwood

Lying on the cool terrazzo floor of his kitchen, Adrian watched the dance of moths around the yard light outside his window, and waited to see if David would pick up the phone. At the seventh ring, he did.

"Hello?"

"Hi there. It's Adrian."

"How are you?" said David. "*Where* are you?"

"I'm fine. I'm in Omaha. How are you?"

"We're good," David said. "Have you been there all summer? We haven't heard from you."

"Yeah, I stayed when school got out, and got a job with the city of Council Bluffs."

"Doing what?" David asked.

"Working for the department of parks and recreation," Adrian said. "Riding a lawn mower most days. Fetching bag worms out of trees. That sort of thing."

"I wondered when we'd hear from you. I thought maybe you were in hiding. That you'd flunked out of Creighton or something."

"Well, actually...."

"Actually what?" David asked.

"I avoided calling for a while because I didn't want to tell you," said Adrian. "I'm changing course again, and taking a leave of absence from law school. Yes—I'm going back to the seminary."

"Get out of here!" said David. "At La Crosse?"

"I talked to Father Moriarty, and he said I could return for a fifth year at the minor sem."

"I didn't know there was such a thing."

"It's something they'll contrive for me—somebody too confused to either take the plunge into the major seminary, or just call it quits."

"So, you'll be a student there again?" David asked.

"Well, Moriarty doesn't care, of course, if I do anything *academically*, as long as I'm back in formation. He barely passed Latin himself for four semesters. He thinks the whole purpose of the minor seminary is to clarify your calling," Adrian said. "Who would argue about *my* needing clarification? I'll pick up some credits in something, go back to my old work-study job as sacristan, hang out and breathe the air for a while."

"So," David asked, sighing heavily, "how did this come about?"

"I don't know, exactly," Adrian said, wrapping the telephone cord in nervous circles around his finger. "I've missed the seminary more than I expected. And this spring, I was getting more and more depressed. I really don't speak the language here at law school, you know."

"I can imagine that," David said. "But wow, man. Holy Name? Isn't there another place to go besides there?"

"I don't know. Much as I complain, I can't seem to let go of it."

"Why don't you consider coming to United?" he asked, referring to his own seminary.

"Protestants!" Adrian said, "You have it so easy, never cursed with belonging to the *one true Church*. You can shop around until you find some denomination to embrace, maybe even one that will ordain you despite your 'lifestyle.'"

"You insist on holding on to those Roman Catholic credentials, huh?"

"The thing I said about law students not speaking my language?" Adrian said. "It's just about the same with non-Catholics. If you guys speak Latin, the dialect is sure foreign to me. I just want to be with my own people."

"Did somebody break your heart? Is that what this is about?"

God love David for his directness.

"Not hardly!" Adrian said. The thought of his neighbor, a law-yer named Terry, flashed through his mind for an instant, but even that was not the thing David had in mind. "I know it might seem like I'm diving again for the cover of celibacy, but deciding to go back doesn't really provide me with much shelter in that regard. It creates as many problems as it solves."

"Well, diving for cover is pretty much what comes to mind. What do you mean, 'it creates problems'?"

"For one thing, I've started having nightmares again, and they're not getting better since I decided to go back," Adrian said. An awkward silence passed while Adrian thought of this morning's dream, weighed possibly sharing it with David, and finally decided against it. "I'm quite aware how much I'm swayed by missing all the guys at Holy Name," he said. "It kills me, knowing that when I get there, my own class and the one after it will all be gone, off to do theology."

"Hey, communal showers are great, but they're hardly enough reason to entertain the priesthood," David offered.

"They're not exactly communal, anyway," Adrian said. "I think you're trying to oversimplify this."

"But you get my point."

Adrian was ready to steer the conversation in another direc-tion. "I can't get used to how craven the folks in my law school class seem," he said, in his own defense. "You know, I'm used to the image of myself as a minister."

"And not a craven minister at that—you were always going to be more in the poverty, chastity, and obedience mold," David said.

"Well, right," said Adrian. "You have the expectation of com-forting people, becoming their confidant, their confessor, ban-daging their boo-boos. Law school is full of people who seem to actually enjoy being cutthroat and adversarial."

"What can I say?" said David. "I didn't recommend it. I just think you should come meet the people in my congregation in Uptown. They're very progressive."

"How are things for you at Union, by the way? Are you still lik-ing it? Does your internship start soon?"

They went on to discuss the subjects of David's classes: sacramentalism, comparative Christology, homiletics—the stuff of divinity school. David was enthusiastic about his studies, and about his seminary in general. He waxed celestial for some time on the subject.

"How is Ted?" Adrian asked eventually, bringing the discussion back to personal matters.

"Good. He's on vacation next week, and we're heading up to the Boundary Waters."

"Cool," said Adrian. "Just the two of you?"

"Yes! None of our friends are that butch."

"I think of the two of you a lot. If I swing up to Minneapolis for a day or two on my way to La Crosse, do you think we could catch an afternoon of sailing?"

"That sounds great. Just let us know. I'm free a lot more than Ted is, but maybe we can work around it."

"I know you might be disappointed that I haven't taken root here at law school," said Adrian. "I can't say that I understand it myself. But *patient endurance to all things attaineth*, right? There's one creed I fully subscribe to."

"You'll be alright," David said. "You used to be a distance runner, didn't you? We'll just be patient with you."

"Look, it's late as hell, guy, and I have to work early. Sorry I called at this hour, but I hadn't been able to reach you."

"Yeah, we've been sailing a lot of evenings," said David. "It'll be great to see you soon."

Adrian was more awake than ever. He sat in the narrow kitchen, arms wrapped around his knees, feeling churned up by how blunt David's remarks had been about men and sex. His dream from that morning did nag at him, a kind of worrisome unsolved riddle. At Holy Name, the really conservative guys—who foreswore even masturbation—used to refer to wet dreams as "legal dreaming nights," because they could get off without breaking any rules. Was his subconscious even more reactionary than theirs, rousing him from any such indulgences? He'd had a vague feeling that all of this might, in fact, relate to his feelings for Terry. The dream was the same as before: He and Father

12

Sweeney were in the Halloran Lounge eating popcorn late at night, and he was feeling a lot of desire for the young priest, who lay on the floor on his side, rolling his head back in laughter at something Adrian had said. In the dream the man was Fr. Sweeney, yet his laughter had something characteristic of Terry about it, as well. Just when Adrian moved in to kiss him, they heard the rector's footsteps on the stairs and they separated, catching their breath. Father Moriarty came into the room, a disdainful smile on his face as always, and chatted. When Moriarty turned to leave, he said, "Don't stay up too late, gentlemen," and Adrian could swear he shook the dust of the room from his feet as he departed, walking between the two of them toward the door to the refectory. From that point until he woke up, Adrian reeled with guilt, sinking through the floor, descending into blackness and a vacuum. He came to consciousness with such a wave of despair it took him several moments to realize he was here in Omaha in his own bed, derelict in nothing more than his duty to get up and give the cat some food and water. The experience reminded Adrian of how he and his brother Charlie used to walk into the darkness at night to turn off the water softener at their dad's store, then race back toward the light of the house, because the darkness behind them felt like the devil in pursuit. The end of the dream was like that, like falling into Satan's minions, breaking into pieces for their consumption, and Adrian woke up from it in a sweat. No such thing as a legal dreaming night for him.

There were times when Adrian thought he'd made some peace, belonging to a Church that condemned homosexual acts but not homosexual orientation. Then this dream, or some close variation on it, would start recurring. As he found a glass and poured it full of milk by the light of the refrigerator door, a fragment of prayer from the breviary was coming to him. What was it? The last words of night prayer: Lord grant us a restful night and a peaceful death.

Amen, he thought. *Amen*.

2

Sr. Eileen O'Rourke

Throughout her adult years, Eileen had known that whatever her failings, she was at least steadfast in her calling to religious life. Now another summer was coming to its end, and along with it, her own thirty-ninth year. She was driving her old black Volkswagen down Route 61, past the sumac reddening, past the blackberries ripening to ebony on the sides of the hills, and quite possibly into a future where she would no longer be a nun.

Rounding a curve and watching the gorge open before her, its lush green extending for miles downstream, Eileen recalled a favorite fantasy of her childhood, in which the river was the aisle of a vast cathedral, and the hills on either side the pediment supporting the vault of the sky above. As a girl she would drive this highway with her mother, and wait for the sudden revelation of the view here at Lake City, where the dammed Mississippi filled the entire plain and the road clung to its edge along the bluffs, the very best vantage. Passing this way, she felt as though she could lean out through the mist and touch an imagined bride who would pass at any moment, trailing a veil and petals in her wake as she made her way to a distant sanctuary.

Now Eileen inhaled the dampness of the place once again, feeling a bit of the awe she remembered from her childhood, a time when she lived a few blocks from the river, in the little house on Bennett Street in La Crosse. The fog often would move into their yard from the Mississippi, and linger there in dense banks, full of mystery but not fearsome, like a quiet elderly relative to whom one was accustomed.

Eileen put her head partly out the window as she drove down the highway. Her foot left the accelerator and she felt the car glide easily down the road. Just now, it seemed that memories like these were enough to have brought her to La Crosse for the year, that she had been tracking them down intuitively, until the recollections struck her full force. It was true that the business of selling her mother's house brought her back here, but couldn't that have been accomplished with a couple of short trips and the help of a real estate agent? Indeed, her decision to move back to Wisconsin had not been really logical. Eileen had followed a whim, not exactly thinking how it was right, only feeling that it was so. Her spiritual circumstances, she finally knew, were ones she could not *think* herself out of. She was determined to sense and to honor her feelings in a way she never had before. Perhaps she could justify this year away from the convent if it were full of moments like the present one. The river was a nearly spiritual presence in her memories of it, and seemed so again as it greeted her today.

Entering the town of Lake City, Eileen pulled the car into a gas station at the side of the road and up to the self-service pump. Stepping out the door she smelled petroleum fumes and the strong odors of river grass and mud as they wafted across the highway.

"Do you have any 10-30?" she asked the teenager in the booth. He looked up briefly from the muscle magazine he was reading and nodded, then he blew a bubble in gum he was chewing and popped it on his nascent moustache.

"Jus' a second," he said, pulling the gum from his lips and reaching to the floor for a can of oil and a spout. He came out the side door of his booth and offered them to her. "Need more than one?" he asked.

"No, thanks," she said, and turned toward her car hood with the oil. Two or three years ago he might have offered to add the oil for her, despite the "self-service" sign. Now he was an adult himself and wouldn't jump to do it out of deference. Unlatching the hood and hoisting it Eileen smiled, suddenly remembering that a mere two or three *days* ago she would have been different, too, and would have been tucking her habit or her pectoral cross into her collar as she leaned over an engine. Even other customers often offered to pour her oil.

In a minute Eileen was back on the road, marking off landmarks as she neared her destination. Her departure the previous day from the convent back in North Dakota had been bittersweet, in the end. Sister Vincent Thomas and Sister Anastasia, however stoic and selfless as their calling (and their German upbringing) might dictate, had surprised her with tears as she prepared to go. Sister Anastasia had baked her a great bundle of things to eat and had stashed them in the back seat of the Beetle without a word, yet when Eileen came out of her bedroom with her last pieces of luggage, the two gathered at the doorway like some kind of conspirators.

"We want you to know we like you very much," said Vincent Thomas.

"We've been praying that God sends you back to us," added Anastasia. "We're afraid of what'll happen to us without you here."

Eileen chided them slightly. "You'll be just fine, I'm sure of it. It's only for a year, after all."

"I know, it's silly," said Vincent Thomas. "But after all this time I feel as if you're our child." And with that, tears came to her eyes, and she moved to hug Eileen. Sister Anastasia stood by, fishing for the Kleenex in her sleeve.

Eileen was moved in a way she hadn't expected, saying goodbye to these elderly nuns. She had often thought of them as immune to needing her, drawing what little they required from the respectful "Good morning, Sisters" they received every day as they moved about the halls of the hospital, taking prayer cards to the dying. Now she felt frail bodies inside these big Ursuline habits and was aware of them more than ever as being small, and full of feeling. All the way across two states, until she stopped for the night in St. Cloud, the two of them had been on her mind as she drove, perhaps more than they ever were in the years she had lived with them.

Yesterday marked the official start of Eileen's year of exclaustration—a year "out of the cloister," although she didn't actually live in one. Eileen had gone to the convent after eighth grade, in 1962, when such things were still done. She was fourteen at the time. In its twenty-four years of vicissitudes, the experience had dwindled, somehow lost its center. Back at the beginning, her order had clung to tradition longer than most, and Eileen had been one of a majority reluctant to change that. At one point in her twenties, she had been asked to serve the order as provost, a position that could have easily led up the line maybe to superior and to moderator, but she felt very unsuited for all that, and turned it down. What emerged in her community eventually was leadership favoring change, and then the motherhouse was divided—literally. Nuns went to live in communities of two or three in various towns, most of them teaching in parochial schools, returning to Eau Claire only twice a year for retreats. Eileen found herself regretting, then, that she had not come forward to take a leadership role, possibly to avert such dissolution.

This break with tradition took place in 1978, and Eileen stayed at the motherhouse at first, clinging to what was, teaching at Bishop Halloran High School and living with the retired nuns who remained in Eau Claire. How she had stumbled into the next phase of her life, she wasn't sure. One autumn she had packed up and moved to the Standing Rock Reservation. It wasn't so impulsive, of course. She'd seen an advertisement for teachers needed on the reservation, written away for the details and gone to North Dakota to interview. But she hadn't stopped to think of how extraordinary it was—or to question her deliber-

18

ate choice—to take herself away from the Sisters of Bonaventure. She'd arranged to live with a few Ursulines in Fort Yates and to undertake a mission, teaching what she thought of as the most neglected adolescents on the Plains. This was the purpose she saw at the time. Seldom would she reflect on what *she* was becoming.

At Standing Rock she was countercultural—eccentric, even—a missionary from some other way of life trying to give sight to the blind, a glimpse of something new to children who mostly saw drink and joblessness and a rapid end to youth. Perhaps she closed the door on her old life more easily, feeling that she could go back any time she wished, just by leaving the reservation. The fact was that Eileen couldn't go back, that her own culture had dissolved from under her, had become a mere remnant of itself in every place it survived, even in Eau Claire. To the schoolgirls there it was a revelation that the Church was ancient, and that the pop singer Madonna's use of its symbols was an afterthought, a whimsy. It was a battle just to give them a sense of perspective. Eileen knew this, yet somehow she imagined going "home," should she ever tire of Standing Rock.

As it was, for several years she hadn't tired of it. She lived off her sense of conviction, and became increasingly ironic. She bought round-toed black shoes from one of the last suppliers of women religious, in Pittsburgh. She learned CPR and taught it to her students, then earned her emergency medical technician's certificate so she could ride with the volunteer fire department. She opted always to retain her short veil, even while starting intravenous catheters and calling out for saline in the back of an ambulance.

Once she saw a faucet hanging in midair in a display at the North Dakota State Fair, pouring water apparently from nowhere until she put her finger into the flow and discovered a clear tube, which supported the fixture and conducted water up the middle of the downspout. This was her, she thought, existing in midair with no apparent source of support, just her feeling of God and of righteousness.

Such isolation ultimately became a cause of disappointment to her. If she'd been born to Protestantism it might be fine, but she was theologically ill-suited for this; she missed feeling that she rested like a stone somewhere in the pyramid of the Church, below the top but nonetheless secure. Now she relied on her own conscience and was startled at times at how much bitterness came from inside her.

Earlier today she'd been overtaken by an Oldsmobile with one of those evangelical Christian bumper stickers claiming, *God said it. I believe it. That settles it.* The elderly man behind the wheel did not look at her when he passed, nor did he appear to have looked at oncoming traffic, as he slipped back into their lane perilously short of colliding with a northbound truck. Eileen entertained a wish to flip him the finger—if only she remembered how!—as the truck passed, and she sailed nearly bumper-to-bumper with the Oldsmobile down the highway.

She wouldn't have been so irritated if it weren't for the smugness of the old man's bumper sticker. The early years of Eileen's religious life were simple, like that. The Church of the '50s taught that a spiritual life consisted of acts prescribed for her, devotional acts offered up to God, habits constructed for her by religious living. At some point the focus shifted—outside her, perhaps inside her as well—to her motives, the personal meaning of her chosen path. Eileen suspected then that she was a fraud, an imposter in religious life who could be found out, found empty of the necessary spiritual pith. Perhaps her move to the reservation had been an attempt to earn this, to forge a purer soul, invest herself with higher motives. Only recently had she become convinced that the effort had failed. Her wishes for the old man were certainly unseemly, but one benefit of her growing sense of isolation had been less concern over outbursts of feeling. She was so alone now that even her veil was packed away in storage; she felt accountable to little more than herself. It depressed the hell out of her, if you wanted to know the truth. Sometimes the word *exclaustration* sounded like treatment for claustrophobia, or a way to rid cow's milk of bacteria.

When she'd made the decision to leave, her spiritual adviser seemed resigned, even diffident. He was a Jesuit at Standing Rock, who may have been barely hanging on himself, although he didn't want to show it. Father Zimmerman had found a devil to fight in Reaganomics, and although Eileen didn't vote Republican, she had no faith in any alternatives, either. In her fantasies these last years, she saw herself like a figure of the Old Testament; she felt most connected when reading Psalms from the Breviary or reciting the Confiteor at Mass: *I confess to Almighty God that I have sinned through my own fault, in my thoughts and in my words, in what I have done and in what I have failed to do....* Why was it that she would resonate with being a sinner, with wandering outcast in the desert, but not with being forgiven? Her thoughts would drift when the readings were taken from the letters of Paul. How could anyone have his kind of certainty? He seemed hardly a man of her own religion. Protestants of the born-again variety left her dumbfounded. Their conviction that God spoke personally and definitively to them made her feel like God's stepchild. She was a Christian who wondered too often what it was like to be a Jew.

Sometimes her students, to be provocative, would ask her outright if she didn't miss getting laid. How could they know that thoughts of "getting laid" were foreign to her, like thoughts of joining the Homemakers Club, that group of white farm women from lands bordering the reservation? What she really missed was the will to carry on with her own life, the energy to propel herself forward in any direction from where she stood. That was her longing.

Eileen's mother had died in November 1984, and Eileen had gone to La Crosse for a week to bury her. The two of them, frankly, had not been close. In the last few years, as her mother's senility grew worse, Eileen seldom went to visit her. Brigid O'Rourke had remained self-sufficient to the very end, although increasingly hostile and paranoid. She cursed the actions of her neighbor and lifelong friend, Mrs. Seaman, who only meant well and continued to take Brigid to Mass every week, despite her behavior, up until the Friday Eileen's mother had a stroke bringing in the clothes from the line. Elsie Seaman was a bit doddering herself by then, and apparently trotted out to check Brigid's pulse before returning to the house to call the hospital. She told the operator that an ambulance was probably not necessary, as she was quite sure Brigid was dead. Elsie turned out to be quite right—Eileen's mother had bled into her brainstem and never took another breath.

Because the end of a semester was coming on, Eileen had packed her mother's things into boxes, moved them to the attic, and postponed dealing with them. She met with a realtor, got his agreement to rent the house furnished and keep the taxes paid, and returned in a flurry to the needs of her students. Her custom had always been to keep her summers filled with commitments, maintaining her ambulance shifts, teaching adults who sought their GED, and tutoring students who failed classes during the school year. Months passed and Eileen kept herself busy, leaving the need to better conclude her mother's affairs hanging in the back of her mind, an unread footnote to which she must return.

Her own unhappiness remained a separate problem, seeming to grow steadily out of control. She saw herself take on a sharper and sharper edge with her students and co-workers. For years she'd seen a certain salvation in her ability to touch even one student, to find in the throng of uncomprehending eyes a single pair that lit with recognition when she lectured on periodicity, the way in which the table of elements illustrated the filling of nature's every niche. Now Eileen began to focus instead on the dozens of dull expressions, the feet fidgeting for class to be over, on Barry White Bear passing cigarettes to Lonnie St. Pierre in anticipation of going to the parking lot for a smoke. She felt a discouraging sense of failure. And when she made her usual self-deprecating remarks to the other teachers or to Cookums Yellowknife, the postmistress, she felt herself lose modulation, saw them wince slightly at her words. She eventually told the women of the altar society she was taking a year off for herself, and she felt a bit disheartened, if not surprised, at the knowing glances they shared and their immediate endorsement of it.

The opportunity had come this March, when she was beginning to feel the most deranged. She saw a printed advertisement in a newsletter from the Bonaventures in Eau Claire. Beckett High School in La Crosse was looking for a science teacher to fill in for one of their lay faculty, who was taking a year's sabbatical to finish her master's degree. Practically the moment she saw this, she knew she would get this job, take leave of the Ursulines in Fort Yates, and move for a year, not to any Bonaventure community, but into her mother's house.

Father Zimmerman had been skeptical, asking her in his awkward way about her having prayed over this move, as if *he* suddenly believed in prayer more than action. She'd prayed that a path would be made clear for her, one that drew her along almost of its own necessity. Practical or not, this path appeared, and she regarded it as the answer to those prayers. She would move to La Crosse, take time to sort her mother's stored things and disperse them in a thoughtful way, and fix the house up to sell it. The outside stairs needed to be rebuilt, and every surface needed repainting. She greeted the plan as if it were a first burst of air after holding her breath, as she had in contests with her sister Helen when they were both in grade school. When the job came through, and Rome granted exclaustration, she knew she had as much confirmation as she could hope to find. She acted as if this job opening were a sign from God. What did she think it meant? It was a change of direction. It might lead her to new answers to what God required of her. It might give her new questions to ask.

She'd slept poorly all that spring and early summer, with troubling dreams, and worries about her students or her lesson plans. One dream in particular she remembered; it was the day after she received permission from the Apostolic See for her departure. In the dream she was a girl and got a cat from a farmer at an orchard where they stopped to pick apples. It was initially playful when she took it home, but it eventually became fierce and turned on her, and she had to take it back. She awoke just as she was handing the cat back to the man, feeling relieved of terror yet full of sorrow, thinking that the man would now kill it. She felt full of shame, a child a kitten could not love.

As Route 61 took her past the town of Dakota and nearer to La Crosse, Eileen found an unfamiliar configuration of exits. She picked out the ramp to downtown, then crossed the river and wound her way carefully past Eversole's auto lot and the towers of G. Heilemann Brewing Co., eventually finding South Avenue where it headed into the residential neighborhoods downstream. Driving past the industries along the river, she thought for a moment about the house key in her pocketbook, untagged yet recognizable to her by its feel, ever since her mother gave it to her in 1972. Eileen felt the urge to make a pot of tea, coming over her suddenly like the impulse to sigh or to remove her shoes. She almost missed a four-way stop, anticipating relief for her thirst and tension when she reached the house and could put the water on.

Turning at last up Bennett, she noticed the topmost branches of the crabapples even from this end of the street, pendulous

24

with their fruit and swaying in the breeze, and beneath them the deep red shingles of the house, beautiful and shimmering in the sun. Why was the air suddenly so pungent? A neighbor's grass, new-mown, was intoxicating, and even the first-fallen leaves of the trees seemed succulent, mashed like cast-off produce under the tires of her car. Eileen pulled the Volkswagen quietly onto the pea gravel of her mother's drive and watched a tabby cat scurry along Mrs. Seaman's lilac bushes, then out of sight behind the garage. Vegetation everywhere was ruffling slightly in the wind as Eileen stepped from her car. Her throat felt a bit parched, and she wished for a drink of water even before the tea could brew.

The lock tumbled easily on her key, and the bell on the back of the door jingled once as she stepped inside, pushing the door closed behind her. Eileen stood in the hallway for a moment, taking in the expanse of red floor tiles leading into the kitchen. The quiet seemed strange, as if she had entered a museum when she passed the threshold, with every detail recreated in perfect verisimilitude, but spooky in its desolation.

In the kitchen now, she saw a single hint of movement, the afternoon sun coming through the tattered leaves and trumpet-like blossoms of hollyhocks outside the window and playing on the counter in splashes of light. The shadows danced like images in a silent movie, grainy actors on a battered screen. Eileen focused finally on the counter, which was full of marks left by knives over the years as her mother cooked, cut into the linoleum in a scrawl as familiar as her mother's handwriting.

Suddenly a dull congestion filled the bridge of her nose, and her face screwed up of its own accord, as if she were about to sneeze. She put her thumb and fingers to her eyelids, wondering for a moment what in the world had come over her. Perhaps a vessel was about to burst, or this was the aura before a seizure. She fell upon an image, then, of her mother standing here, her back to the room, kneading bread or cutting up vegetables for dinner, and she felt tremendous sadness. The memory wasn't a singular one; in fact it could have been from any of a thousand days she watched her mother cook in this kitchen. Eileen began to sob, although she felt at the same time slightly outside herself, a person watching from the hallway and asking, "Is this really me, crying?" Like the tin man, discovering his heart. She coughed a few times, gradually believing the news that death would affect her so much. Then she took deep breaths and wiped the tears from her eyes with the heels of both hands.

"Oh, Mother," she said softly, to the room. "You really are gone."

An aluminum teakettle sat on the stove, the only implement left in the kitchen when the renters departed in June. Now the thought of tea no longer appealed to her, and Eileen walked into the downstairs bathroom. She stood at her mother's bathroom sink and scooped cold water from the faucet onto her face.

"I'm just being emotional," she said to herself, as if to dispel the belief that she was crumbling physically. Just now she wasn't sure which was worse. Outside the window in the wind, roses bobbed and dove on their tall white trellis.

-3-

Home, Where the Hearth Is

Ryder, Iowa was a town just shy of five hundred souls, on a flat stretch of State Highway 9. There was no river or creek to intersect the railroad here, and from a distance it seemed the most improbable stand of white clapboard houses, rising from the plain. A water tower announcing the town's identity in tall black letters stood above the dwellings, looking like a mosquito, its proboscis sunk deep into the aquifer below. Adrian had packed his things back home to Ryder from Omaha, and now his Chevette sat in the driveway next to his parents' Wagoneer, the back end low to the ground with a burden of books, records, and clothes.

Sun was streaming through the sheers at the living room windows as Adrian came out of the kitchen with his coffee. His mother was arranging herself next to an arm of the couch with a cup of tea, seeking comfort like a cat preparing for a nap. "Why that priest doesn't take a stronger stand, I don't know," she said. "The school board would take notice if the whole parish were calling to state their opinion." At the moment her dudgeon happened to be up over a teacher who taught about contraception in home economics class.

"Calling to express whose opinion, mother?" asked Adrian's older brother, Charlie, keeping his nose in this week's *Kossuth County Gazette*.

"You!" said Eleanor Underwood. "You ought to be supporting your mother, not aggravating her."

27

The family was gathering at the big house on Main Street for the occasion of Adrian's brief visit home. Adrian's sisters, Carol and Beth Ann, were coming later in the day, and Charlie lingered around the breakfast table under the pretense of having tea before heading out to the farm.

"Did Dad say anything about the septic company coming today?" asked Charlie.

"He was gone by six," said Eleanor. "I don't recall him saying anything."

"I figure if they're going to be in town, they might as well stop by our place," said Charlie, who lived with his wife only five blocks from the elder Underwoods. "Hey, Ayyy-drian. Here I thought I'd come to Omaha and you'd get me tickets to Blue Jays basketball. Now Mom says you're not even going back to Creighton this fall."

"Unhh-uh," Adrian acknowledged, his cup in his mouth. He picked up a *Newsweek* and found a corner chair to sit in.

"Didn't care for law school, huh?" said Charlie.

"Maybe I should call Ernestine and her mother," Eleanor said, continuing with her own thoughts. "They have no kids in school, but Mrs. Martin is a first cousin to Bill Crouch, who sits on the school board."

"Hey, Mom," said Charlie. "Have you reported old man Burns to the bishop yet for selling rubbers at his service station?"

"I'm not that interested in what Bud Burns does in his garage. What the school board does with a bunch of minor children is an entirely different matter."

"Old Burns," said Charlie. "Selling rubbers every Saturday, then sitting in the front pew at Mass on Sunday. Shameless of him."

Adrian burrowed into his magazine, ducking for the moment any further questions about his latest change of plans. Not that anyone was ever very probing. He imagined his parents and his sisters had rolled their eyes exactly once at the letters he sent with the news, then returned to their lives with little thought of it.

They were accustomed by now to his making these decisions without their input.

Adrian had always been the skittish and independent type, resisting the least advice from anyone in the family. By accident and design, he defied comparison to anyone else his age. Charlie, who was once full of adolescent bluster about flouting everyone's expectations, apparently got any piss out of his system early by marrying a girl from the country, a farmer's daughter from "the Coulee" as they called it, and now had settled down to farming with his wife's father and hanging around his parents' house like a frayed chair set on the back porch. The family regarded Adrian, on the other hand, as unrelated to the known universe—however prodigious he might be in a parallel one. His mother would make a stab at connecting him to Ryder when he was home, reporting on marriages and births, suggesting phone calls to high school classmates he didn't make a move to see. The efforts met with little enthusiasm from Adrian. After high school he had taken a year off, working at the farm supply store and going as far as smoking pot a few times with the guys working there, who were mostly Charlie's age. Next had come his foray into the weirdness of the spiritual writers—or rather, the weirdness of an eighteen-year-old reading the spiritual writers, the likes of St. John of the Cross and Teresa of Avila—and then came his bound forward into the seminary, which no one in his public-school background had ever dreamed of. Adrian remembered the times he tried to catch up with friends from Ryder who had gone to college, and the befuddled looks he got as they tried to comprehend a trajectory like his. He'd never been any good at explaining why he went to the seminary, or why he left it. He cringed at the thought of trying to tell anyone he was going back.

There was a certain community where Adrian's initial decision to go to Holy Name was understood. He'd made a retreat called *SEARCH for Christian Maturity* during his senior year in high school, and went back to be on the staff of subsequent retreats. It invested him with some vision of himself as part of a religious culture, not just a secular one, and shortly thereafter as a natural leader in it. There was quickly an expectation—not only his own, but others' as well—that his role in this community would be the role of priest; somewhat in the way it was known in his high school math department that he would lead the team for the national math contest, or in band that he would play first chair in the trumpet section. It did not surprise him that once he volunteered for the next season's SEARCH, the vocations director was talking to him about enrolling at a seminary. But once he got to Holy Name, the ground seemed to shift. He'd assumed when he went that the seminary would foster a spirituality well beyond the concreteness of the catechism—that the faces of his peers and advisors would light with recognition when he talked of what St. Teresa had to say in *Interior Castle*. Such was never the case, however. Holy Name seemed a culture entirely consumed with authority, and one's proper relation to it.

The problem of whether or not to be a memeber of the clergy, and if so, exactly how, occupied Adrian's thoughts all through his years at Holy Name. The problem of how to be a gay lay person in the Church was one he'd hardly begun to fathom.

Did his family ever think of him as being in any trouble? At certain moments, he felt that being gay was like being one of the Catholic girls in high school who'd feared they might be pregnant—envisioning their plans for their lives, the demands of their conscience, and the practical realities of the world about to collide fantastically, with something sure to give way, to fall to the ground in tatters. He had counseled more than one friend through just such a crisis. At other times, he chose more or less not to contemplate his situation in the Church. Like those girls, hoping their period was just late.

"Adrian, do you think I should take this carpet up and replace it with a shorter pile?" asked Eleanor. "I keep asking your sisters, and they just want to leave everything the same. They don't have your father to clean up after. Or Charlie, with those infernal boots he wears now for the country."

"I don't know, Mom," Adrian answered. "Maybe you'd better keep Charlie out of the house. It sounds like he mostly gives you hell, anyway."

"You hear that? Someone notices!" she said to Charlie. Charlie smirked slightly. "Can you bring some cream in from the farm when you come tonight? The girls are bringing pie and I'd like some for whipped cream. Ask your mother-in-law."

Charlie eventually left for the farm and Eleanor went to her room to dress for the day. Adrian took his coffee down to his old basement room. His stay in Ryder this trip was going to be very short, and there was little to do except eat solidly, perhaps get some reading done. On every previous pass through Ryder he had repacked the belongings in his room, taking things out and putting things back in, finally leaving less and less of himself at his parents' house. Last summer, before he headed off to Creighton Law, he had gone through boxes of scrap, saving some but burning much of it in the barrel behind his father's store, as if he'd elected a certain identity and was shedding others, by process of elimination. Newspaper clippings, track ribbons, pictures given to him by the yearbook photographer—he suddenly wondered why he'd ever saved them, as he ditched them into yellow flames one July afternoon, with no one in the sleepy town paying much notice. His actions then had a certain resolve, which now, after just a year, seemed lost again.

In a corner of the unfinished half of the basement there stood a table with one of Adrian's junior high school creations on it. It surprised him that no one else had gotten rid of it by now, although he himself had spared it in last summer's purge. It started life as an air hockey game given to Charlie when he was nine, and then stood neglected in the basement for years. Their sister Carol had discovered Adrian in the middle of transforming it into a toy of his own, and demanded to know whose permission he had. Adrian hadn't understood his own shame at the project, or why he'd kept it hidden. What he had done was paint over the markings on the rink to make it appear like a landscape on the moon, and then to fashion a tiny city in different grades of Styrofoam and tempera paint, which would float above the ground when the air blower was switched on. He once viewed the project as the final embarrassment of his childhood, the last time he'd been caught "playing dolls," although certainly not the first. Just about all of his youthful fantasies and games he'd regarded as some form of this shameful business, so he'd sequestered his make-believe worlds, trying to keep them a secret from others.

Still today he didn't wish to destroy it, and in fact he felt the opposite—a pang for the innocence it represented. He ran a fingertip over the tiny turrets and peered into the dusty cellophane windows. He found a sheet to cover it up, and returned to the bedroom, where he dug into his canvas laundry bag and started sorting clothes into piles of colors and whites.

Harvey Underwood was waiting on a customer choosing thread from the glass case of sewing notions in the back of the store when Adrian came in. The store was otherwise empty, and the humming of the tall coolers full of milk and produce was the only sound, aside from the quiet suggestions being made by Harv to the woman.

"Hi, Dad," Adrian said.

Harv raised his eyebrows toward Adrian, and Adrian helped himself to a bottle of pop from the old red Coke machine. He took a seat on one of the stools near the cash register and fidgeted with the bottle while he waited for his father to finish. The woman paid for her thread and some flannel and left.

"So how's the party coming?" Harvey asked.

"Mom's busy peeling potatoes. I guess Carol and Beth Ann are bringing some things with them. You been busy today?"

"Slow, slow, slow," he said. "I was about to dust the plants."

This was just his father's turn of phrase. The pots of sanseveiria in the window hadn't actually been touched in years.

"Anything I can do?" Adrian asked.

"You could stock the candy bars with me."

Adrian fetched the boxes from the cooler and began to restock.

"So what's the latest gossip?" Adrian asked.

"Ain't no gossip. No, no gossip at all," Harv said. He took a pen from behind his ear and started jotting down notes to himself about brands to reorder from the distributor in Fort Dodge. Two farmers tromped into the store looking for bait to go fishing. Harv waited on the men while Adrian found a bottle of Windex and began to clean the two display cases that partitioned public space from the niche where his father tended the cash register. Maddy, his father's long-term bookkeeper and assistant, came back from the bank, carrying the cash purse.

"Hi, Ade," she said, opening the register and filing rolls of change.

Adrian bristled a bit at her breezy informality. He wasn't quite sure why he'd always disliked this woman. "Hello, Madeleine," he said.

"I hear there's big doings up at the house tonight. Everybody coming home. That's nice."

"Yes, nice," he said.

"You don't need to do that," she said of his cleaning.

"Well, Dad got busy or I'd have gotten him to lock up the store and go fishing with me."

"Fishing! That would be the day," she said. She closed the drawer and headed back to the coffee-stained office to return the cash purse to the safe.

Adrian kept up efforts at the plates of glass in front of him.

Flatware clattered against dishes and voices rose and fell around the dinner table.

"Louise said to me, 'As far as I'm concerned, half the people at that school would be *better off* practicing a little birth control. There's plenty of their kind already,'" Eleanor related. "I'm ashamed to say I laughed, despite myself. So I guess we can't count on her vote."

"Who is she to talk?" asked Beth Ann. "That snob."

"Remember the time her girls got white ribbons on their dresses for 4-H, and Louise couldn't figure out how *her* daughters could do so poorly?" said Carol.

"By using fusible interfacing on their hems!" said Beth Ann, laughing.

"Girls, enough," Harvey said.

"Well, she married that Lutheran husband, you know," Eleanor said. "I suppose she won't part company with him on this one."

Adrian saw Carol's eyes go to her sister, and then to Harv. Carol was avoiding any discussion with her mother about the guy she'd been dating from Ames, who was a Presbyterian.

"Parting company. I think that's the contraception technique the pope says is okay. Isn't it, Mom?" said Charlie.

The conversation continued, and dishes at the table were emptied one by one. Beth Ann got up to cut the pies she had brought. Cynthia, Charlie's wife, got up to help her.

"Mrs. Mooney said Liz had her baby," Eleanor was telling.

"What was it?" Beth Ann asked.

"A boy. She named him Prescott."

"Who ever heard of that?" said Charlie. "Poor kid."

"Sounds foolish to me," Harv said.

"Oh, shush," Eleanor motioned to him.

"I think it's a nice name," said Beth Ann. "Sort of WASP."

"WASP and obscure—so it's pretentious on two accounts," said Charlie. "Don't the Mooneys know they're plain old Catholics like us? Whatever happened to Matthew, Mark, Luke and John? Poor kid."

"Well," said Adrian, "it's not like the child has to grow up in Ryder, after all."

Laughter burst from the three Underwood women, although Adrian hadn't meant to be funny. "Liz lives in Minneapolis, you know," he tried adding, but he realized what he'd already betrayed. He stopped short when he caught his father's face, which looked confused and smarting. Harv had lived in Ryder all his life, whereas Adrian's mother had not. Eleanor was anchored in her childhood back in Mankato, and in her sprawling English family there. She'd happily packed Carol and Beth Ann off to

34

apartments in Des Moines after nursing school, and paid the long distance bills to keep up with their lives, just to have them out of Ryder. Adrian occasionally glimpsed what Eleanor could never see: Harv's disappointment when she dismissed his feelings like some waft of fumes, curtly waving her hand and forging on. Harv, for his part, would never have stayed in business running the general store if *he* didn't convey that he truly belonged in the community.

Soon the conversation was back to Liz Mooney what's-her-name, and her baby shower. Adrian focused on something in the living room, and his mind wandered. He remembered an airport somewhere, and himself standing with his shoulder bag in hand, gazing up at a Calder mobile. It must have been Kennedy Airport, and that band trip he'd taken to Frankfurt. He felt slightly dizzy.

"You alright?"

It was his father, at the head of the table to his left, drawing him back to the moment.

"Yeah, I'm fine. Just a little tired, I guess," Adrian said. "I had a long drive yesterday. I think I'll get up and put on some tea."

-4-

Cradle, and Dawn

Eileen's trunk rested on the threadbare rug, splayed open where she had left it the night before when rummaging for sheets and pillowcases. It was the first thing in her line of sight as she awakened. She thought it looked like an old vessel wrecked upon a beach, sitting where it did in this slate-colored room where she slept. She had come to consciousness in her mother's bed, huddled beneath one of her own quilts and grasping the lumpy pillow from the hall closet as if it were something she had wrestled and subdued during the night. How long had she been awake, staring like this? Minutes, perhaps. At first she worried she might spend an eternity lying here, depressed. Now she grew assured that rather than paralyzed she was merely pensive, and would spring back to action soon enough. She just needed time to collect her wits.

Her mother's room had always been this color, a deep blue-gray, as far back as Eileen could remember. There was a time when it seemed exotic, a note of mystery in her mother's generally prim and dignified life. That was when her mother was full of vigor, storming around the world full of righteous purpose, raising her daughters. In later years, it had only seemed dark, a pall her mother wore willingly about herself, especially when she withdrew so often to her bed. Eileen found herself wondering for the first time what she'd do with these walls as she got the house ready for sale. Surely this color must go, but she dreaded the thought of painting over it, and knew she'd leave it for last, after repairing the exterior and painting the other rooms.

A pair of grackles started a spat in the branches of the elm tree next door, and Eileen got up to close the window against the racket they made. Standing there, she felt at last free from the gravity of the bed.

In fifteen minutes she was showered and dressed, and went out to unload the rest of her belongings from the car. She poked around her parcels until she found a box of tea. Soon the kettle on the stove was puffing steam, and Eileen poured water over the leaves in her tea pot before heading upstairs, pad of paper in hand, to survey the house from top to bottom. The filth she found everywhere! Often-touched surfaces were grimy, while untouched ones were laden with dust. The wallpaper peeled in various places and the plaster of the bare walls was chipped and flaking. How much had her mother let the property go, she wondered, and how much of this had been the tenants? Eileen could not remember the condition of the house at the time of her mother's funeral—she could scarcely remember being in it that trip, although she did sleep here and stay to pack her mother's things. The upstairs hallway looked particularly dreary as she stood in it. The light was dim, the rug underneath her feet was dull and soiled, and jutting into the space from above was that cumbersome trap door to the attic, a cord hanging down so one could open it and pull the retracting steps down from the ceiling. The contraption had always seemed to her ill-designed, and unstable. And the work that lay beyond it for her! Boxes of junk up there, needing to be sorted, and either saved or sacrificed. She couldn't think ahead that far. First she needed to make the place livable. She peeked into the two bedrooms under the gable, and made a note to buy ammonia to clean the windows. Back in the kitchen, pouring her tea, she began to feel like herself once more, a woman in possession of a plan. She would get ready to go to the store and feel she belonged in the world.

Driving to the market Eileen passed by Beckett High School, its rows of windows reflecting the glare of the mid-morning sun, and its white statue of Mary holding her arms in supplication on a pedestal out front. Schools in summer always seemed to shout their emptiness at her, to proclaim the utter dispensability of what went on in them the other nine months of the year. She would need to get the key and go in next week, to look over the books in her classroom and take stock of the laboratory facilities. She did not relish such tasks, particularly carrying them out alone in there like some ghost haunting the place. That would occupy her soon enough.

She slowed and looked for the correct cross street for Quillen's Market. As she put on her turn signal, a motorcycle sped past her.

"Bitch, you lost or what?" the young man riding it shouted, veering across the center line to get around her.

Well, for heaven's sake, she thought.

In the store, Eileen pushed her cart through the gleaming aisles and marveled at the newness of everything. Most of the items on her list were easy enough to find, the bakery and dairy in their logical places, the cleaning supplies gathered in a single aisle. The regional brands she remembered seemed to have disappeared from the shelves, replaced by the same fare she'd seen in the supermarkets in Mandan. There was something slightly jarring about this—deflating an unknown wish, to come back to La Crosse and find it ever the same. La Crosse was no longer her home, even if none of the places she had been keeping herself had ever taken its place.

There was a slight drizzle falling as Eileen lifted paper bags of groceries into her car and wrestled with where to situate the handle of a mop she'd bought. By the time she slid into the front seat, the drops had started to fall faster, and she reached for the windshield wiper control.

She returned to her mother's house by way of the coulee road, under the branches of the cottonwoods lining that drive. She arrived at the house to find a casserole on the side porch and in it, potato salad, full of mustard and onions. She recognized that Elsie Seaman had left it, not by the dish but by the gesture itself, which was identical to one Elsie made at the time of Brigid's death, in the days after the funeral when Eileen remained in the house to pack things up. Eileen brought it in and set it on the counter, and had no more than shaken the raindrops from her head than she heard a soft tapping on the screen door. She walked out to the hall and there was Elsie, thin as a bantam hen and stooped on her failing old spine, but Elsie nevertheless, without any cover on. Eileen opened the door.

"Oh, I'm so glad you've come!" Elsie gushed. "Those renters were okay, I suppose, but it didn't seem right to have them in here with your mother's belongings, with no regard for the place. I was so anxious for you to come back."

"Elsie, it's nice to see you. Thank you for the dish. You didn't need to," Eileen said, ushering her into the kitchen.

"I thought you wouldn't be prepared to cook, just getting home and all," said Elsie.

Eileen automatically reached into the cupboard for a cup and poured Elsie some tea from the pot in its cozy, which Elsie took, remaining standing.

"Sit, sit," Eileen said, pulling a chair out from the table. Elsie sat.

"Elsie, it's been so long! How are you managing?" The image of Elsie's wiry legs climbing the steep stairs of her old house entered Eileen's mind.

"Well, I do miss her," Elsie said, of Brigid. "But it's all I can do these days to take care of *myself*, really. The arthritis has slowed me down a bit. Still, it's a little lonely over in that big house alone. Arlene and Jack left Dubuque for Kansas City, and hardly come home any more except for holidays," she said of her son and his wife. "The renters were not the type to be around, working so many hours, both of them."

"Oh, you poor thing," Eileen said. "I'll have to take you out. Is there anything you lack? I imagine you have trouble lifting. You should make me a list, and we'll get to it."

"It's so nice to have you back," Elsie said. "What about the end of the year, when that other young teacher comes back? Will you return to the sisters?"

"I don't know," Eileen found herself saying. Did she really *not* know? The plan was to go back, but she had gone the extra step of obtaining formal exclaustration, which would give her up to three years to make a decision about returning.

"Well, I imagine the house will sell quickly if you put it up. So many new people have come into town—they say buildings are springing up all over lately. I felt so bad you couldn't stay when your mother died. There wasn't anyone but you, you know. The realtor has done the essentials, but there's more than that. There are things at my house I think you should have. Some of your mother's things. If you don't want them, I'll take them to the Lutheran Home."

"Sure, Elsie," Eileen said, taken aback by the immediacy her mother had in Elsie's thoughts. "Let me get settled, and we can look them over."

"Of course," Elsie said, draining her cup and rising to leave. "I won't keep you now. I'm sure you need to rest."

"I'll serve you a proper tea when I get the house clean and can bake some scones," Eileen said. She gave Elsie a hug of reassurance, then Elsie was off, out the door and across the grass to her big yellow house, nearly a replica of Brigid's, on the next lot.

The hallways at Holy Name Seminary smelled of old books and furniture polish, mixed with more than a hint of lingering frankincense. Eileen arrived for Mass just a few minutes before nine, as the rector had instructed her over the phone on Friday. She was looking for a place to make her liturgical home this year, and the seminary was not far from her mother's house. She had been here only once before, for the twenty-fifth jubilee of a priest from Holy Trinity, the parish of her childhood, but she still remembered where the chapel was, in the center of the clustered seminary buildings. The structures were all built of the same white stone, and were inscribed with mottoes picked by Bishop Halloran himself: *The promise of the harvest is in the sowing,* read the arch above the main entrance.

Sliding into a rear pew of the chapel, Eileen noted the uniform dress of the seminarians kneeling in the rows in front of her—their sweaters, dress slacks, shirts and ties—and the high, crisp cut of their hair. Soon the *schola cantorum* was filing in for the start of chant. The rector here ran a tight ship, and it showed, as the ceremony coalesced just at the arrival of the hour. The voices of the young men in the choir broke into a Gregorian processional and ascended the nave, resounding from the tiles of the ceiling like notes from a carillon. The officiants came up the aisle—what looked to be a couple of associate priests, two acolytes with the gospel and processional cross, and then the rector. Eileen felt a thrill, to be back in the presence of what was once called "the Church triumphal"—Bishop Halloran's vision of the Church, which was still preserved here even after two decades of Bishop Simmons's lower-key reign over the diocese. Fr. Moriarty, the rector, presided at the service. It was the feast day of St. Monica, mother of St. Augustine, and Fr. Moriarty spoke about the special meaning of Augustine's conversion in the history of the Church. Moriarty seemed a very likeable man, with a soft, melodious voice and a delicate primness of gesture. The Mass ended with songs by the St. Louis Jesuits at communion and the recessional, sung with no verses left out.

Eileen was surprised to find one of the seminarians waiting at the door for her as she exited the chapel. "Father Moriarty would like to invite you to join the community for breakfast, if you'd like," he said. He was gangly, bespectacled and nervous, although he looked to be one of the senior seminarians, by his age.

"Thank you," Eileen said. A moment passed. "How do I proceed, then?" she asked.

"The refectory is this way," he said.

Eileen noticed two nuns now, coming out a side door from the chapel. Apparently they had been sitting behind her, in the last pew.

"The nuns eat in their convent," the seminarian explained, "after Sister Stanislaus has finished serving breakfast."

Breakfast was proceeding lock-step, just like the service that morning. The seminarians might be orderly, but they were also young men, and the press of their appetites could be seen in the briskness of their movement down the hall toward the smells of coffee and frying bacon. Eileen felt herself swept along in a dash toward the seats at the tables. The brief melee ended when everyone was seated, and the seminarians were once again composed and silent. The priests entered, and Fr. Moriarty said a brief grace before sitting down. Immediately the young men dug into baskets of toast placed on the tables. A certain number of white-coated seminarians strode to the kitchen, returning in moments with bowls of food. Soon the seminarian on Eileen's left addressed her.

"Is this your first visit to Holy Name?"

"Well, the first in many years. The last time was 1967, not long after the seminary was built," Eileen said. "I'm a lot older than you young men. I'm sure a lot has changed since then."

"Oh, I wouldn't count on that," said a Hispanic boy across the table. "Things still seem pretty tight around here to me."

"Your name is...?" said Eileen.

"Louie," he answered. "Louie Lopez. Quad Cities. Bettendorf most of my life, then Dubuque in junior high and high school. Man, my friends still can't believe I'm here. This is too wild, man."

Louie was a freshman, in his first week at the seminary.

"They gotta loosen up around here. Can you believe these waiters?" He nodded toward the boy near their table, who stood at rigid attention while his peers ate and talked.

"And you?" Eileen asked the first seminarian.

"Alan. Alan Hennessey. From Portage. I guess it's about what I was expecting. I visited last year and met with the vocations director. I knew about the dress code and all."

"They sent me a letter with all that, but who reads that shit?" said Louie, with no notion of excusing his language.

Eileen was used to the profanity of her students at Fort Yates, but it surprised her to hear it here. Fr. Moriarty's work was apparently not so easy—she should be more impressed at how seamless this morning's liturgy had been.

"Just a week ago I got my hair cut," said Louie. "Man, I was so wasted from the going-away party my friends threw, the old man had to haul me out of bed to go to the appointment."

Louie seemed somehow mistaken, thinking the seminary was like a tour of military duty.

"I'm majoring in music," said Alan. "I'm not sure if I want to be a priest, or a director of liturgy. I play the organ. I've had eight years of lessons."

Eileen did not mind the *non sequitur.*

"I wasn't even planning to go to college," said a thick, crew-cut boy at the end of the table. "But since it's the seminary, my dad said it was okay. I don't know how I'm going to do in Latin. English in high school was bad enough."

Eileen remembered reading somewhere that less than a quarter of recruits at the minor seminary were eventually ordained. Seeing the mix of cultures at her own little table, she began to understand how this might be.

The boy on her left finished off the eggs in the serving bowl, and he'd hardly put it down when the waiter swooped in and made away with it to the kitchen.

"Do you want to go walk by the river after breakfast?" Alan asked the boy in the crew cut.

"I got dishwashing duty. I can later, though."

Breakfast was winding down, and Eileen rose to dismiss herself. Fr. Moriarty had already left the room, so there were no formal goodbyes to say. She made her way out of the refectory and down the hall. Outside, she walked along a row of sheared arborvitae lining the path to the parking lot. Passing what must have been the convent, she saw one of the two nuns from earlier emerge and approach her.

"Good morning," the woman said, sunnily. "I'm Sister Florence. Comptroller for the diocese. Sister Stanislaus and Sister Bede and I live here on the grounds. We're a motley crew—I'm Augustinian, Bede is a Sister of Mercy, and Stanislaus is a Sacred Heart. It's the times, you know. Our work brings us all here. It really is a special place, this community."

"Hello," said Eileen. "I hardly noticed you at Mass. Let me introduce myself. I'm Eileen, with the Bonaventures."

"I think I know your superior. Peggy."

"Yes. You may know her better than I do. It's been a while since I've seen her. I've been out at the Standing Rock Reservation."

"Yes, of course. That is such important work, and so difficult, I'm sure. I have to go, but we must have you over for dinner some Sunday. That's when we're most at liberty. If you can manage."

"Sure," Eileen said, not feeling at all certain. Did Florence take her lack of a habit only as informality? Her exclaustration meant more to her than she realized, and she felt uncomfortable at the thought of being among other nuns.

"I'm sure I'll see you again at chapel," Eileen said, declaring how they might meet again. She waved as she made her way toward her car waiting in the lot.

-5-

Days of Silence

Adrian's return to the seminary was remarkably uneventful. On the surface, he blended almost imperceptibly back into life at Holy Name. He checked into his room, one of the nice corner ones with two windows, which came with seniority. He knew by now how to live in one of these seminary cells, had picked up all the tricks over the years for mounting pictures on the tiled walls with putty and doubling the storage space with stacked rattan trunks from the Pier 1 in town. Ben Miller's graduation last May had left the job of sacristan open again, and Adrian took up the duties as if he'd never left them. He resumed the daily rhythm of morning and evening prayer, of rosary and benediction, and fell in with the order of seminary life with simple efficiency.

His feelings, perhaps, were another matter. When he'd driven up to the seminary the previous Saturday evening, his senses had been flooded with things he loved about this place: its cool, well-kept vegetation, luxuriant in the approaching dew, and the stillness, imperturbed by traffic anywhere nearby, broken only by the sounds of crickets and mosquitoes on the forested side of the grounds leading down to the river. The white limestone blocks of the buildings themselves were luminescent in the twilight, and seven huge elms, undoubtedly three times as old as the seminary, lifted their leafy arms to preside over the comings and goings below them. Bishop Halloran had hand-picked these trees for amnesty when clearing the land for the buildings, and his vision in this, as in so many things, endured.

The priests of the diocese were winding up their annual retreat when the senior seminarians arrived, a day ahead of the others. On Sunday morning, as a send-off, all one-hundred-seven priests had concelebrated Mass in the chapel. Adrian had watched, with the same excitement he'd felt when he first beheld that sight. It was the first image he'd loved at Holy Name—all these priests in matching albs and chasubles hand-sewn at Blue Cloud Abbey, filing into the sanctuary, while he sat in thrall in his pew, a witness, a man among men. This vision still gripped his imagination more than any other, attended by the most inexpressible of his feelings about the seminary. He yearned to belong to a holy brotherhood, had clung always to some hope of it, whatever the apparent obstacles. Why *had* he ever left the seminary? he asked himself.

Well, for one thing, there was the seemingly perpetual skepticism with which he and Fr. Moriarty regarded each other, the enduring failure of any connection between them, however close Adrian might have felt to his fellow seminarians. Moriarty had the most responsibility at Holy Name for defining what "call to priesthood" was supposed to be. Although Adrian had huge intellectual differences with Moriarty, Adrian always assumed these were ultimately trivial. More important to him was his sense of never getting any validation from the rector. The seminary operated mostly through a system of unacknowledged rewards and punishments from Fr. Moriarty, ranging from the assignment of work-study jobs to the awarding of liturgical roles. Cleaning bathrooms was plebe work, but no disgrace unless one pulled it as a sophomore or later. Choice prizes were turns at the lectern, especially on feast days or at Masses with ranking clerics present, like the bishop or the odd visitor from a major seminary or from Rome. Elevation to head prefect in senior year was the highest honor, and no one ever doubted which member of the junior class was most anointed, come selection time. Adrian had not been head prefect, of course, but he also hadn't been singled out for humiliations like a second year as dishwasher—where some others had. Mostly, he felt neglected, unnoticed, which seemed pretty damning in its own way. Did he underestimate the importance of his intellectual waywardness? Fr. Moriarty's sole comment on that subject, when Adrian pulled a 4.0 for yet another semester, and this time with twenty-one credits, had been to suggest that Adrian *neglect his spirituality less.* Adrian continued to think it possible he had dreamed up the idea he was unwanted in his own Church. There were many rooms in his Father's house, were there not? He remembered his first interview with the vocations director in Des Moines, and telling the priest about his wish to be present in the middle of life's great events, the sacramental moments of baptism and marriage and death, to help articulate their inherent sacredness. What had happened to that? It had simply evaporated.

Fr. Sweeney had been sent back to Dubuque, and a new priest from that diocese had come to join the seminary staff. Fr. Herman would certainly not present the distraction the handsome Sweeney had, and Adrian rather welcomed this. The absence of his classmates, however, since his return to Holy Name, was crushing to him. No sooner did his heart leap at seeing the familiar face of the seminary than he began to feel grief at his loneliness, the ineluctable sense that he swallowed most every utterance that came to mind, for lack of ears that would understand it. The circle he'd had—Carl, Bill, Danny, and Ben, the ones who'd elected third-year Latin with him—were now their own little diaspora, in Rome, Emmittsburg, St. Paul, even one in Japan. This year's senior class had been just sophomores when he left, and now their numbers had dwindled from ten down to six. Paul Nice was head prefect, as anyone could have predicted, and from that perch he seemed more relaxed than ever before. A choice of the major seminaries, from the American College in Rome to the "local" St. Paul Seminary, was Paul's to make. Still, his every word was measured, and he fussed interminably over the details of how things appeared. Paul was a striking man who dressed impeccably and was regularly put in charge of the choreography for special services and celebrations. Adrian, as sacristan, came nearly up to Paul's standards, which is more than one could say for the rest of the community. Such perfectionism, coupled with Paul's discombobulation whenever confronted with anything other than a literal interpretation of doctrine or scripture, seemed to Adrian to be somehow inimical to spirituality. (Paul was stumped when a fourth-grader in catechism class asked if purgatory was between heaven and earth, or farther away.) But Paul thrived at Fr. Moriarty's Holy Name, and Adrian was left trying to make sense of it.

The seminary's relation to Assisi College was one of genial co-existence. Holy Name had closed its college in 1975, and had sent its men to Assisi for their bachelors' studies since then, retaining only its role as a formation community. Fr. Daimler was the only priest at the seminary with a faculty position at the college, in Religious Studies, and he taught the introductory theology course which first year "sems" were required to take. Assisi was run by Franciscan nuns, who were vaguely tut-tutted by Fr. Moriarty from time to time, as sowers of discord in his world, the diocesan Church. He had euphemisms for liberal Catholic thinkers that enabled him to avoid use of the word *liberal* entirely, often just referring to "that element" or "certain parties in the Church." The notion that the religious orders in general were a lot of restive children was more or less taken to be established fact.

Adrian had been in many ways the Franciscans' darling, a serious student of philosophy and classics at what was still predominantly a nursing and teachers' college, despite its liberal arts mission. When he wanted to come back and audit some things this fall, he simply called Sr. Rose, the registrar, and asked for the okay. Since he was in no-man's-land regarding financial aid, she told him, "I think we can consider it a scholarship. Let me

know what you're taking, and how many credits. For the books."
He was grateful for such connections.

This morning Adrian was on his way to see Ernie Jenkins, a
professor in the English department, for permission to audit his
course on Shakespeare's history plays. He rode his bicycle up
Wilson Avenue to the college and locked it in the bike rack outside Marian Hall, the main academic building. He had checked
with the departmental secretary for Jenkins's office hours, so he
found the man at his desk in his third-floor office.

"Hello. Dr. Jenkins?"
Adrian had seen him around campus and knew his name, but
had never been introduced. The man turned and took a pair of
reading half-lenses off his face.
"Yes?"
"Adrian. Adrian Underwood. I came to ask if I could audit
your Shakespeare course—422."
"Underwood. Yes. Your reputation precedes you. I thought
they got you out of here, finally, with a triple major or some-
thing."
"Just a double, sir. In philosophy and classics."
"So what are you doing back?"
"Trying to find myself, I guess."
"And your lost self just might be in *King John*, you think?"
"I guess so," Adrian said, and smiled.
Jenkins was dressed rather formally, and he talked without
exactly making eye contact, keeping his attention somewhere
between his visitor and the work on his desk.
"What English have you had?"
"Um, Advanced Comp, Chaucer, Nineteenth Century—and
Shakespeare's Comedy and Tragedy from Dr. Shelbe. I got an
A."
"Yeah, you can come," Jenkins offered. "If it's not cancelled.
I'm having to twist a few of my English majors' arms to get them
to take it, but it looks to be still on." He finally looked Adrian in
the eyes. "Is that all?"

"Yeah. Sure. Thanks," Adrian said, and turned to go.

"Say," said Jenkins, discovering he had another question. "Are you still 'finding yourself' at Holy Name?"

"Yes, sir."

"I see," he said, with the slightest of chuckles. "Well, good luck to you." With that he turned back to his papers. For a moment Adrian surveyed the man and his office, the stacks of papers and the posters of Virginia Woolf and a National Theatre production of *Hamlet*, then he left.

Out on the main college quad Adrian mounted his bicycle and headed in the direction of the Romanesque convent chapel, *Mary, Queen of Heaven*, to pay a visit. Soon into his left vision strode a familiar figure in black. He knew the gait even before fully looking that direction.

"Father!" he said, lighting up.

"Well," said Fr. Keenan, looking up from his path. "If it isn't my young logician." Every former student, to Fr. Keenan, was his "young logician," since he met them by teaching Logic in the core arts curriculum. Adrian had never been addressed by the man in any other way during his four years here. It was usually the start of a riff, a signal that some intellectual skirmish was about to ensue, but sometimes—like now—it was merely "hello." Fr. Keenan looked genuinely pleased to see him.

"To what do I owe this privilege?" he asked.

"I'm back on campus, at least a couple days a week," said Adrian. "I came back to Holy Name."

"That would be *irregular* now, would it not?" Keenan said.

"Highly!" Adrian said, and laughed. Keenan was perhaps the only cleric Adrian thought truly liked him. To Keenan, the mind was absolutely no enemy of faith. He was famous for standing in front of his classroom with a logical puzzle on the chalkboard, and exhorting his students, "Think! Think, my children!" He had zoomed in on Adrian a hundred times in that course, demanding logical precision, and Adrian had never failed him. Keenan seemed to love Adrian's calm authority under duress, the way he could return the priest's intense gaze, when others averted their eyes. The philosopher was a Sulpician Father, in many respects a lone wolf, but revered by all the lay professors in the philosophy department. He was recognized even throughout Holy Name and the chancery downtown as a priest of tremendous vision.

"Perhaps the world of laws failed to satisfy the hunger of the mind?" Keenan ventured.

"It's more like I have unfinished business here," Adrian said. "I think I had to get away before I could see the question of priesthood with a clearer eye. I can't say that there's ever been a job description in the Church for a career smart aleck, and that's about all I was aspiring to fill before. I guess I'm back to find out if there's anything more in it for me." As simple as this was, Adrian hadn't articulated it until this moment, when admitting it to Fr. Keenan. The goodly priest was a touchstone for the logical coherence of any assertion, but he tended to elicit honesty from a person as well. Adrian knew Fr. Keenan's opinion about his return to Holy Name mattered.

"Well, time is the great teacher, no doubt," Keenan said. "And here," he gestured broadly to the edifices around them, "what have we to share, but our time?"

God bless him.

"I'll see you in the cafeteria some day then, perhaps," Adrian said.

"That you will," said Keenan, who resumed his stroll toward St. Joseph Hospital.

A group of sophomore seminarians was shooting pool in the basement rec room when Adrian came in from storing his bicycle in the garage at Holy Name. Adrian greeted them, then dashed upstairs to shower before dinner. This was Wednesday night, and after the meal they would all convene for Fr. Moriarty's weekly formation talk.

If liturgy and homilies at the seminary were not quite suited to a didactic purpose, Moriarty made up for it in his formation lectures. There he countered disparate influences of the culture around them, from over-spirited academic inquiry on the one hand to the tone of left-wing periodicals like the *National Catholic Reporter* and *Sojourner* magazine, on the other. The evening would extend, after the talk, into a soiree with tea and cookies, and end with night prayer.

The Bishop Marsh Room was set up in its usual fashion, with rows of folding chairs facing a portable chalkboard. Adrian sat in the back, knowing tonight's talk would be familiar, since it was the first of the new year. The rector sauntered to the front of the room, smiling and handsome. His salt-and-pepper curls were cropped tight and he wore his pressed clerics with natural grace. In the moment before he spoke, Moriarty would often stroke the tip of his tongue under his front teeth, where one tooth over-lapped the other just the slightest bit, and he would beam at his listeners.

"Tonight, gentlemen," he said, "we will talk about being *holy* in the *world*. This is the state to which we are called by Jesus, and it is the opposite of being *wholly in the world*." He wrote these two words, holy and wholly, on the board as he spoke, to clarify their distinctiveness, then erased them. He followed this with his classic gesture, the drawing of a chalk line down the center of the board. The discourse proceeded, and soon the board began to fill with contrasted opposites—selfish versus other-centered, material opposed to spiritual, this world against eternity. Adrian wondered why this annoyed him so much, when in content it was just Christianity 101. He had never warmed to this aspect of Moriarty, year in or year out, his division of the Church from the world. Year in or year out—you're in or you're out. Adrian's mind was bored already, and making word plays. While the new seminarians sat with rapt attention, Adrian started to look forward to the tea that would follow, weak as it was.

He usually tried to disregard Fr. Moriarty's religious politics, the way he would his mother's. Perhaps he'd been obstinate, actually, writing his college theology papers on topics like liberation theology instead of more favored subjects, like the return to devotional practices among the Catholic laity. With Eleanor, he hardly brought up the subject of the Church, except to discuss their shared social justice concerns, like the rights of migrant farm workers or the diversion of federal dollars into military spending. Any part of a religious vocation that might have to do with his longing for brotherhood was miles from his mother's imagination, he knew. *She* never understood the need for anything but rectitude, and might very well covet the prospect of being the only "good" Catholic in Kossuth County, or maybe the whole state of Iowa.

When the lecture ended for the evening, Adrian latched onto one of his favorites among the junior seminarians, in hopes of striking up a conversation about bicycling. The fellow was happy to chat, and they headed toward the table of refreshments together.

On Thursday morning, classes were finally starting, and the table of freshman seminarians Adrian waited on at breakfast was full of chatter about the prospects facing them at Assisi. The discordant note was being sounded by Louie Lopez, who was in turn being ignored by his peers.

"Man, I need to get out of here for a smoke!" Louie said.

"I heard that as long as you pass all the weekly quizzes in Latin I, he won't fail you on the final exam no matter what."

"You say that like it's easy. I hope he doesn't take things too fast."

"You've got to study, that's for sure. I had Latin I in high school."

"Lucky for you. You'll book through this."

"Man, could I use getting laid," Louie said. Eyebrows were raised involuntarily around the table, but no one addressed him.

"I'm more worried about Logic. I hear Fr. Keenan singles you out in there like nothing in the world. I choke under pressure like that."

"He's tough, that's what I hear. But it's a general ed class. We won't be facing him alone."

Louie's eyes scanned the table, and he let out a dramatic sigh. Adrian had seen this trajectory before, with Tom Dillon in the class below him, and with Jeffery Hanifl, who would have been among the current seniors. After a week of relinquishing control over everything, from his clothes and his hair length to his curfew and even the *word* for curfew ("quiet"—as in "shh, it's past *quiet*") Louie was casting about for some support in opposing it all. No one else had reached the same point of psychological meltdown—at least not yet—and he found no one to join him. Adrian could see what was coming, that Louie's brittle bravado could not last, and his would be the first departure from the seminary among several in this year's freshman class. *Ouch*, Adrian thought to himself, watching it unfold. For the moment he was relieved to wear the stony affectation of a table waiter. He felt sorry for guys like this.

On Thursday afternoon Adrian got back from campus in plenty of time for a run, and slipped into his gym gear right after tossing his Riverside Shakespeare on the bed. The aroma of sauerkraut was coming up the stairwell from the kitchen, where Stanislaus was doctoring it in German fashion with mashed potatoes and bacon, as Adrian loped out of the building. The grass of the seminary grounds was spongy under Adrian's feet as he charted a course heading downstream. With his current light schedule Adrian expected to increase his running and exceed his previous weekly distance. He'd looked into his community service assignment today, stopping by the nursing home on Earle Avenue. It was hardly out of his way on trips between Holy Name and campus, and he'd fit his volunteer work in easily. He'd get excused from dinner at the seminary one day a week to accommodate it. Soon he was out on Mormon Coulee Road, heading in the direction of Mt. La Crosse to the south. He ran all the way out there once, but today he would settle for a fraction of that distance. As he settled into his stride, a couple of pheasants flew up from the grassy berm ahead of him, both brightly plumed, and rose in diagonals over the trees and telephone wires along the road. Adrian established a rhythm, a ratio of strides to breaths, and watched the fenceposts file past him, only to be replenished on the distant horizon, endlessly.

His thoughts turned to his runs last year in Omaha. He was feeling a bit homesick for the place, for the catalpa trees and the broken sidewalks and Queen Anne's lace—it surprised him, actually. He missed the familiar smells of the stockyards, of milled grain and roasting coffee. Of course it was his neighbor, Terry, the man who'd become his running partner there, that he missed the most. Crazy Terry—*Terry of the Insufficient Goodbyes*. He'd given Adrian a breezy wave at his departure, as though Adrian would be right back in a day or two. Adrian could hardly believe Terry felt so little.

The two of them had lived in the same apartment building from the start, and saw each other coming and going for several weeks, even met each other running on Twenty-Eighth Street a few times, before Terry one day came upon Adrian hauling his bicycle up to the landing outside his apartment door, and introduced himself. Terry was older, in his early thirties, and an attorney in the D.A.'s office downtown. Their first meeting had ended with Terry suggesting they could run together sometime, which Adrian doubted would happen. But it did, since the two of them kept the same late hours, and often one would be stretching just as the other came home for the evening. "Wait up," one would say to the other, and then they'd set out for the streets of the city together.

Their route became standard—across the interstate, then all the way down Twenty-Fourth Street, over the Howard Street Bridge, and back up Twenty-Eighth Street to their building. They would pass through the ethnic neighborhoods of South Omaha, through the dust of the Purina Chow mill, over patched asphalt and under the gaze of multiple Virgins Mary sheltered in bathtub grottoes in front yards.

Besides their running, Adrian fancied the idea that he and Terry would someday have the law in common. Terry's career, however, had more than just a head start—it was stellar even among his contemporaries. Terry was decidedly, if not openly, gay, although between him and Adrian it had never really been discussed *per se*. Terry had just let it drop one day that his ex-boy-friend worked in a certain building they passed, and Adrian took it in stride, literally and figuratively. Adrian asked his name, and how long ago they'd broken up, but didn't take it much further than that. Although Adrian's own orientation was never brought up, he felt unmistakably taken under Terry's wing after that. He was invited along for drinks with Terry's friends, and included on hiking trips once or twice on Saturdays. When the friends were gay men and began to ask Adrian questions that were prying, Terry would intervene to shield Adrian as soon as he sensed dis-comfort. "You mind yourselves," he'd say, and his friends would obey him.

Not that Adrian was defenseless. There had been no pretense in his own mind that he would be *straight* if he left the seminary—the seminary itself being a world of neuter status. There was little room to question his own proclivities after the tremendous crush he'd had during sophomore and junior years on a boy from the dormitory at Assisi, whom he met in Shelbe's class. Vince read Schopenhauer just because he was interested in his writing, and batted tennis balls across the court outside the fine arts center on sunny afternoons after class. Adrian would drop by and invite Vince to meet in the library, where they would study Shakespeare together and mock their classmates' Puritanical reactions to bawdiness in the text. The two of them were good Elizabethans, they'd tell themselves, to account for what set them apart from the others. Maybe what they were were simply gay boys, inclined to a bit of subversion.

It had been quite a jolt this spring for Adrian to learn that his friend Terry was ill. They were on a weekend camping trip to Wind Cave at the time with a group of Terry's friends, and sharing a tent for the night.

"You'll probably hear my alarm go off at four a.m., so I thought I'd go ahead and tell you before hand. I get up to take AZT, a drug my doctor at the University of Nebraska is helping to study. It's for HTLV-III."

Adrian read the papers, and knew what AZT was.

"I'm very sorry to hear that," he said.

"Yeah, it's a bummer."

"How long have you known?"

"Greg and I were together at the time. When the test came out, we both took it. I was positive, he wasn't. It was pretty much no sex after that."

"Jesus," Adrian said.

"Nah...more like Mary Magdalene," Terry said, squeezing Adrian affectionately on the shoulder. It was the only time Terry ever touched him.

Long after Terry had gone to sleep, Adrian lay awake, shaken, feeling like he might join the keening of the wind, blowing through willows outside the tent. Adrian propped his head up on an elbow and stared at Terry's features, caught in the little bit of light thrown by a lantern in the middle of the camp. Terry looked boyish, angelic, his chest rising gently with every breath. Adrian could hardly believe this man was mortal, much less dying.

For David, Adrian's friend up at Union Theological in Minneapolis, whom Adrian had met at a religious studies conference in Chicago, the urge for sex was simple, and led pretty directly to action. The fact of sexuality thus established, David would reckon with whatever obstacle it presented to his being a minister. For Adrian, nothing was nearly so clear. He was smart, and had insights, but lacked any kind of resolution. What was this discipline of his, that he thought things through so much, put aside his feelings, and obsessed about what was fair, or logical, or intellectually consistent? Would the Church really nourish his mind, he asked himself, and if it did, wasn't that enough? Fr. Moriarty didn't have to *like* Adrian, did he? Adrian possessed no theology in which *sex* mattered, except in its avoidance. His greatest fear right now was that this entire year would pass and that things wouldn't change, that nothing would get resolved in his own mind.

Adrian finished his run, then bounded up to the fourth floor and showered up. He waited distractedly on dinner, then ate with the group of seniors who shared table-waiting duty with him. He spent the evening reading *King John* for Jenkins's class. Later that night, too restless to sleep, he padded down to the telephone on the second floor and placed a call to David. "Just catching up," he said, when David asked about the reason for the call. It was a bad time to talk, David said. He and Ted were fighting. No, nothing serious, but it was an argument they'd been needing to have. Could he try tomorrow night? "Sure thing," Adrian said, returning the phone to its cradle.

-6-

A Badge to Wear

The evening shift of nurses had just come out of report when Eileen arrived for her first day volunteering at St. Francis Nursing Home. Dinner had been delivered to the floor, on melamine trays in a tall rolling cart, although it was only 4:30 p.m. An aide in pastel pink scrubs was sliding trays out and placing them in front of the residents, most of whom were tied into geriatric chairs with vest-type restraints. This was the skilled nursing wing, and the food on the trays consisted of assorted purees in various colors.

"Some nice macaroni and cheese, Mr. Bostert?" said the aide, to a grizzled old man who was busy fiddling with the volume on his hearing aid. She coaxed him toward a pool of yellow on his plate.

"What did you say?" he boomed at her.

"Macaroni and cheese!" she shouted.

The purple pool next to it Eileen guessed to be boiled beets, by its tint. The aroma coming from the cart was not much of a clue.

Eileen had been told that she would find Cindy, the head day nurse, here on "C" wing, finishing the paperwork from her shift. Cindy was supposed to give her an orientation to the ward. Presently an obese woman all in white, including a crisp nursing cap and heavy support hose, marched out of the nurses' station with a tray of Dixie Cups sprinkled with pills.

"Is Cindy here?" Eileen asked.

61

"I'm Cindy," the woman said. "I'm supposed to be off, but the night nurse is on the phone to a doctor. Miss Adelaide is spiking a temp again. Can I help you?"

"I'm a new volunteer," Eileen said.

"Oh, yes. We were expecting you. Just let me pass these and I'll be right with you."

She began going chair to chair, pouring shots of grape juice and helping her charges wash down their medications.

A young man raced in just then, slinging his backpack into a chair and proceeding immediately across the room to help a list-less woman in grey braids. She had slid half out of her chair under the tray table, and he pulled her upright before taking a seat next to her and beginning to scoop spoonfuls of her meal up to her. He was undoubtedly a student, although not likely an undergraduate. The adolescent in him was thoroughly gone, given way to an earnest, purposeful manner. He was fair and ruddy, with a slightly roman nose and thick reddish-blond hair. Apparently Eileen was not the only Thursday night volunteer, unless this young man were that woman's grandson.

Soon Cindy was finished with her rounds, and she motioned Eileen over to her.

"Volunteers help feed the residents, of course," she said. "If you're able to stay past dinner hour, I'd suggest you visit some patients over on 'A' wing. Most of them don't have Alzheimer's, and they really miss having company. Have you volunteered in senior care before?"

"As a postulant, years ago," Eileen said.

"Well, it's pretty simple," Cindy said. "I'll point out to you which residents need to be fed. There are quite a few on this ward."

"Pupa! Pupa!" shouted a distressed old woman as they walked past.

"Yes, Trina, I know," Cindy said to the woman, giving her a pat. Then she turned to Eileen. "Do you know what that means?"

"No, what?"

"It's Polish for hiney. She's saying her hiney hurts. Been saying it for years. The doctors can't find anything wrong, though."

Cindy directed Eileen around the room, indicating the men and women she'd be feeding, and eventually steered her toward the young man, who was just finishing his assistance to the lady in braids.

"This is our other volunteer, Adrian. He started here last week."

"Hello," Eileen said. The young man stood up, wiping food from his hand onto a paper napkin, and extended a handshake.

"This is Eileen," Cindy said.

"Yes, I know," the boy offered.

"How...?" Eileen started.

"You were at breakfast, at Holy Name," he said. "You wouldn't have noticed me, in the crowd. I was waiting on another table. But you were introduced."

"You're a seminarian," Eileen said.

"Yes," he answered.

"How long have you studied there?" she asked.

"Too long," he said, with a chuckle. "And not long enough." He smiled, a bit enigmatically.

"Well, I'm pleased to meet you. I was so impressed by my first service there. You have a lovely home."

Cindy asked the young man, "Did Angela take you over to the other wing when you oriented last week?"

"No," he said, turning toward the nurse. "She was planning to, and then there was some kind of emergency."

"A bowel incident, I suppose," Cindy said. "Well, why don't the two of you come this way. I'll show you over there and have you meet some of our chickadees. They're such precious little things. I just love them."

Eileen raised her eyebrows, casting a glance to see if the seminarian was startled at the nurse's way of speaking. He just shrugged his shoulders, and began to follow Cindy down the hall.

Estelle Haney was parked in a wheelchair in front of *Jeopardy!* on the television when Cindy ushered Eileen and the seminarian into the day room on "A" wing.

"Hey, sweetie. There are some volunteers here I want you to meet." She took the handles of Mrs. Haney's chair and turned the woman to face the center of the room. "Were you watching the show?"

"Who is Aaron Burr," Mrs. Haney declared, a moment before a contestant on the set said, "Who is John Wilkes Booth?"

"Sorry," said the game show host. "The correct answer is 'who is Aaron Burr.'"

"Estelle, this is Eileen, and this is Adrian. They're volunteering here on Thursdays. Maybe they're fans of *Jeopardy!* too."

"That body shop owner is beating those two school teachers," Estelle said, and smiled. Her head was listing to one side, apparently from an old stroke that left her neck weak.

"Nice to meet you, Estelle," Adrian said.

"You must be the latest boy from Holy Name," the old woman told him. "I can tell. Corduroys and buttoned shirts. No one else at the college wears them. The Sorenson boy, last year, he explained it to me. You must know him."

"Yes, I do," Adrian said.

"My little bunny here doesn't miss much," Cindy said. "Did you know Estelle was a lawyer? The first woman lawyer in La Crosse County."

"That's fascinating," the seminarian responded.

"She's got it wrong, of course," Estelle said. "I was the first woman lawyer anywhere between St. Paul and Dubuque."

"*Wherever,*" Cindy said. She called to two other ladies ambulating toward the day room. "Margaret. Sophie," she said. "Come meet some folks. These are fresh recruits. Just off the boat."

More than Mrs. Haney, these two ladies seemed to warm to Cindy's cuteness. They smiled broadly, teetering with the cargo of their pocketbooks over to where Eileen and the seminarian stood.

"That was sort of fun," Adrian said to Eileen as they headed down the hall at the end of the evening. "Estelle is quite a character."

"What did she say?" Eileen asked.

"She wants someone to bring her books from the library. Says she's bored silly with these old ladies. While she herself is ninety-six."

"I guess she's a different breed, if she was a lawyer way back when."

"She founded the local League of Women Voters, she'll have you know. She asked me if I could recommend any historical novels," Adrian said.

"You'll find her something," Eileen said. "You've got the whole Assisi library at your disposal, don't you?"

"Yes," he said. "Have you been there yet? They don't have much popular literature. Maybe I can bring her something about politics."

Soon they were out the front door of St. Francis, standing under a large cedar portico supported by pillars of buff stone. Adrian lingered there.

"Will you be here every Thursday?" he asked.

"Yes. It'll be my regular night."

"Great. You said you just came to La Crosse from...."

"A little North Dakota town, called Fort Yates. On the reservation."

"And you taught science there? I was never very strong in science, myself. Just not that interested, I guess. I did the traditional seminary things at Assisi—philosophy, Latin, Greek."

"Did them?" she asked, wondering what he meant.

"I graduated, once. Then I did a year of law school," he said. "Now I'm back, treading water, trying to decide whether to go on to theology."

"Oh, I hope you do," she found herself saying, prematurely. "I mean, we need priests so much."

"The question is whether that includes me, I guess."

"Why wouldn't it?" she asked.

"Oh, I don't know. I could be just a troublemaker. You don't know."

"That seems doubtful," she said. He seemed so clean-cut, and kind. "Are you studying for a diocese?"

"Yes, for Des Moines," he said.

"I haven't met the new bishop there. Is he a nice man?"

"I guess so. My mother likes him because he's conservative, like all of this pope's appointments. Mostly I've dealt with our vocations director, Father Zaino. The bishop came straight from Philadelphia, where he had been an auxiliary. I think he's still adjusting."

"To a rural diocese?" Eileen ventured.

"A rural diocese, Scandinavian farmers, rodeos on Sunday after Mass...."

"I see," she said. "I think he's from an old Italian neighborhood, am I right?"

"Yes, he is. So we're a new part of the world for him. Fr. Zaino says the chancellor went pale when the Knights of Columbus asked the bishop if he could say Mass at the state fair. I guess he figured the bishop would be a fish out of water there."

Eileen laughed. Her first thought about this young man had been right. He was not jokey and awkward, like her teenagers, or even like the freshman seminarians she'd met at breakfast, for that matter. Something had polished him. Surely Fr. Moriarty must be eager to see him at a major seminary.

"And you wouldn't be?" she said to Adrian. "A fish out of water?"

"No, to the contrary. I'm practically a hog in mud. I spent nine years in 4-H, and capped it off winning the state demonstration day when I was seventeen. I showed how to re-cane a chair."

"Did you grow up on a farm?" she asked.

"No. But '4-H ain't all cows and cookin',' as our club T-shirt used to say. I grew up in town. A tiny town, but a town. It was zoned against livestock, with an exception for chickens. It was called Ryder."

"Why did you leave North Dakota?" he asked.

"I inherited my mother's house when she died, and came back to La Crosse to get it ready for sale."

"You're must be a handy person, then."

"A little," she said. "I picked things up, even without 4-H. Lots of years living in old convents—a person doesn't have much choice but to become handy."

"Where is the house?" he asked.

"It's in southwest, by the river."

"Do you know what year it was built?"

"Gosh, I'm not sure. Twenties, maybe. My parents weren't the first owners. I take it you know something about houses."

"My grandfather was a builder—of churches, actually. I guess that's where I got an interest."

"Maybe you can be my consultant," she said. "Left to my own devices, I could lower the property value."

"I'm not that expert," he said. "I just like buildings. Grandpop's father was a stonemason in England. When grandpop came over, he originally farmed with one of his uncles, in the Archbishop Ireland colony at Minneota. But he didn't know how to farm, and pretty soon he left for a job cutting stone in the quarry at Mankato. He worked his way up, to where he was the project foreman on all their church buildings. I'm named for Adrian, Minnesota, and its patron saint. Grandpop built St. Adrian's church when my mother was still a girl, and she always loved the place."

"He cut Mankato stone?" Eileen said. "He may have built this portico."

"No, this is Winona stone. You can tell by the color."

"Oh, of course," she said, smiling at him.

A nurse's aide peered at them through the glass front doors, then left. Night was starting to fall.

"Would you like to go somewhere and get some coffee?" she asked.

He looked at his watch, seeming to consider.

"There's a Bridgeman's over on South Avenue," he said. "What I'd really like is a grilled cheese and a malt."

"Very well, then. Did you drive?"

"No, I'm on my bike. What do you say I meet you there? It's just a few blocks."

In a minute, Adrian was at the bicycle rack crouching over his lock, and Eileen cut across the lawn to her Volkswagen. The air was starting to cool, and Eileen was reminded of the summer evenings of her girlhood, when she and Helen would linger outdoors until their mother would call them in for bed. Boys playing baseball could be heard to shout on a field near the nursing home, and a group of swallows sped by, in search of mosquitoes rising out of the grass.

The waitress at Bridgeman's wore a large button on her uniform urging Eileen to "Ask about our Lollapalooza Sundae." Eileen thought she would pass on that. When it came to Adrian, she wasn't so sure, since he scarfed the halves of his grilled cheese sandwich in three bites each. When did boys stop being so ravenous? He emptied nearly half his malt in one continuous draft on the straw. None of this, however, appreciably slowed his conversation.

"The windows at Holy Name were done by the same art glass company that did Queen of Peace in Austin and St. John the Baptist in Mankato," Adrian was explaining.

Eileen had voiced her admiration for the chapel at the seminary, a topic on which Adrian proved eager to elaborate.

"They're unusual, I guess, in that they show the different vestments of priesthood, rather than pictures of saints or scenes from the life of Christ, like one usually sees," he said. "My favorite is the one depicting the maniple. The bottom of the window reads, 'May I always wear the badge of weeping and of tears.'"

"Why that one?" Eileen asked.

"I don't know. It's hard to put into words. Maybe it's the paradox—in wanting to bear grief. But if you're able to bear grief, then people who suffer can bring theirs to you."

"I see," Eileen said. An unusual young man, this one.

"I suppose that seems morbid," he said. "But I've spent a lot of hours kneeling in that chapel, looking at those windows. And at least some of the time I was thinking about what I was supposed to be thinking about—whether or not I had a calling to be a priest."

"To comfort the afflicted," she said.

"Yes. I just wish I were as confident about the other parts of the calling."

"What in particular?"

Adrian frowned a little. "I wish I could say." He gathered crumbs from his plate on his fingertip, and lifted them to his mouth. Four girls in the next booth were giggling and debating what songs to play on the jukebox.

"How old are you?" Eileen asked, abruptly.

"I turned twenty-four in June," he said. "Why?"

"Just wondering."

The waitress arrived to bus their dishes, and asked if they needed anything more. Adrian assured her he was satisfied, and she slapped a guest check on the table before loading up her arms and gliding back toward the kitchen.

"I may not be going back to religious life, myself," Eileen said. Adrian looked up at her, and nodded that he was listening.

"I got an indult of exclaustration, although the Beckett job is only for a year. I've been increasingly...what could I say...discontent? I never expected to find myself having doubts like this. The two of us might be in places that are similar."

The boy looked at her soberly, and said nothing, probably unsure if he should question her further. She was fifteen years his senior, after all, and a professed religious.

"I don't know what it is. I used to have a lot of confidence that religious life had an intrinsic spirituality to it—that the discipline, and praying and wanting it, were enough. Anymore, I fear you can do all that and still come up empty-handed. That *I quite possibly have*."

"It's uncanny you would put it that way," he said. "I think about hands, often."

"How is that?"

"The idea of spirituality I can relate to is being the hands that hold the wheat, as God blows away the chaff—the wheat being what is sacred, what is saved, what is divine in each of us, and in living day to day. The essential task then is to hold steady, to let go in the right way and hold on in the right way, to be the container God needs one to be. That much I know I can offer. The rest? Well, I don't know what it is. If more is needed, I may not be your guy."

"Hearing you describe it, it sounds like it should be enough," Eileen said.

"I've never gotten the message at Holy Name that it's enough," he said. "It's easy to get focused on what my spirituality is not. It's not 'feeling' the spirit, at least in the way the charismatics talk about it—and they'll be the first to tell you, you don't have any spirituality at all if you don't have what they have...."

"Tell me about it!" she said.

"It's not being pious, or ascetic...."

"You should be thankful to have one image, if it's one you truly believe in," she said.

"It is," said Adrian.

Driving back to her mother's house, Eileen hummed the beginning of some song—a hymn, actually. *For the beauty of the earth, for the glory of the skies, for the love which from our birth over and around us lies, Lord of all to Thee we raise, this our hymn....* She sang the words to herself. She felt invigorated, pleased just to be behind the steering wheel, driving her car from the pool of light under one lamp post to the pool of light under another along the curvy road, like a trout ascending a brook. Why was she elated like this? It must be the prospect of making a friend in this young man. He had said to her, "I'll see you Sunday," as he took his leave from the restaurant. Eileen found herself looking forward to their next meeting enough to feel a bit foolish. But how long had it been since she'd known someone in the same boat as her? They might find a lot to talk about. She didn't really understand his references to dissension and being a troublemaker—but no matter, probably. It was likely he just lacked self-confidence, or came from a troubled family. Some times the brightest ones had no notion of their own worth. Arriving at her mother's house, she was still humming the song. The faint smell of mothballs greeted her as she happily hung her sweater in the coat closet.

-7-

Reverberation

A ritual was performed at entrances to antique shops everywhere. Over time it became almost as familiar to Adrian as dipping fingers into Holy Water at the vestibule of a church. As he walked into the Antiques Marketplace on Main Street in La Crosse this balmy Saturday, it was repeated.

"Anything special you're looking for today?" said the shop owner, lounging in a sofa chair behind the counter.

"No. Just looking," Adrian said.

"Well, you'll know it when you see it," the owner remarked.

That was it. Adrian had played a part in this exchange all across Iowa, southern Minnesota, and southwest Wisconsin, thinking it was meaningless, until finally he came to appreciate what the shop owners knew: they were purveyors of objects that already had a place in the customer's memory, whether the customer knew it or not. Forgotten lines and shapes, colors and textures—smells, even—a whole storehouse of the sensual world resided in these emporia, squatting in former department stores in the centers of small towns, lying nestled in hay lofts strung along the minor roads to Tomah and Hokah, Winona, Waseca, Fort Dodge and Fort Atkinson. (Wasn't that a cookie jar just like Aunt Susan's? Didn't Uncle Saul have a chair just like this?) Over a period of years wandering these places, mostly indifferent to the Red Wing pottery and Eastlake furniture, Adrian gradually discovered the pattern of his own purchases. He learned to skip browsing the booths entirely, as he always found himself at the back of a store, amid the bins of prints and engravings, scanning for tabs that said "local interest" and "architecture." He'd established quite a little collection of such prints in his room—a private gallery of architectural styles and methods—before it dawned on him that his underlying purpose was to lay hold of his grandfather's life, or at least to lay hold of his grandfather's life's work.

It started with fascination for stone buildings in general, until Adrian began to find prints of his Grandpa Jude's actual churches—St. Francis of Assisi in Rochester, the Church of the Blessed Sacrament in Hibbing, Queen of Peace in Albert Lea. He thought it accidental when he discovered the first of these prints and purchased it, yet over time he began to see the method to his own behavior, the real possibility that he might document his grandfather's career with these renderings—even if the motive for doing so still eluded him. Finally, even this broke through. His antique expeditions were quite a habit, and from time to time from the corner of his eye he would catch some form, some image suggestive of something cherished and lost, which on closer look he would find instead to be something ordinary, nothing he actually wanted. Finally, one day in a little shop in Goodview, he stepped into a niche full of old books to find an elderly man stooped in the corner, the back of his tonsured white head turned to Adrian. Adrian felt his breath stolen away for a moment, until the man stood and revealed himself to be just another stranger. Adrian had found the bathroom then, and sat on the toilet lid welling with tears, shocked at the momentary rush he could feel in taking this man to be his Grandpa Jude, returned from the dead.

Jude Heaney had died when Adrian was six, and Adrian's memory of him seemed faint. His mother's version of her father and his legacy was a begrudging one, at best. Depending on which story Eleanor was telling at the moment, Jude was either an annoyance to her, or merely absent. Her mother, on the other hand, Eleanor loved passionately—unnaturally, it sometimes seemed. Alice Heaney survived Jude by twelve years, and the parlor of her Mankato house remained the center of Eleanor's world right up until Alice's death. Even afterward, it seemed the hub around which Eleanor and her sisters moved, their abiding point of reference.

Adrian had gradually discerned his own sense of his grandfather, one that departed substantially from his mother's narratives. It started with his few memories of the man—one of himself sitting on Jude's lap at a table in the kitchen, and another of himself walking in Jude's footsteps on a rainy visit to the quarry, feeling wonder that his grandfather should have carved such a great canyon into the earth. Other than these little snatches, his longing for the man seemed almost to have arisen from nowhere. His mother told Adrian that by the time of his birth Jude was already retired, living with old photographs of his work and stewing in his envy and worry over modern church architects and their use of non-masonry construction. Nevertheless, Adrian fostered his own regard for the man, immune to his mother's dismissals, and skeptical of her certitudes. He thought of Grandpa Jude, in fact, as the person with whom he had the most in common. Perhaps that was something he'd mostly invented himself.

His trip to antique row today had been spurred by his conversation with that nun at the nursing home, Sr. Eileen. She'd indulged his enthusiasm for church architecture rather graciously, taking an interest even in hearing about the interior woodwork at Holy Name, the screens and stations and the wood-coffered ceiling. He thought of buying her a print of something local—a picture or even a postcard showing Holy Trinity, her childhood parish, if it were possible to find one. The thought was inappropriate, actually, since he hardly knew the woman. He must be feeling pretty isolated even to be thinking of it. He should make a call to his parents and see how his cat was adjusting to living at their house again.

Something about his current status at the seminary seemed very odd. His assigned partner for night prayer on Wednesday was a newcomer, Alan Hennessey, who managed to make Adrian feel quite old. Alan was obsessed with how he was being sized up by Fr. Moriarty, an effect freshman year had on most everyone. The loss of all personal control seized a guy's attention—it had to be given credit for that. Adrian wanted to say the impossible to Alan, which was *just relax*. Alan was in this for the whole ride, from minor sem to major sem, and on to diaconate and ordination, if only he chose to take it. How could Adrian know this? He just did. Alan was the right type—obedient, smart enough, naturally possessed of tact—a sure bet for priesthood if he wanted it. Yet Adrian would never convince Alan of this, even if he tried. It was a commonly remarked phenomenon, among upperclassmen at Holy Name—how obvious these things became when they applied to younger cohorts. But within one's own? No one ever felt sure. The head prefect wrestled with traces of doubt, while even the hopeless among them maintained some hope of ordination. And every man had to decide for himself when and if he should call it quits, what portion of discouragement was too much to bear. "Relax, Alan," he wanted to call after the guy, seeing him race off to class after drying the breakfast dishes. When it came to the prospects for his own progression, Adrian sensed that the ball was finally in his own court, that Moriarty would not prevent it. Moriarty hadn't been compelled, after all, to let Adrian come back to Holy Name. Having such knowledge set Adrian apart from the group of other seminarians this time around. Did he miss feeling under siege, like Alan and the others? For the sake of the camaraderie, perhaps. But he found himself looking forward to more conversations with the exclaustrated nun. To acknowledge this seemed like knowing he was no longer a child, was truly emancipated. He felt pretty good about that. He continued to flip through a stack of engravings from the turn of the century, finding nothing that really interested him. There was a certain comfort, always, in the act of looking.

"Maybe another day," the owner said, as Adrian left the store.

Adrian was on the schedule as lector for Mass on Sunday. He'd delayed looking over the readings until the last moment, and now he checked Ezekiel 37:1-14 for any unfamiliar names he'd have to pronounce. Thankfully, there were none. It was a simple text from the prophet, actually—the allegory of the dry bones—and one he found captivating, now that he re-read it: *Dry bones, hear the word of Yahweh. I am going to make the breath enter you, and you will live. I shall put sinews on you, I shall make flesh grow on you, I shall cover you with skin and give you breath, and you will live....* * Adrian would take pleasure in delivering it.

Watching the processional come up the aisle from his spot in the sanctuary, Adrian noted Sr. Eileen sitting in the rear of the chapel, behind the faces of the seminarians. The freshmen were seated together in a group, while the upperclassmen were spread throughout the pews and the ranks of the *schola cantorum*. He felt a bit anxious, suddenly, about reading today. Would he breathe deep enough to project his voice? Or to sustain it for whole sentences? Adrian usually enjoyed the fact that liturgy brought the energies of the seminary into intense focus. It seemed odd that he should be nervous now. Perhaps being chosen to read this early in the year compounded his usual sense of being scrutinized. After the processional, Fr. Herman completed the *Kyrie* and *Gloria* and the opening prayer in short order, and before Adrian knew it, he was on.

Milling in the hallway after Mass, the seminarians were enjoying a somewhat celebratory mood while they waited for the breakfast bell to ring. Adrian had only a few moments to store

---

The Jerusalem Bible.

the lectionary and catch Eileen's attention before he had to join his peers moving to the refectory.

"Sister," he said, coming up behind her. She was talking to Alan Hennessey near the carved chapel doors.

"Hi," she said, upon turning and seeing him. "Very nice job."

"Oh, thanks," he said.

"I was just saying to Alan how much I enjoyed the homily. Is Fr. Herman the assistant rector?"

"No, that would be Fr. Daimler," Adrian said. "Fr. Herman has too much of a sense of humor." The bell sounded.

"We can't stay long," Alan said. "Moriarty waits for the last sem to take his place before he'll say grace."

"We'll get you invited to breakfast again before long," Adrian said. "And I'll see you Thursday?"

"Sure," Eileen answered.

Adrian counted on Carol being in on a Sunday afternoon, unless she had a weekend shift at the hospital. She was indeed home when he called.

"Hey, kid."

"Hi," she said. "I didn't expect it to be you."

"Yes, it's me. I thought I'd call for the low down on the family gossip."

"Yeah, right. I am the family gossip," she said. "You haven't heard?"

"No, I haven't. Does it have to do with your Presbyterian?" he asked.

"Yes—I finally told Mom about him," Carol said with a sigh.

"And what did she say?"

"What do you suppose she said? 'There's no hurry, now. You're really too young to be serious.' I mean, who's ever said that to a twenty-six-year-old? The Victorians, even? Is she for real?"

"You know she doesn't want to come right out and say it, that a Protestant isn't good enough," he said.

"She will to Beth, knowing that Beth will tell me."

"She didn't! Really?"

76

"Yes! He's a resident in radiology, for cripe's sake," Carol said. "What does she want? I can't marry a priest, after all."

"Now, I'm sure there must be a nice Catholic proctologist or something around the hospital, Carol. One of those guys with a pocket protector full of pens in the front of his shirt. You just haven't given any of them a chance."

"Oh thanks, Mom. It's such a treat talking to you."

"Seriously, now," he said. "You aren't going to let her stop you, are you?"

"I don't know...."

"Just go for it. It'll prepare her for the bigger shocks later on."

"And she should just be grateful I'm expanding her horizons? I guess you'll point that out to her," Carol said.

"That should come from Charlie, actually," he said.

"Charlie's help is all I need!"

"What's he done now?" Adrian asked.

"Nothing new. He's just always so tactless."

"And you notice how she's kicked *him* out of the house," Adrian said.

"But Charlie's Charlie. The rules are different for him."

"So, use him to your advantage."

"You're so irreverent, I can't believe you."

"Yes. It is the cross I bear," he agreed. "But you know it's only with you I talk this way."

"I find that hard to believe," Carol said. "But really.... She and I are going to have a lot of uncomfortable scenes. I'm not sure it's worth it. I'm really not trying to make trouble."

"Well, it's easy for me to talk, I suppose. I only date Jesus, after all."

"Gad!" she said. "You're hopeless. Do all the seminarians talk that way?"

"No, not really."

"I didn't think so." The buzzer on her clothes dryer sounded. "Can you hold on while I take the laundry out to fold?" she asked.

"Sure thing," he said.

That evening, Adrian got out his Greek dictionary and started reading Euripedes' *Medea*. His old adviser, Dr. Flood, had convinced him that if he were coming back to La Crosse he should take advantage of the tuition reciprocity Assisi enjoyed with Carleton College in order to do an independent study with the renowned classicist at that school, Professor Gundersen. Tomorrow Adrian would make his first trip up to Northfield to meet with the man. Over the phone, they had agreed that *Medea* was the work to start with, so tonight Adrian got to work construing the first lines spoken by the nurse at the beginning of episode one, just as a warm up. By the time he'd wended his way through the summation of events leading to the present action, of Jason's quest for the Golden Fleece and the killing of Pelias by his daughters, Adrian was about ready to wrap it up for the night. He looked up the word *philei* at the end of nurse's speech and finally ferreted the correct meaning: Medea's sons had no thought of their mother's troubles, for young minds *are not used to* dwelling on grief. *Nea gar phrontis ouk algein philei*. Adrian marked his page and reached to shut off the lamp on his nightstand.

8

Row the Boat Ashore

The last time Eileen lived in La Crosse had been in the middle of the '60s. The population of the town was 24,000 then and declining, because of a general exodus from the town. Young people, especially, left in great numbers for better prospects somewhere else. No one anticipated—or could wait around for— the later growth booms at the state university or in the medical industry that would redound with employment opportunities. Eileen was no exception, just well ahead of the curve, when she departed the place at the start of her teens. Her schoolmates at Holy Trinity Elementary would eventually end up in places like the Twin Cities, Madison, or farther-flung capitals. Eileen knew of only a couple who were still around, one who worked at the brewery, and one who had his father's refrigeration business. If she were to run into them in the post office or the grocery, she supposed they would remember her. But escaping into the Church—now, that was not a common thing, at least for girls. A significant number of boys, of course, would eventually enter the seminary because of the Viet Nam war and the draft. But there was no selective service to propel women into the convent, and furthermore, no great emphasis placed by the Church itself. The director of men's vocations had a prominent office at the chancery, while women's vocations were left to the independent efforts of the several orders in the area.

Eileen was not the least concerned at the time she took it up with whether or not her vocation was popular, or even seen as consequential. Prior to sixth grade, she herself had no vision of her future at all, beyond wrangling with her fretful mother through junior high school over whether or not she and her sister, Helen, could go on overnight field trips with their classmates. Any notion of a religious vocation was surely fleeting, although Eileen and Helen had never talked much about boys or marriage. That was only because their mother was herself a widow. Eileen's father, Frank, had been stricken by a neuromuscular condition, later diagnosed as Lou Gehrig's Disease, when Eileen was an infant, and had died in a nursing home when she was three. She didn't remember him, and knew that her mother had kept her away from the nursing home and eventually the funeral, fearing what effect they'd have.

Helen remembered him. She would sneak his shirts out of the attic and wear them around the house, along with his boots from the basement, at times when their mother left the girls at home alone. This was not often, as Brigid did not have a job. She mostly made do with her husband's railroad pension and social security, and took in alterations work she did at the house. Helen also loved the garden, which had been their father's. It was the one thing their mother preserved intact from that era. The roses and bleeding heart had actually come from Frank's mother, in Milwaukee, many years before. Evidently Brigid saw these as the only part of an O'Rourke legacy worth preserving, because she never took Helen and Eileen to see their grandmother on that side, and seldom wrote to her. Brigid had married into the O'Rourkes late in life, and everyone had been surprised when she bore the two girls in the middle of her forties as she did. She did not have a strong connection to Frank's family before he left her a widow. Grandpa O'Rourke, like Frank, had died fairly young, before Eileen's mother had gotten a chance to meet him.

Brigid had bounced back from Frank's death, finding a life for herself in the altar society, in keeping house and in handmaking her two daughters' clothes. She carried on more or less as the mother Eileen had always known. Yet it must have taxed her more than was obvious, for when the next calamity happened, she simply never recovered.

Helen was Brigid's pride and joy, and her favored child. Helen cheerfully greeted the birth of her younger sister when she was three, or so they were told, and had bravely accepted the loss of her father, holding to the certainty that he was living with God in heaven. She was smart and popular with her classmates—this Eileen had seen herself—and was always full of enterprise when it came to social opportunities or learning adventures. South La Crosse lacked a Girl Scout troop until Helen persuaded the lay science teacher who lived around the block to start one, and it was Helen who decided they should set out to learn the names of all the native plants they could gather on their camping trips to Barron's Island and along the Root River.

Helen developed leukemia as a high school freshman, and died before finishing sophomore year, with Eileen still in sixth grade. This funeral Eileen had attended, and along with the details of the illness, it was burned into her memory. She remembered the trips back and forth to the Mayo Clinic, the attempts at chemotherapy, and the inexorable dissipation of Helen's energy and curiosity, even the dissolution of her very flesh. Eileen remembered Helen, wrapped in a woven blanket and sitting in the rocking chair in the front room, looking like she was being swallowed slowly by the chair. A week later she would be gone, as if the chair had finally gulped and taken her.

The funeral was an utterly alien event to a twelve-year-old. A previously insular world was suddenly invaded by neighbors, all laying some claim to pain that was incontrovertibly private. How could Eileen have anticipated, at her age, the rituals of food-bringing and poem-sending and facile comparing of her tragedy to others that would come at the illness' awful end? She still thought of it with abhorrence, probably more so because her mother *could not* share with Eileen *her* pain.

It was as if whatever contact they'd had, before this, ended absolutely with Helen's death. To Brigid's view, Eileen's pain was nothing like her own, if she considered it at all. Brigid was inconsolable, and in turn unconsoling. She took to the rocking chair herself for months on end, holding the old blanket Helen had used, in the way a toddler clings to his even as it disintegrates into rags. Eileen coped by trying to carry on for both of them, urging her mother to return to her usual routine—even by the slightest increments—and cooking meals, which her mother wouldn't eat. These efforts only added futility to Eileen's anguish. When Brigid refused even to go see her doctor at the Skemp Clinic, Eileen gave up, to a large degree, and found a way to move forward alone. She relied on familiar habits, excelling at her schoolwork and cultivating piety in the systematic ways the Church provided, with novenas and rosaries and the spiritual and corporal works of mercy, fabricating hope out of the promise of rewards in a life to come. Finally, in eighth grade, she went on a visit to the Bonaventures' convent in Eau Claire. She found a sense of momentum and purpose in the life the nuns lived there, and decided she would go join them.

Was it possible to will one's heart never to mend? That was how Eileen saw her mother's life. Her mother had chosen to be crushed by her tragedies, and Eileen's choice was to be unlike Brigid. Eileen had been out of the house and busy doing something ever since the day she went to join the convent. She had never looked back.

Brigid did carry on, eventually, resuming attendance at the altar society and being coaxed by Mrs. Seaman to take up sewing again. The two of them had little projects—a quilting circle, and green stamp books, which they saved up until they could get a new sewing machine together, the commercial type with serger and seam binder and button hole attachments. Clearly, to Elsie, Brigid had remained a friend. Eileen knew that she might exaggerate her mother's collapse, might be uncharitable, finding fault with her as she did. Nevertheless, to Eileen it would always seem her mother taught her many things early in childhood, and after Helen's death had lost her hold on sanity, could only teach Eileen through example what not to do.

Taking up residence in her mother's house, Eileen found herself springing into a flurry of animation—how else was she to cope with the sad emptiness of this place? She drew up plans for how to rebuild the stairs and marked the cracks in the interior plaster that would have to be chinked and refilled. She pruned back the growth on all the perennials around the yard, and generally set about being even more active than usual. She looked through the fall schedules at Assisi and UW-La Crosse for a late afternoon or evening course she could take. She inquired at the diocesan offices about volunteer opportunities, and chose from the list she was given the names of a nursing home and the Franciscan Hospice Program. Life was about being out there, living, which was something Eileen knew how to do. Heaven forbid she let this lonely house take away her will to live, the way it seemed to have taken her mother's.

This particular morning dawned without a cloud, and Eileen found herself feeling buoyant as she made her way to the college campus near downtown. As it turned out, Assisi offered a course on medical ethics on Wednesday evenings. Eileen was on her way to see Professor Brannigan, the course instructor, about adding the class at the last minute. His door was open when she found it, although there were two men conversing in the office as she came in. One sat in the desk chair and the other was near him, half-sitting on a corner of the desk. When they saw Eileen, the man perched on the desk stood up.

"Dr. Edward Brannigan?" Eileen inquired.

The man in the chair smiled and nodded. "Yes?"

"I'm Eileen O'Rourke. Sister Eileen O'Rourke. I came to ask about your class. In medical ethics."

"Sister.... Would that be...Franciscan?"

"No, Bonaventure. Out of Eau Claire. I teach biology and chemistry, this year at Beckett High School. I was hoping to pick this up as a continuing ed student."

Brannigan rifled through papers on his desk for a class list.

"I think there are a couple of openings in that. This is Ernie Jenkins, from the English department."

"Hello," Eileen said, extending her hand.

Jenkins took it, tepidly. "Hello," he answered, and turned toward the door. "I'll see you, then?" he said to Brannigan.

"Yes. Saturday. At eight?"

"Yes," Jenkins said, and departed, directing nothing more toward Eileen.

"So, are you new in town?" Brannigan asked her.

"Yes and no. I grew up here. I'm here covering for a teacher at Beckett who's on sabbatical."

"We get a lot of Beckett students here," Brannigan said, "especially in nursing, I think. Their preparation in science is generally good."

"Well, I can't take credit for that," Eileen said. "I just got there."

"So they pulled you in from the prairies somewhere, did they?"

"From North Dakota. The Standing Rock Indian Reservation."

"Fascinating," he said. "I've been looking for a contact out there. We send a group of students in our 'Contemporary Issues' class up to Minneapolis every winter, to experience living on the street for a night with the homeless. I've been looking for other opportunities like that. I've often thought the reservation might be ideal."

"Well, I've been there for a night, and for six years. Maybe you can give me credit for 'relevant life experience.'"

"Ah, but in your line of work," he said, "it can't count as extra credit. It's all included in the vows, isn't it?"

"I guess that's fair enough," Eileen said, enjoying the man's ease with her, the bit of insider's humor. "So, are you going to sign my add slip, to let me *earn* these credits?"

"Sure thing. Give it here," he said. He hunted through a cup full of pens for one that would write.

"How long have you been at Assisi?" Eileen asked.

"The Franciscans and I go back seventeen years. I came here fresh out of my doctorate at Loyola. I've been busy teaching 'Intro to Moral Theory' ever since," he said. He found the right instrument at last and applied his signature to the paper. "They're a good bunch. Hearts are in the right place."

"But...?" Eileen said.

"But...nothing," Brannigan said. "You'll hear nothing but unqualified praise from me." He was a diplomatic sort, apparently.

"Is it just that you don't share their religious zeal, then?" Eileen asked.

Brannigan cocked his head ever so slightly. "You're very attentive, aren't you?" he said. "That's excellent. I always look forward to a student in class who will keep me on my toes."

"It's just natural curiosity, I think," said Eileen.

"Yes, natural, but uncommon."

"So, I'll be seeing you?" she said, turning to leave.

"Wednesday. 6:30 sharp," he said, clucking his tongue twice against his teeth.

Elsie put a placemat down in front of Eileen and patted it smooth before setting a teacup and saucer on it. It was what a ladies' page writer would have called "a riot of color"—pieced together of thirty-two scraps of cloth, each one gathered around a Mason jar lid. It was the kind of handiwork that very well might have been Eileen's pastime had she not taken her detour into religious life. With alacrity Elsie poured boiling water from a monstrous kettle into a flecked china pot, and brought it to the table, beaming.

"Red rose is O.K., I hope?" she said.

"Yes, fine," Eileen answered.

"Never mind my sewing. It's taken over the kitchen since I've started doing my cutting on this table."

Indeed the fabrics had encroached, somewhat fantastically, on Elsie's downstairs space. Portable clotheslines next to the walls were draped with swaths of fabric, woolens on one, cotton prints on another, pastel flannels on a third.

"When the children move away, you never know what an old lady will find to stand in," Elsie said. "I've been cutting patches for my own quilting circle, and also for the woman who comes to teach at the Lutheran Home. That's who the flannels are for. She likes to have the residents making baby blankets—I think because the flannel is softer for those old ladies to work. Polished cotton slips through their fingers too much."

Elsie was able to regard the ladies in the Lutheran Home as "old," and herself as something short of that. It came down to distinctions like this—not only of who lived alone, but who could still manipulate broadcloth. Elsie bobbed the tea ball in and out of the pot a few times, checking the strength of the brew.

"Every Monday and Wednesday I go there for the afternoon," she said.

"Are you still picking the bins at the Salvation Army?" Eileen asked.

"Yes, and other sources. I get around, you know. The woman at Penney's and the one at the fabric store in the mall both save me a few remainders. And I get the leftovers of what people donate to the poor box at Holy Trinity—Bess Meier tosses a few things my way. They won't let me volunteer, myself. They say they can't trust me not to tear the wearable clothes into rags. It's the truth, of course," Elsie said.

Elsie suddenly thought of an idea. "Can I give you some of my jam, with toast?" she asked, hopping up to fetch a jar.

"Sure. I'd love some, Elsie," Eileen said.

Elsie disappeared through the door to the cellar for a moment, and Eileen heard a shuffling of jars on the ledge beside the stairs before Elsie reappeared, with a jar of pale green jam.

"The gooseberries were very sweet this year—I guess because we had a lot of rain," Elsie said.

Elsie sliced bread and put it in the toaster, then pried the lid from the jam. "Father Alvarez said to greet you. I asked him to say a Mass for your mother this week."

Should she know Fr. Alvarez? Eileen asked herself. Perhaps he had been a concelebrant at her mother's funeral. She found herself wondering if Father Hurley was even the pastor at Holy Trinity any more, or if he had been moved since her last visit.

Elsie, for her part, picked up this conversation as if Eileen had never been away.

"I think he'll say the Mass Saturday evening, if you want to go. He was saying the Wednesday Mass for the Stanczak twins," Elsie said.

It had always been a bit like this, with Elsie assuming Eileen's familiarity with her world, and knowing more in turn about what Eileen was doing than Eileen could account for. Elsie would comment on someone like Fr. Zimmerman, and Eileen would wonder, *Did I tell mother about him?* If she had, it had not seemed to engage her mother's interest. And yet there he would be, alive in Elsie's imagination.

Elsie waited for the toaster to pop up, knife in hand.

"Do you know how to adjust the humidity on one of these new furnaces?" Elsie asked. "I can't figure the thing out. I probably shouldn't have let them add it. But *salesmen*, you know. I just want to turn it down a bit."

"I can take a look at it," Eileen said, uncertain of how the furnace was even a concern, in August.

Soon the toast was presented on a plate, and Eileen poured tea into two cups on the table. Elsie took a wedge of toast for herself, but after a single bite rested it on the side of her saucer and sprang up from her chair. She continued to putter as she talked, interrupting her own sentences, if necessary, when her voice went out of range in another room. It was the way Eileen remembered Elsie talking to Bud, her husband of thirty-odd years, until his death—an everyday way of being in someone's company and still getting business done.

"Did you know Elouise Jackson died?" Elsie said. "It's probably for the best. She had that cancer for so long, she'd wasted down to eighty pounds. And Agatha Beniek, too. You may not remember her. She stopped coming to church when her husband died. Pretty soon I may be the only old-timer in the parish still alive."

Elsie rummaged in the refrigerator for something, sending a grapefruit rolling across the kitchen floor in the process. She picked it up, rinsed it, and sliced it into quarters, as if that were what she'd gone seeking all along.

"I shouldn't even buy these grapefruit, they're so expensive," Elsie said, biting into a piece. "But they still *agree* with me, which is more than I can say for a lot of foods."

"You can afford the little splurge, can't you?" Eileen asked.

"Oh, yes. I don't know what I'm saving my money for."

Elsie prattled on. Watching the old neighbor engage in timeless habits—plucking dead leaves from the wandering Jew growing on her window sill, bringing her copy of *GRIT* in from the mailbox, punching down a pan of bread dough rising near the stove—Eileen started to feel a kind of sadness, moving all through her, like some echo of failure. She watched Elsie's movements and for a moment felt how much she had really missed this woman all these years, years she had spent in the world, failing to create any other home for herself. She'd missed Elsie Seaman, whose Christmas cards she many times hadn't got around to answering.

"Elsie, let's take a look at that humidifier now," Eileen said, rising out of her seat and swigging the last of the tea in her cup.

"O.K.," said Elsie. The old woman untied her apron and hung it on a hook by the stove.

Back home that afternoon, Eileen got a measuring tape, pad, and pencil, and went out to get specific lumber dimensions on the wooden back steps. Could she find boards in the right dimensions to restore them identically? Perhaps she could simply re-use these vertical posts. The longer she looked at it, the more she began to reconsider whether the whole thing truly had to go. Most of the deck boards were loose, but the joists weren't failing.

Maybe her plan to rebuild them was unnecessary, and too ambitious—a diversion, even, from the really important tasks at hand. She could get in her own way at times, with all of her list-making.

In the house now, Eileen washed her face with a washcloth at the downstairs sink, and decided it was time to call the principal at Beckett High School, just to touch base. Lifting the hand set on the living room phone, she saw that the receiver had a tiny card inserted, with telephone numbers written on it. They were still in her mother's script: just four names, although there was room for as many as ten. Fire, police, Elsie, Eileen. And then blank spaces.

9

Second Look

The cafeteria at Assisi College covered the whole second floor of the student center, and the tables on either side looked out on the sunny streets below. Adrian deliberately avoided a mass of sophomore and junior seminarians and their coterie, who typically gathered along the north wall. The type of person on campus who fell into being a seminary groupie had always given Adrian a slight case of the willies. Most of these hangers-on were girls who dressed in sweatshirts with "Precious Moments" figures and other juvenalia on them. (Adrian expected they would dress that way for the next two decades, as if someone had cued them to go through life as permanent schoolchildren.) They would join the seminarians in taking Religious Studies 101, Fr. Daimler's introductory theology course, and meet the sems in the library before dinner to get help with the slightly confessional essays Daimler encouraged his students to write. They'd cultivate "safe" crushes on the celibate seminarians, and their crises of infatuation, coming and going, would be the subject of furtive discussions and late-night phone calls to each other. ("I'm so confused. I think he'd be a really *super* priest. But I *like* him.") If heterosexuality in general held little interest for Adrian, this permutation of it horrified him. His abhorrence undoubtedly stemmed from fear that he might be anything like the young men at the center of all this attention—who were more or less stalling for time at the seminary, and would eventually drop out to take up real dating. At the very least, Adrian could choose not to sit with them at lunch.

His group of guys, now gone, had hung in a crowd near the coffee counter, drawn partly by the drive to compete with each other and partly by the need to commiserate. Adrian recognized similar clusters of sems dotting the cafeteria now, but knew he didn't really belong with any of them—he'd passed his course in Modern Philosophy several semesters ago, and would hardly blend in to a discussion of what essays to expect on the mid-term. There were tables of frat boys and sorority girls, and contingents of grizzled blonde hockey players, speaking whatever dialect it was hockey players spoke. Adrian spent an uncomfortable moment standing there, without a destination.

He eventually joined a table filled mostly with faculty, near the south wall of windows. The ones Adrian knew best were Dr. Shelbe, and next to him one of the junior literature professors, Thad Benson. Fr. Keenan often joined them, although he wasn't there today. Keenan, Adrian knew, viewed this lunch gathering as part of his educational mission, a place to draw certain bright students into the intellectual life of the college. Adrian generally hadn't joined them in the past, despite repeated invitations. He'd felt it would be disloyal to the seminary in some way. In retrospect, that seemed a pretty foolish idea. Today Adrian took a seat next to Molly Powichroski, a classmate of his who'd taken a job in the dean of students office after graduation and was still at Assisi, looking for her own place to fit in.

"Hi, Adrian," she said, as he scooted his tray onto the table beside hers.

"Hey, Molly."

"I heard about your coming back," she said, "from Paul Nice."

"I'm back alright. How are things in the dean's office?"

"The new dean is cool. Kind of an old hippie, actually. We get along."

"An old hippie," said Thad Benson, mimicking a toke. "Yeah, dude."

Molly swatted him on the arm.

The rest of the group had been in the thick of debate prior to Adrian's arrival, and barely missed a beat on his account.

Brother Phillip, from the theology faculty, was speaking. "The view of America taken by Rome is based on this tiny minority of reactionaries, who write letters to the curia more often than the moderates in the Church. The mainstream isn't indignant at the National Conference of Catholic Bishops, and it isn't writing over there to complain."

"So what do you advocate?" asked Thad, sitting next to his fellow literature professor. "That the American bishops should get proactive in Curran's defense—that they should persuade the moderate and liberal lay people to write letters in his support to Rome?"

"By all means!" said Brother Phillip. "Be a little political. You've got to play the curia's game by the curia's rules. Those guys over there are not shepherds of flocks, they're a lot of jackals. And if you shun their methods, they'll simply use them against you, unopposed."

"Well," said Jim Coughlin, the chairman of the political science department, at the other end of the table, "when the pope reprimanded that Brazilian theologian—what's his name? The Franciscan. *Alphonso Boff*—the Brazilian cardinals went straight to Rome and took him to task for it. They played every card they had. And in the end the pope lifted the sanctions."

"Yes. Exactly," said Verna Luckritz, one of the philosophy professors. "The national conferences don't have to take this sort of thing lying down." She was the hard-edged, wry type. Adrian admired her, and had taken her seminar in existentialism. "Good grief," she continued, "Hans Kung. Joseph Curran. Edward Schillebeeckx. Pretty soon, what theologians will be left, except for a couple of Polish Thomists?"

Adrian understood the discussion they were having. It was prompted by the charges of doctrinal error being brought against a Dutch theologian, Schillebeeckx, by the Congregation for the Doctrine of the Faith. For the past couple of years this pope had been on a roll, making all the liberal theologians knuckle under with threats of excommunication. Americans were preparing for one of their own, Joseph Curran, to get the same treatment.

"Where did you read that, about the Brazilian cardinals?" asked Dr. Shelbe, whose doggedly romantic view of the Catholic Church was once again under assault.

"In a column in the *National Catholic Reporter*," Coughlin said. "The Brazilians were willing to withdraw their financial support from Rome, if need be. So Rome listened."

"I read that article, actually," Verna said. "More than the financial threat, I think they persuaded John Paul II that Boff was *not* divergent from the larger Brazilian Church. That he was mainstream."

"You politicians," said Shelbe. "I don't know about you—any of you."

"So what's really at stake here?" asked Verna, spreading peanut butter on her wheat toast. "That's what puzzles me. Is it really truth that concerns them? If not, then why bother with the censure in the first place?"

"I think it's very clear, that if you silence all dissent, power accrues centrally, to Rome," said Coughlin. "Why wouldn't Rome seek that? These are not nice boys, who will share their toys if they don't have to. It's about power for its own sake."

"I don't think we have to be that cynical," said Thad.

"Why can't everyone just get along?" said Molly. "I think they're all immature." Molly might hang out with the brothers and priests on the faculty, but such a discussion taxed her patience. She was less of an intellectual than a shameless flirt, and here at the table she found the presence of a clerical title not so much an obstacle as an irresistible challenge. She was known to have actually succeeded in seducing one of the brothers who worked in the computer center during junior year.

"Any less cynical," said Brother Phillip, "and before we know it we'll end up like teams of plodding oxen." He mimicked a docile animal, hooves lifted and head cowed.

This was not the kind of conversation Adrian was used to having back at Holy Name, to say the least. He wondered if he might be seen here as someone conspicuously in league with the hierarchy, but the group didn't behave that way. They munched their salads and proffered their opinions happily. Adrian sipped his milkshake and said not a word.

The rec room in the basement at Holy Name was hung incongruously with wallpaper in a nautical theme of starfish and ships. Kevin Meade, one of the junior seminarians, was dancing to Simon and Garfunkel on the stereo, singing along to "At The Zoo."

Kevin had been in Adrian's room to borrow his Cassell's Latin Dictionary, and had taken the opportunity to thumb through Adrian's album collection as well. Now the two of them were in the rec room, having already listened to *Wednesday Morning 3 A.M.* and worked their way nearly through the *Bookends* album. Kevin thought it was cool that Adrian was in possession of such ancient fare, and couldn't wait to listen to them. Adrian remembered Fr. Neimeier, the priest of his childhood, the one who gave him his First Communion, singing these songs at a parish festival one summer Sunday long ago. Ryder was a mission church of the parish at Fort Dodge, entrusted by the pastor there to the young Fr. Neimeier, perhaps contrary to the bishop's better judgment. The long-haired Fr. Neimeier rode a motorcycle, on which he always packed his guitar, ready for any lull when he could strike up an impromptu sing-along. It was Fr. Neimeier who first introduced Adrian, all of six years old, to the songs of Simon and Garfunkel, and it was at a parish festival between Adrian's second and third grade years that Neimeier eventually pulled out "At the Zoo." Adrian remembered as if it were yesterday the delectation he felt in hearing the mischievous priest sing about the zookeeper, so very fond of rum.

Adrian propped his feet up on the arm of the sofa and watched Kevin raise his arms and sway to the rhythm of the song. He thought of himself as a child, bopping from foot to foot in front of Fr. Neimeier, perched with his guitar on a folding chair in the school gym between the cake walk ladies and the high school boys lined up for the free-throw toss, and he felt a sudden surge of happiness to be back at Holy Name.

"They are *so* cool," said Kevin. "Did you really sing these songs at Mass, after Vatican II?"

"Oh, I think it was only 'Bridge Over Troubled Water' that got sung at Mass," Adrian said. "And I remember hearing 'One Tin Soldier' a lot."

"Was that Simon and Garfunkel?" asked Kevin.

"Oh, no, that was Jinx Dawson, of Coven," Adrian said.

"How do you know that stuff?"

"I don't know. Where were you during those years? It's not like I'm that much older than you."

"I was at the Cathedral parish in Dubuque," Kevin said. "We never went in for that sort of thing."

"Then you lost out, guy," said Adrian.

Kevin grinned and gyrated.

When Adrian and Kevin made their way back upstairs to bed with the albums under their arms, the hallway on the first floor was dark except for a light on the bulletin board. A fresh square of white paper captured the light beaming down on the otherwise empty expanse of cork, a sign which by now was familiar to both of them. As they approached it, the bottom of Adrian's stomach fell.

"After prayerful reflection," it began, as it always would, "Aloysius Lopez has decided to discontinue studies for the priesthood. He will leave the Holy Name Community on Tuesday morning. Please remember him in your prayers."

So it was that the first of a new crop perished. Adrian and Kevin shared a glance. Neither of them commented on Louie's decision.

"Good night," Kevin said, glumly, handing Adrian back his albums.

96

"Good night," said Adrian, watching Kevin disappear into the stairwell.

Adrian lay in bed, trying in vain to get to sleep. He couldn't get the notice on the bulletin board off his mind. Louie had seemed unable to relinquish anything in order to become a part of Holy Name. It was clear to Adrian that he himself would relinquish sex, that in this regard he would live by the bargain that was struck. But had he ever relinquished his rebelliousness? He was aware that he'd left Holy Name the first time for a lot of the wrong reasons. Had there been any right ones? Holy Name seemed more benign to him this time around, less ominous than he'd remembered it, and a guy like Louie seemed merely silly, and impatient.

A song from one of the albums kept going through his mind, infectiously. The sweet voice of Art singing about innocence, and confidences. Preserve your memories. They're all you have.

The Hour of Our Need

"Let me get into that dresser drawer," Estelle Haney said to Eileen. "I've got some clippings in there in a scrap book, I'd like to show you."

She positioned her wheelchair to the side, so she could pull the drawer out. The contents of her bureau were atypical for a resident at St. Francis Home; there were no afghans or crochet in there, only notebooks and letters and dried-up pens, newspapers and paperback books.

"Here it is," she said, wobbling a bit as she lifted the book onto her lap. "I want to show you the clippings from the Beaudry trial. Only rape case tried in La Crosse County Court in four decades. I won it at the last minute because a bailiff in the courtroom recognized the defendant, and brought his wife in to contest the man's alibi." Mrs. Haney paged through the book, then pointed an atrophied finger at the first in a series of yellowed clippings. The headline read *Trempeleau Man Indicted*.

"He claimed he'd never been in the bar in Holmen that night, and he got his relatives all to lie for him, to say he'd been somewhere else all evening. But the bailiff's wife remembered seeing him there. She'd been to that bar only once in five years, to celebrate her wedding anniversary, and remembered the date precisely," said Mrs. Haney. "Nailed him, we did. I thought she might be in danger for her life, after showing the Beaudry clan to be a lot of liars in front of the whole county like that, and sending Gil Beaudry off to jail for twenty years. But she didn't care. For me, I guess that's when my reputation as a ball buster got started." She grasped the corner of the page and turned it. "I hope my language doesn't offend you—I've never been one to tailor it for religious folk."

"It's fine on my account," Eileen said. She could see Estelle got quite a lot of enjoyment out of her reputation, whatever term it went by.

"See... 'Assistant State's Attorney Mrs. Estelle Haney opened arguments on Wednesday, with an account by the victim of the alleged assault in an automobile outside Germano's Road House....'"

Eileen read the lines of type over Estelle's shoulder.

"You must have been very courageous," Eileen offered.

"Me? Achh," Estelle protested. "That girl, now, there's the brave one. She couldn't have been more than fifteen. And Gil Beaudry was a big tower of a man, six-foot-five and two-hundred-some, with a snort like a bull hoofing the ground. The bailiff's wife, she was full grown, older than Gil, even, but still just a slight little thing, wearing a dress in the single sizes. A man ever hit her he'd break her in half."

"But not you?" Eileen asked.

"Nah. Whatever man thought of hitting me thought better of it, I guess. Rumor was I was a better shot with a pistol than any man in the Bar Association. Truth be told, I'd never even picked up a gun. I wasn't Agnes Vinson, after all."

"Who was Agnes Vinson?" Eileen asked.

"This old pioneer from out toward Coon Valley. She kept a pet bullsnake under the porch of her house to keep the mice away. Rode roundup with her men every spring, and cussed with the best of them. Now there was a woman no one dared cross. My mother used to threaten me, saying I'd end up like Agnes if I didn't watch my ways. Agnes was my heroine, actually."

There was a soft knock on the door, and Adrian poked his head in.

"I thought I heard you in here," he said. "You're missing *Wheel of Fortune*, don't you know?"

"Thank goodness!" said Estelle, shooing the notion with her fingernails in the air. She turned back to her scrapbook. "How's the handsome priestly one?"

"Please, don't make me a priest yet," Adrian objected.

100

"I was showing Sister here some clippings from my infamous career."

"Your days practicing law? Great!" Adrian said, pulling up a chair.

"So what's next here?" Estelle asked herself, turning pages. "Oh, right. That bribery trial of Desmond O'Neill." The face of a very fat man with a cigar stared up at them from the page, scowling. "My son was in his daughter's class at school, unfortunately. So was the son of the judge in that case. Terrible, trying time for everyone involved."

"Did they ever consider making *you* a judge?" Eileen asked.

"Oh, they were hardly ready for a woman in front of the bench, much less behind it," Estelle said. "This was Wisconsin in the thirties, after all. Once or twice I actually had the defense counsel ask the judge for reassignment, on the basis of some cockamamie idea that as a woman, I'd unfairly prejudice the case for the jury. Fortunately, Judge Bick supported my practicing. His mother was a midwife, you know. I wish she hadn't already passed by the time my own children came along."

Cindy came in, bringing a pitcher of water.

"Half full of ice, just the way you like it, Stelly Jelly," she said.

"Yes...of course," Estelle said, rolling her eyes slightly. Cindy poured a glass full and put it in Mrs. Haney's hand.

"When did you retire?" Eileen asked Estelle.

"My husband died early, and I worked some all the way up to my seventies, when I decided I'd make do on the widow's pension he left," she said.

"You didn't have a pension of your own?" Eileen said. Estelle looked at her askance.

"Now what do you suppose?"

Cindy was peering into the wastebasket in the corner. She lifted the liner and tied the top in a knot, before tossing it toward the door. "You'd better not hog these two all to yourself, now," she cautioned Estelle. "Sophie will start talking about *them* the way she talks about those two daughters who never visit her."

"If Sophie could only forget who comes to visit, like all those other poor fools, she'd be a happier woman."

"Estelle! That's not nice," said Cindy.

"But it's true, all the same. I never waste time brooding about the children who never visit, myself. I never thought they liked me much in the first place."

"That could hardly be so," Eileen said to her.

"Well, they certainly don't go out of their way to look in on me. It's not like they moved away anywhere, to have careers. They're right here in town."

"How many children do you have?" Adrian asked.

"One son, one daughter," Estelle said. "My daughter, in particular, stays away. She 'prefers the company of others.' Her exact words, mind you."

"That's a shame," Adrian said.

"No matter, really. She and I never took a shine to the same things, nor to one another. Her father understood her better. She was such a homemaker, or whatever. I was relieved when she married and had a mother-in-law to discuss all that. It bored me to death."

"I'm sure she'd come by if she knew you wanted her to," Adrian suggested. "How could she really not?"

Cindy was forcefully fluffing the pillows on Estelle's bed.

Eileen noticed condensation dripping from Estelle's water glass onto the scrapbook. "Let me get that." She turned to pull a tissue out of a box on the dresser, and lifted the glass out of Estelle's hand.

"Put it over there," Estelle said. "I'm finished for now."

Eileen found a coaster for the glass, and picked a framed photo off the dresser. "Did you show Adrian the picture of you when you went to Milwaukee and got to meet FDR?" She handed it to Adrian.

"Let me see," Adrian said, eyes wide. "You were a good looker, Mrs. Haney."

"Five more minutes until seven," Cindy said, pulling the bedspread back and patting it down. "The aides will be in for your bath, Stelly. You'll have to send your visitors away until next time."

Eileen rose to comply, and Adrian handed the photo back.

"Well, next Thursday, I suppose," he said to Mrs. Haney.

"Whenever," said Estelle.

Eileen squeezed past the wheelchair and flashed a smile to Estelle. "Yes, next Thursday," she said.

Eileen looked at the invitation sitting on her mother's library desk. Someone must have simply highlighted every name starting with the title "Sr." on the college enrollment list when mailing them out. How else would she have been included, and where would they have gotten her home address? The Franciscans were holding a reception to kick off the new year, with an art show in the fine arts center and a talk by an Eastern provincial. The honor of Eileen's presence was requested. Her first thought was to hope it wouldn't be modern art they were displaying: anything after the Impressionists, and she couldn't begin to comprehend it. This was the sort of event Eileen knew she really ought to attend, so she'd marked the R.S.V.P. in the affirmative and returned it. But now the day had come and she really didn't relish going. What did one wear to this kind of thing, if not a habit? The answer was simple, she guessed, since most of the Sisters there would be in street clothes, in shades of brown or black. Eileen washed her face and toweled off before walking to her closet. She gazed at her clothes, finally pulling a fresh charcoal pantsuit out from under its bag from the dry cleaners.

Motes of dust glimmered in the red and amber light coming through the stained glass windows of the fine arts center as Eileen entered the cavernous room. The buzz of women's voices filled the air, some of them laughing or calling out to acquaintances spied at a distance. Eileen quickly ascertained that no men had been invited—which figured, since the title of the evening's talk, by a Sr. Francine Davis, was "The New Franciscan Spirituality for Women." What was wrong with the old one, Eileen couldn't help thinking. A few of the women were in veils, and Eileen soon gravitated toward a cluster of four of them by a table of refreshments. They were fully engaged with each other as she drew near, so she veered and approached the table instead. There she found boxes of wine, and trays of cheese cubes with caraway seeds and bits of jalapeño in them, supplied by the college cafeteria. Eileen used a toothpick to deposit a few on a Styrofoam plate and poured herself some lemonade from a carton she found among the wine boxes. She listened in on the conversation of the nuns standing near her.

"...I heard her at the conference in Detroit in May. She didn't address the topic of *stewardship* as much as I'd have liked. I'm not sure the Eastern provinces really endorse the idea."

"I understand there's a papal encyclical devoted to it coming out soon, to build on the *Populorum Progressio* of Paul VI. If that happens, I think it will settle the issue of endorsement."

"Or else fuel some sort of backlash. Suddenly it will become important to talk about 'solitude' and time for 'reflectiveness,' and social action on natural resources will be eschewed as a male agenda, as if it elbowed women's issues out of the way!" They shared a laugh, and one of them turned to set her drink on the table.

Eileen averted her gaze, dabbing her forehead with a napkin. She meandered toward the folding chairs arranged at one end of the hall. The chairs all had "Assisi College" stenciled on the back, in white spray paint.

Thankfully, one of the more elegant-looking Franciscans, in a brown tailored suit with a gleaming silver cross pinned to the lapel, stepped up to the microphone and asked for everyone's attention. The women at the gathering found their way to chairs, and soon the program commenced. The woman introduced Sr. Francine, who came to the podium and launched into her presentation. The room became respectful and engrossed. Eileen was glad the show was on the road.

Sr. Francine outlined a spirituality resting on three bases: service, prayer, and community. Service and prayer—nothing was novel in what Francine had to say about them. The new spin was evidently in her definition of community, and Eileen strained to understand the point. Just at the moment, Francine was saying something about "honesty, openness, and *the mystery of the other.*" Eileen tried to picture what the nun had in mind, but felt herself groping about for something that would stay in focus. The nun directly in front of Eileen was nodding her head as Francine spoke, in recognition. The woman's silver coif bobbed above her suit collar, and Eileen could see her lean to murmur something to the nun on her right. Eileen flashed momentarily on a meeting that happened years ago, during the controversy about sisters leaving the Bonaventure motherhouse. There was a memory of Sr. Immaculata, the provincial, angry and in tears. Had she been angry at Eileen? Funny, Eileen couldn't recall. It was so many years ago. Why did it come to mind? Sr. Francine next spoke a sentence with the word "intimacy" in it, which in a former era would have been a reference to lesbianism, and a code word for the most abhorrent of perils in religious life. Apparently the word had been recast, but Eileen was baffled as to how. She looked around at the nuns to her left and right, viewing their reactions; they seemed imperturbed. Eileen was no longer tracking the discourse she was hearing. For her it was somewhat like viewing the art on display, which although not abstract (thank heaven!) had turned out to be a series of sculptures made of square nails, welded together into representations that seemed basically Native American, of horses and spears and shields. What was the point she wasn't getting? Sr. Francine's tone grew more emphatic as she continued to speak, but Eileen was hardly listening. By the end of the talk Eileen's head throbbed, and she felt queasy. The applause in the room assaulted her when it came, and she looked for a sign for the restroom.

Ensconced in a stall, she cradled her head and tried putting pressure on her temples. She was not going to make it through any long reception today, that was a cinch. If she'd had any wine, she'd have attributed the headache to that. She knew she found these events very stressful. Eileen left the bathroom, found the sister who had planned the event to thank her, and made her way to the exit. The cool air outdoors went a great distance toward relieving her distress, and she loosened her collar to get more of it as she strode down the sidewalk, away from the gathering.

Hixon Forest was poised on the brink of autumn as Eileen parked her car along the entrance road and ambled into the woods. The first acorns were making their ardent fall to earth, and the percussive pops they made as they hit the undergrowth joined the twitter of birds and the faint whisper of leaves ruffling in the copse. Eileen found a place under a tree, sat herself down, and leaned against the sloping trunk. It was a hickory, very common in this county, and a great, mature specimen. The air was crisp and fragrant, tinged with wet leaf humus and juniper, and Eileen knew she would quickly forget the tensions of the day as she sat here. Her mother used to bring her and Helen to this park, sometimes on an afternoon like this after school, for no special reason. They would hike, she and Helen picking up sticks in succession until they found the perfect walking stick, and then bear them through the woods, imagining themselves to be scrappy old prospectors, heading through the mountains in search of a stream to pan for gold. Their mother believed in exercise, at least back then, and would traipse a good mile into the woods briskly, before turning around and bringing them back. Then they would jump into the car and drive into town as if the hike had been any other errand on a busy day. They would stop at Quillen's and buy spaghetti and sauce—the thin, meatless kind—and go home to cook it for supper, which was still on the table by 6:30.

Eileen looked out to where the hill dropped off to the ravine and the creek below. The opening bars of an old song came to mind, a William Blake poem set to music: *Memory, hither come, and tune your merry notes. And while upon the wind your music floats, I'll pore upon the stream where sighing lovers dream, and fish for fancies as they pass within the watery glass.* Funny thing to remember, that. Her grandmother used to sing it long ago, in her house up on the hillside in Fountain City. She would stand doing the ironing, looking out the picture window at the Mississippi and its valley, while Eileen and Helen played dolls on the day bed. *I'll drink of the clear stream, and hear the Linnet's song, and there I'll lie and dream the day along.* And then the song had an odd ending. *When night comes, I'll go to places fit for woe, walking along the darkened valley with silent melancholy.* She remembered her grandmother's gravelly alto shifting smoothly into minor key with that last phrase. The woman must have been quite a singer when she was young. Eileen wondered where her grandma had learned the song, as Eileen had heard it nowhere since, except to sing it to herself.

Eileen drove herself home and put on water to boil for spaghetti, for old times' sake. She'd make her own sauce, however, with meat in it this time, and fresh parsley. Some things could be improved upon.

The windows of the house on Bennett Street were rattling in the wind when Eileen awoke. She reached for the alarm clock on the nightstand and peered at the phosphorescent tips of the hour and minute hands. 3:30 a.m., almost. What had awakened her? The room was especially dark, and it appeared the street lamp outside her window was off. Had it just gone out? Eileen had been having a distressing dream and felt relief to have scrambled to consciousness. She turned the switch on the lamp next to the clock, but nothing happened. The electricity was out, she guessed. Eileen got up and felt for her slippers by the bed. She padded out to the landing and tried another switch. No power. She stood there for a moment, deciding what she wanted to do. She could go back to bed, but felt a little too keyed up for that. She went to the toilet and peed, then went down to the kitchen and turned on the flame under the teakettle.

While the water heated, she went to the mantle in the living room and lit the candles in the candleholders there. She moved them both to the end table by the sofa, where she would sit with her tea. She could see well enough to read a book, if she rustled up another candle or two. She produced a couple of votives from the cupboard in the kitchen, and soon she was sitting with her mug, in the glow of several flames like a saint in a votary. Ironic, since what she felt was not the least bit beatific. In fact, she'd awakened with a sense of dread, which had if anything grown as she moved about the house. What was bothering her? Her discomfort around all those Franciscans today weighed on her mind. The talk about community had left her feeling a failure, even more than usual. Those women so obviously enjoyed getting together like that, while all she had wanted for years now had been to get away on her own. She had often lied to herself, thinking she went to Standing Rock seeking those Indian youth, when what she went seeking in fact was solitude. She could convince herself sometimes that her move to the reservation was high-minded, an altruistic mission, but today what she knew again—the way she knew her own worst profile when catching it in one of those three-way department store mirrors, even if she seldom saw it—was that she had gone to North Dakota to flee her relationship with the Bonaventures. The incident she'd remembered, when Sister Immaculata had been so angry, was over the lack of consensus in the congregation, when some of the nuns wouldn't consent to other members of the order going to live in smaller communities. Eileen had been one of the ones opposed. She did not want the change, and she wasn't going to endorse it. Why did her behavior in that situation fill her with shame? It seemed her exile at Standing Rock was largely a way to punish her order for disappointing her, the way a bitter divorce prolongs a failed marriage. She felt sick, seeing this so evident. She was no saint, no noble counter-cultural hero, she was merely self-congratulating—and alone. She envisioned for a moment those saints in children's stories who lashed and whipped themselves in penitence, and were held up as examples of piety. She'd was no more likely to express her guilt—however intense—like that than she was to approach the shrine at Guadalupe on her knees. She was not the type to go in for dramatics. She lay down on the sofa and pulled an afghan over herself, testing sleep. Minutes passed, and slumber seemed no more likely than it had been earlier. She was anxious for the night to end.

The candles burned, and Eileen tried to vacate her mind. The next thing she felt was fear, building inside her like the symptoms of a dreaded illness. Soon she was thinking truly crazy thoughts, like maybe she wasn't alone in the house, that ghosts of the dead were coming there to join her. Had she finally gone over an edge? The more she tried to dispel the idea, the more elaborate it became. Eventually she imagined they were in the next room, sitting there in all the chairs, lined up on the bench, waiting for her. For what? *I am stronger than you,* she found herself thinking. *I will make you leave this house.* She thought of carrying a candle in there to check, just to reassure herself the room was empty. No. She wouldn't give in to something so irrational. Who did she think they were? Her mother? Her mother's father, more like it, and his brothers and his parents. She could almost see them, lined up, hungry, wanting flesh and some kind of justice. Perhaps she had seen too many B movies. *I am not here to requite you. Go back to the past and howl for eternity, for all I care.* She practically said it out loud. She was really losing her grip on reality, now. Maybe somewhere she had a pill she could take, to get herself back to sleep. Dare she go to the bathroom to search the cabinet? She lost track of what happened next. She felt how cold she was, and curled up tighter under her cover. Sooner or later sleep came.

In the morning, she felt fairly sane. She awoke to a bus revving its engine down at the corner, then heard it accelerate up South Street after the light turned. Eileen sat up and cleared her dry mouth with a swig of cold tea. Whether the electricity was on or not, it was light out now. She hoped there was power, actually—she fervently wished for a hot shower, and the water heater was electric.

What did she know of her mother's father? *This* thought crossed her mind, first thing this morning. He was a cranky, emphysematous old man, who coughed sputum into a coffee can he kept by his chair in the parlor. He was hated by her mother, and yet Brigid had gone there to visit every month or so, because she was a dutiful daughter.

The pipes responded with a satisfying groan when Eileen turned on the water in the shower. Soon the upstairs bathroom was filling with steam. Eileen hit on an idea that made her happy: she was going to write to Teresa. So what if it had been—how many?—nearly *five* years. She and Teresa had been postulants together, right after eighth grade. The two of them were the sole survivors of that group, persevering to take not only their temporary vows but even their permanent vows together. They'd lost touch over the years, but people do that, don't they? She thought fondly of their first year at the motherhouse. Teresa had come from Stevens Point, from a fairly wealthy family, and had found the deprivations of the convent especially difficult. Eileen remembered the two of them exchanging glances one night at the dinner table, when creamed canned peas and potatoes were served for the third time in a week, and Teresa bursting into laughter. They both had gotten their privileges in the library taken away for a month, but looking back, Eileen felt it was worth it. Eileen had always found Teresa to be so vivacious. Teresa had long thick hair, chestnut brown, when she arrived, and Eileen had gaped to see it cut off. They played a game sometimes, where they sat on Teresa's bed with a hair brush and Eileen pretended to comb the snarls out of Teresa's long-gone tresses, and they talked of all the things they missed about home. Teresa's list was always longer than Eileen's, but they pretended not to notice. Their infrequent letters had simply trailed off over the years. Teresa had been in Chicago to do her doctorate at Loyola, and somewhere between her comps and her dissertation, they had lost touch. To Eileen's last knowledge, Teresa was teaching in Milwaukee and living in a house of prayer in the inner city with some sisters from other orders. Now Eileen would send a letter in care of the provincial, and ask her to forward it.

What on earth have I been up to? Eileen thought. She'd taken her self-sufficience ridiculously far, if she'd let even Teresa go by the by. She hoped it wasn't too late to make amends.

After breakfast Eileen got out her toolbox and started to chink the plaster in the stairwell. The crumbling mixture of old plaster and horsehair fell easily from the point of her chisel, sending clouds of fine dust into the air. Eileen stopped and got a mask to cover her nose and mouth. By noon, she had swept up the mess on the stairs and had found a bucket to mix the fresh plaster. She ate a simple lunch and got back to her undertaking. Once she'd mixed up a batch, it was important to work quickly, before it set. She stood on a ladder with trowel in hand and pressed the curd into the fissures that now scarred the wall. She thought of Michelangelo, up there in the space between the fingertips of God and of Adam.

Eileen almost forgot that today was Thursday. She raced at 4:15 to get herself ready to go to the nursing home. When Eileen arrived, Adrian was sitting in the lobby with his backpack. Eileen almost walked right past him, but he looked up from the book on his lap just as she passed.

"Hi," he said.

"What are you doing out here?" she asked.

"Waiting for you," he said. "If I get a jump on feeding supper, there's more work for me. Besides, I'm trying to finish this thesis statement for Dr. Jenkins's class. I have to turn it in tomorrow."

"What's your topic?" she asked.

"Bastardy."

"There's something odd. What class is this?"

"Shakespeare," he said. "The history plays."

"Not my usual bailiwick," Eileen said. Adrian picked up his books, and they started down the hallway. "Did you draw that out of a hat, or is it a subject you chose?" she asked.

"Jenkins suggested it to me. I'm not sure what message there is in that," Adrian said. "We were in the middle of discussing this character, Faulconbridge, and a girl in class was saying how she disliked him—because he was so *impudent*. Yes, he is—but to cast him as an anti-hero, on that basis? So I was defending him, and Jenkins tells me, right in front of the class, '*This* will be your major thesis in this course, Underwood.' I guess he thinks I'm likely to make a good apologist for impudence."

"What thesis?" she asked.

"The bastard, being without an inheritance, has nothing to lose," Adrian said. "So he can see and speak the truth—a lot like the fool."

"I don't know the play," Eileen said, regretfully.

"Well, I won't trouble you further with it," Adrian said, and smiled broadly. He pointed to the book in her hand. "Did you bring that for Mrs. Haney?" he asked.

"Yes, I did. It's about the raid on Entebbe."

When the two of them walked onto Estelle's wing, they could hear wails coming from one of the residents' rooms.

"Damn it, Sophie! Hold still!" someone was shouting.

Just then Estelle rolled her wheelchair out of the day room, into the hall.

"Damn it, if she doesn't want to eat the soup, don't make her," she called, to no one in particular.

An aide appeared in the doorway where the commotion had emanated, replacing a dropper into a bottle. "Good grief," she said to Eileen and Adrian. "If she'd let someone clean her ears now and then, she wouldn't end up needing these eardrops in the first place." With this, the aide strode back to the nurses' station. Eileen shot Estelle a look of reproach for her mischief, but Estelle just winked and turned her chair a bit to face them.

"Is that for me?" she asked, indicating the book in Eileen's hand.

"Why, yes," Eileen said, reluctantly. She handed it to Estelle. "I don't know if you've already read it or not."

"No, I haven't," Estelle said, taking the book and looking at its cover. "I read the review when they printed it in the *Star-Tribune*, a long time ago."

"I thought you might enjoy it," Eileen said.

"Thank you for bringing it," said Estelle. "I've just about fin-ished the one I'm on. I do remember hearing about that raid on the news. Who could forget? It was the day of the American bicentennial."

"Quite a memory you have," Adrian said.

"I suppose you were—what? Not born yet?"

"It's only been ten years, Mrs. Haney. I was about to enter high school."

"Not old enough to vote for Carter, though. Although you Holy Name boys tend to be Republicans, I've gathered."

"I actually come from a long line of Democrats," Adrian said.

"Good for you!" Estelle enthused.

Sophie and several other ladies were seated around the televi-sion, watching Bob Barker host a game show.

"Estelle," Sophie called over the back of the couch. "You'd better take these chocolates to your room, before they're all eaten." She waved the box in the air.

"Go ahead and finish them. You don't have to ask me," Estelle said. "I don't care for any."

"Didn't Frances send them for you?" Sophie asked.

"Read the card. 'To the ladies of A wing.' They're yours," Estelle said.

"Is Frances your daughter?" Eileen asked.

"My daughter? Yes, I suppose so," Estelle said. "She'd claim me if she had to. She'll come for the body when I drop! 'We kept her in the utility closet for you, ma'am. She's a stiffer. We tried to keep her fresh.'"

Adrian let out a giddy laugh.

"Mrs. Haney!" Eileen protested, in dismay.

"Oh, I'm *kidding*," she said.

"It's not funny," said Eileen.

"Tell them ahead of time you want to be packaged and deliv-ered. Federal Express Overnight," Adrian said.

Eileen glared at him, but he was looking Estelle's direction, not hers, and still wearing a grin.

"This young man might want a chocolate, before you've gob-bled them all down," Estelle said to Sophie. "Go ahead," she told Adrian. "They're Fannie Farmer truffles."

Adrian went over and made a game of squeezing one until it cracked, peering at its inside, then pretending to Sophie that he was going to put it back. Sophie held the box out of reach behind her body. To Eileen the canned applause coming from the television was excruciating. How did the nurses and aides not go deaf, working here? Eileen didn't know how anyone could joke about death in a place like this. Especially facing death with no one to care. She began wishing for an excuse just to say goodnight and go. Adrian was sitting next to Sophie, however, engaged in some conversation they took in earnest. Eileen would make the best of it, she guessed. She found the spelling board the nurses used to communicate with the old deaf woman, Rose, and went over to strike up a conversation.

-11-

Counsel of Years

At the start of the year, the freshmen at Holy Name arrayed themselves at the breakfast table like metal filings around magnetic south—all facing away from the place where Louie sat. Now Louie was gone, and a new balance of forces was in the making. Given the pressures the class was under, animosity toward the system was bound to arise somewhere.

"I think he grades too hard," one of them said. "He nitpicks if you don't spit it back just the way he said it in class. Like it's equations we're studying, not theology. He gave me a 'C' on my paper on the sacraments—I guess he didn't appreciate my saying I thought the Church needed to explain to people a practical purpose for confession."

Father Daimler was away for the day, and the seminarians were free for once to discuss his class at the table. Father Moriarty was at a meeting at the chancery, downtown.

"I know what you mean," said another of the freshmen. "I don't think he realizes that when he teaches at the college, no one expects to have to say 'yes, Father, whatever you say, Father.' Not like it is here."

"Now, he's not all bad," said, another. "You have to give him some respect, just because he's a priest."

"A sacrament is a mystery, young man," intoned the first seminarian, mimicking the teacher. "A mystical encounter with the risen Jesus. Jesus is *the* sacrament. Hunh? I'd like to see Keenan dissect that one in Logic class. Does he mean every sacrament is

Jesus? In the way that the bread and wine become Jesus? Or what *does* he mean? And don't say it's just my lack of faith. I don't know how that could be. You can't believe or disbelieve some assertion if the meaning doesn't register."

"That's a slippery slope you're on."

"Why do you say that?" asked Alan Hennessey. "Because we're supposed to believe that the truth about God is too much for the human mind to know?"

"Except for Daimler, to whose mind He reveals it," muttered the first seminarian. "And sends him here to enlighten us. Nonsense is nonsense, if you ask me."

"Don't you guys believe obedience is one of the vows we're supposed to take?" asked the other sem, somewhat shocked.

"Blind obedience? Maybe not."

Adrian was quiet during such discussions. He knew the ropes here, and which ones not to yank on. Father Moriarty's awareness of dissention cropping up, even for a moment, was uncanny, and he had a special weapon against it. Certain seminarians got sent off quietly to the Mayo Clinic for psychological tests. The findings didn't matter, since the stigma of being sent was so effective. Adrian remembered in his own class, how Danny and Carl had gone. Adrian had been smart enough to avoid it himself, as had his classmate, Ben. But the two of them had a running joke about it. They washed dishes together in the seminary kitchen for work-study, and they'd whisper to each other, as Sister Stanislaus stored the leftovers and wiped the counter tops and the spray flew across the pots and pans.

"Heard who's the latest kook?" Ben would say.

"Who?" Adrian would ask.

And they would gossip about the next sem slated to see the psychologist. Ben openly voiced his conviction—well, to Adrian at least—that this was a cynical exercise of power on Moriarty's part. The conclusion was not a hard one to draw, since psychology was never otherwise held in much regard at Holy Name.

"Some day, the kooks will protest," Ben fantasized one day. "There will be so many of them, they'll join in league with one another, and overthrow Moriarty. They'll plan a coup. A *kook coup!*" And then he guffawed at his own joke. "*Kook coup!*"

Burgess Lichter, with her translucent skin and abundant auburn curls, looked like she belonged sooner in a Botticelli canvas than she did sitting in a study carrel at the Assisi library, but this was only one of the intimidating things about her. She was also a 4.0 major in mathematics and German, the second of which she did simply for kicks, with an eye toward doing her doctoral thesis in the first. That she even knew his name came as a surprise to Adrian, although they often sat near each other in Jenkins's class.

"Hello, Adrian," she said, as she passed his desk with her backpack.

"Hi. It's Burgess, right?"

"Yeah. We take Shakespeare together."

"Of course," he said. "How are you liking it?"

"Pretty well," she said. "I went to a Guthrie production of *Richard III* last year, and that's what got me interested in this course. I was looking forward to the chance to read it—I didn't realize we wouldn't get to it till after the midterm. I found myself getting into *Richard II*, by the end. Actually, I'm dying to know what you think about Jenkins."

"What about him?" Adrian asked.

"Is this the first time you've had him?"

"Yeah, and you?"

"I took his seminar on Virginia Woolf. He's pretty cool. I don't find him anti-feminist at all," she said.

"Why would you expect to?"

"Well, some of the women have that notion, because he's gay. It never made any sense to me that it necessarily followed."

"Uh...no," Adrian said.

"You didn't know that...," she ventured.

"What?" he said.

"You didn't know he was gay. I can tell by the look on your face. I thought pretty much everyone knew, but this place is funny about that issue. I guess I only knew for sure because I saw him leaving Marian Hall one day with his lover."

"How did you know it was his lover?" Adrian asked.

"You can just tell. It was snowing, and he was fussing over the guy buttoning his coat. It was pretty obvious."

"Yeah. I guess," Adrian said.

"Anyway, he's a really smart man, and I think he's funny."

"Better than Shelbe, that's for sure," said Adrian. "Have you decided on your thesis topic yet?"

"Not really," she said. "I'm always so last-minute."

"As if it ever hurts you."

"Oh, stop with *that* already. Truth is, if I have to hear one more professor talk about Adrian Underwood and the golden old days, I'm going to retch."

"You're making that up."

"Maybe it was only two or three of them, but still. It gets pretty old. I thought I'd die that first day in class when Jenkins called on you and I realized who you were."

"They're starved for someone who's actually read the text, that's all," said Adrian.

"It's more than that. I get lionized too, but it's different. For me, it's the women professors. With you it's all the men. Or should I say all the bachelors? And they outnumber the rest, let me tell you."

"Any chance I can make my own impression?" he asked.

"Oh, I know it's them, not you. I think they basically idealize youth. It seems teaching attracts that type."

"I know what you mean. What do you suppose that's about?" he asked.

"Beats me," she said. "Professor Schmitz asked me if I wanted to co-lead a seminar on Gödel with her. No, I'd rather spend next semester in Lisbon, thank you very much."

"What's in Lisbon?" he asked.

"Nothing! That's the point. Cheap food. I don't even speak the language!" she giggled.

The reference librarian was giving them dirty looks, by this time.

"Look, I was just going over to the union to get some coffee," she said. "You want to come?"

"Um, sure," he said. "I just have to be back at Holy Name by 10:00, for curfew."

"Get out!" she blurted. "You graduated once already. Isn't there some exemption, in your case?"

"'Fraid not," he told her.

"We'll hurry, then."

The boy at the counter in the coffee bar wore a baseball cap backward on his head. "Need cream?" he asked, pointing his fingers at them like pistols.

"Yes, please," Burgess said.

He brought it, and after she and Adrian poured and stirred, they took seats at a tiny table by the wall. The table shifted on the uneven floor tiles, causing their coffee to slosh over the brims of their cups.

"I could never figure out what part of it was sexual attraction," she said, as if their conversation in the library had hardly been interrupted.

"What?" Adrian asked, pulling napkins out of a dispenser to sop up.

"I was thinking about them making such a fuss over me, as a student. I never knew exactly what it meant."

"I guess I didn't, either," he said.

"I was just giving you a hard time, earlier. At first I thought those men brought your name up because they were smitten, and I was jealous of your being a guy. But then I realized some of them were straight."

"Of course *some of them* are," he said, wondering who else besides Jenkins wasn't. "You get talked about like that, too, you know, when you're not there. Sort of the great female hope, from what I've gathered," he said.

"Like some awaited messiah. Maybe that's it. It's very Catholic of them, in a way."

"Are you Protestant?"

"Yeah, Lutheran," she said.

"And your version of the Messiah is different from ours?"

"No. But there's strictly one messiah in history; none of that business about intercessors, or messengers, or any chosen ones to

119

deliver us," she said. "We hate the idea of anything mediating between God and the individual. It's just us and Jesus. We're a little more afraid of idolatry, I guess."

"Probably a good thing," Adrian said.

"Anyway...let this cup pass from my lips," she said. "I'm a little tired of other people's plans for my life."

"Are your parents like that?" he asked.

"My father is. He's a dean at UW-La Crosse. I thought he was going to kill me when I stayed here and went to Assisi instead of going to the University of Chicago."

"My parents have never gotten that involved," Adrian said.

"Nice for you, I guess. Dad backed off when I insisted on math instead of economics. But then my adviser started dreaming of what destiny I had to fulfill. Ugh! I'm less interested right now in co-leading a seminar than I am in finding a boyfriend! Any suggestions?"

Adrian laughed more heartily than she expected.

"Oh, is that amusing?" she asked.

"It just struck me as funny. Look at the company you keep, after all. If you're going to pick up guys in the library...."

"So, you're a poor candidate, granted. But maybe you can counsel me. Isn't that part of your training, as well?"

"Not at my stage, it isn't. And besides, you know what Sartre said about advisers."

"Sartre?"

"Yes...in *Existentialism and Human Emotion*...."

"I took Verna Luckritz's seminar—she's the best, isn't she?—but I don't remember anything he said about advisers."

"We're human to the extent that we're free to choose, and thereby create ourselves. And we're responsible for all our choices, because even our advisers are the ones we chose ourselves," he said.

"Yes?" she said, quizzically.

"So, if you're asking *me* for advice on finding a boyfriend, how bad could you really want one?" he chuckled.

Burgess started laughing, which made Adrian laugh more. They didn't stop. The boy at the counter dried glasses from the dish drainer with a towel and grinned in their direction, although Adrian wasn't sure why. On general principle, it seemed. Happy to have served up a good time.

Before they parted that evening, by the bicycle rack outside the library, Burgess had posed a question to Adrian. What had led him to want a place at the Church's table, anyway? she asked. With all the back-biting and struggles over doctrine, didn't he conclude that the place was more a hog wallow than a banquet? (Not exactly the metaphor he was expecting from her blushing lips.) What was in it for him? It had taken him until today before an answer eventually had come to him. The Church was truly of the World, but certain moments had the ability to lift one out of the mire of being *in* the Church, and *of* the Church. Perhaps her comment had sent him in search of a transcendent moment, to remind himself of what one was, and the effect they had. He ducked into the chapel after lunch—to pose Burgess' question to God himself, to see if there would be an answer. When he entered the nave, he expected to be there in silence, alone except for the nuns praying on their knees in front of the taber-nacle. Instead, he discovered someone was at the console of the pipe organ in the balcony, playing it full tilt. He or she was play-ing a piece with continuous runs of eighth notes, layered upon each other, in a registration filled with jubilant reeds. Adrian did not know the song or the composer or even the period. But what he felt, listening as the instrument filled the gilded and tiled space of the sanctuary with sound, was awe. Was it faith that inspired this composer, and this musician? Faith which gave birth to such love of sound, such devotion to a discipline, such mastery? Adrian felt small in a moment like this, swept by the current around him, although there were only he and the two nuns and the one organist present. It was an instance in which he felt clearly Catholic, knowing that faith, and a glimpse of the Divine, depended on others, in the here and now. He was moved viscerally in a way that ancient words on a page, or ideas, could only shadow. Was there some apostasy in his saying so? Was he supposed to find the Holy Word an equal source of inspiration? He made a mental note to check some day, just to know where he stood. But faith by the Word alone? His belief would falter, for sure.

The composition came to its magnificent ritard and finish, and the final chords reverberated in the vault. There was silence for a few minutes. Adrian eventually heard footsteps padding down the balcony stairs, and into the light streaming from the rose window to the center aisle stepped Alan Hennessey.

"Alan!" Adrian said, *sotto voce*.

"Oh, hi," Alan whispered, in return.

"I had no idea that was you. You're terrific."

"Thanks," he said, casually. "I stop sometimes to play here, just for fun. They've got a great three-manual, twenty-seven-rank instrument, and it's very underused. Sister Grace told me I could come practice whenever there's not a service going on in the chapel."

"I should think so. To God be the greater glory...."

"Well, I've had a lot of years of lessons. I grew up down the street from St. Mary's Church, and I've always taken playing the organ for granted. Pretty spoiled, I know."

"You'll spoil us, not be spoiled. What's that you were playing?"

"'Final,' from *Seven Pieces*. By Marcel Dupre. He's French, twentieth century."

"Does Moriarty know you can play like that?" Adrian asked.

"Well, he's never heard me, but he knows about it."

"You've got to show him, man."

"Yeah, someday. Speaking of which, I was just about to head back to the sem for dinner," Alan said. "Did you bike?"

"Yeah. It's right outside."

"Join you?" he asked.

"I'd be honored," Adrian said.

Father Moriarty had a predilection for images of the physical world in states of corruption, and the human person was far from exempt from this. The rector would refer to the seminarians' duties of daily hygiene as "cleaning up the carcass," and he felt particular indignation at any failings he detected in their attention to it. Once he spent the first twenty minutes of their weekly formation lecture dwelling on how grossed out he'd been to hear someone blow his nose during the consecration at Mass several days earlier. "Please take care of that problem before you come to chapel," he pleaded, derisively. Adrian wondered where Moriarty found transcendence in the world—or whether he simply suffered gloriously his privation of it. For his own part, Adrian pedaled his bicycle next to Alan down Jackson Street, through the various scents of autumn clematis and of Concord grapes overripe and dropping from the vine onto sidewalks, and he felt truly blessed, indeed loved by God.

It was Wednesday night, and Adrian filed into the Bishop Marsh Room for formation lecture with the others. The chalkboard had been rolled out as usual.

"We are surrounded by a world of *babies*, not a world of *adults*," Fr. Moriarty began.

Oh, not this dichotomy, Adrian thought.

"The baby world is one of *instant gratification*. While the Christian world, the world of adults, is one of gratification foregone for a higher purpose. The baby world is one of thinking of *me* first. While in a Christian world we think of others first...."

Fr. Moriarty never managed to convey very much hope that faith or works or anything could move a person across this great divide—or to convey much interest in seeing anyone bridge it. It seemed unlikely that the man believed in a concept of moral development so much as predestination. Adrian wanted to be somewhere else right now. Might he find Fr. Keenan at lunch tomorrow? he wondered. He'd see Eileen in the evening at St. Francis Home. He wanted to talk with her about an opportunity he'd discovered, while talking to Sr. Beata in the campus ministry office, to go build housing stock in Appalachia over spring break. He daydreamed the hour away, waiting for the end of the lecture.

Father Keenan showed up in the cafeteria line a few persons after Adrian. He was with Lloyd Hecht, the editor of the campus press.

"Meat loaf or barbequed chicken?" a voice asked.

The cafeteria lady rapped her metal spoon impatiently on the steamer pan, dislodging a morsel clinging to it. Adrian shook his head no and scooted past her station. He dawdled over the salad bar, waiting for Keenan and Hecht to catch up with him.

"Good day!" Keenan said to the cafeteria ladies, with their hair up in nets. He asked for the macaroni and cheese, and one piled a plate for him.

"Good day, my young logician!" he finally said to Adrian.

"Hello, Father."

"Can we convince you to join our roundtable today? Or will you insist on being square?" he asked.

"I'll gladly join you. Which round table will you be taking?"

"Pick any. Even a square table, when we take it, will be a roundtable. Isn't that right, Professor Hecht?"

"I'm not a professor," Lloyd said.

"Yes of course," said Keenan. "Editor Hecht. In the cafeteria, with a pen. Or was it Mrs. Peacock, in the study with a rope?"

Adrian looked at him, a bit puzzled.

"Don't mind him," Lloyd said. "I edited a manuscript of his— at his insistence—and now he's calling me poison pen. The great blood-letter."

"Red ink flowing everywhere," Keenan said. "How was I to know what a cruel heart beat in a human chest!"

"There's a difference between sound logic and effective prose, that's all," said Lloyd.

"Ah! He plunges the blade again," said the priest.

They found a table and sat their trays down.

"So how are you finding your recent stay with us?" Lloyd said.

"I'd hardly consider myself company, at this point," Adrian answered. "I'm making myself at home. I have too much time on my hands. I read most of the time. And search my soul, of course, but that's not much territory to cover—I have to pace in that little cramped space," he said.

"Oh, pshh," said Keenan. "I could suggest some things to read, though, should you run out. Come by my office."

"Really?" Adrian asked.

"Certainly. What interests you? Martin Buber? Karl Rahner? Or a little Andrew Greeley? Come peruse my shelves and see what you like."

"Okay, I'll do that," Adrian said.

Thad Benson saw them as he left the food line, and came over.

"Professor Benson!" Keenan announced.

"Hey, everyone," Thad said, sliding into a seat.

"Do you know our student here?" Keenan asked him.

"I think we were introduced," Thad said. "You're a seminarian, right?"

"Yes," said Adrian.

"Not a calling I could see myself following. But bless it, someone has to. Right, Father?"

"Mr. Underwood is back after a little sojourn in law school, in Nebraska," Keenan said.

"You have my sympathy," Thad said. "No one should be forced to live there."

"Have you ever been to Nebraska?" Adrian asked.

"Well, no. Wisconsin is the farthest west I've ever made it. I've never really adjusted to it. I can only imagine it gets worse the farther you go."

Lloyd turned to Keenan. "I thought I'd see you at the planning meeting for the Feast of the Immaculate Conception," he said. "Aren't you celebrating Mass? You're usually a fixture at those things."

"No," said Keenan. "I can't preach at an Immaculate Conception service."

"You're going to be out of town?" Lloyd asked.

"No, I just don't have enough Marian devotion to be the man to do it, that's all."

"How can that be?" asked Thad.

"How? I've never found the Marian tradition works for me, personally."

"You can't just say that, can you?" Thad protested.

"Say what?"

"That a part of Catholic tradition doesn't suit you. You can't just pick and choose."

"Do you believe in it?" Keenan asked Thad.

"What? In the Immaculate Conception? That's neither here nor there. I'm not a priest."

"Am I not also human?" asked Keenan. "If not all humans are priests, does it follow that not all priests are human? I ask our student of logic."

"But to be a priest you have to believe what the Church teaches," Thad said. "Aren't you afraid of corrupting a seminarian, talking this way?"

"I imagine Mr. Underwood understands me when I say that there is no theology of Mary in the synoptic Gospels, or in Johannine or Pauline texts. Is that right?"

"Yeah. You're right," said Adrian.

"So I hardly think I'm corrupting him," Keenan said.

"Johannine?" Thad said.

"The witness and writings of the Apostle John," Adrian explained.

"And the other thing...synoptic?"

"Taking the same point of view," said Adrian. "Mark's Gospel was written first. Matthew and Luke had access to the Gospel of Mark in writing their Gospels, and shared a common additional source, usually referred to as 'Q.' Thus they form the three synoptic Gospels."

"Pauline refers to the writings of St. Paul," said Thad. "I knew that."

"Glad to see they taught you *something* out East," Keenan said. "Didn't you study at Fordham?"

Thad went into a slight pout. "Yes," he said.

"I never took much comfort in the idea of Mary laying requests at the foot of God for me," Keenan said. "I always figured I'd rather just take my chances with the Man himself. But then, when my daddy said no, I was never one to go asking Mommy. She and I never got along that famously."

"I can't believe you just said that," Lloyd confessed.

"What do you suppose the gift of personal faith comes from, if it's not mediated by our experience? If Marian devotion were central to Christian faith, I suppose I'd have to reconsider whether I was a Christian. Fortunately for me, it's not."

"I've never known you to be so flip about these things," said Lloyd. "How do you stay in the good graces of Sister Margaret?"

"Perhaps because Sister Margaret has had the good sense not to ask me exactly why I won't preside. I say the noon Mass over at *Mary, Queen of Heaven* three days a week, and two Sunday Masses forty-eight weeks a year—I don't think she's about to look a gift horse in the mouth."

Ernie Jenkins came past their table with his tray.

"Hi, Dr. Jenkins," Adrian said.

"Oh—hello," Jenkins said.

"Join us?"

"Uh, I'm meeting someone...over there. But thanks," he said, and ambled toward the other side of the cafeteria.

"Well, this discussion has taken a detour from the intellectual into the personal, hasn't it?" Keenan said. "Our student will feel we've not lived up to our reputation of providing food for the mind. Can't we do better, professors?"

"That's why Jenkins went looking for other company," Lloyd said. "He doesn't want to live with that much pressure. It's our lunch break, after all. Who wants to be responsible for intellectual discussion?"

"Somehow I doubt that's the whole story with Jenkins," Thad said.

Adrian looked across the room to see if he could pick out where Jenkins had ended up, but didn't see him.

A couple more students joined them at the table. One was Molly Powichroski, and the other was Anthony Wahlgren, one of the senior seminarians. Anthony was exceptionally quiet, gigantic, and gaunt. He majored in political science and was quite a maven of geographic and sociopolitical trivia. Adrian suspected Anthony, having gone fairly unappreciated at Holy Name, would not go on to the major sem.

"Hey Anthony," said Lloyd, "what do you have to say about the fall elections?"

"Not too much excitement there," Anthony said. "Just the congressional seats up for grabs. Most of the interest comes from people trying to read the electorate, to see if Bush will face a credible challenge in '88 when Reagan's second term is up."

"I should hope so," Lloyd said. "Although Bush isn't quite as maddening as Reagan."

"Maddening?" said Molly. "Why do you say that? I think he's a great president."

"Oh, not *this* conversation," Lloyd said, eyes cast heavenward. "Government by invented anecdote, that's what I find maddening. He's got to be the single most anti-intellectual president we've had this century—if not ever."

"He really feels what most people feel," Molly said.

"And if they feel it that makes it the truth?" Anthony asked.

"I think he holds the same values most people hold, morally," Molly said. "Lloyd, you're always thinking that the pope should follow more closely what average people think. So why not the president?"

"Because it's not people's basest, most irrational prejudices, immune to reason or evidence, that I'm asking the pope to consider. I'd just like him to listen for once to people's experience. At the other extreme, I don't think the president of the country should be making shit up just to pander to the popular prejudices of the majority. That isn't leadership, either."

"What has Reagan ever said that wasn't true?" Molly demanded.

Lloyd looked around at the group, incredulous.

"Does this even merit an answer? Pick any press conference, any interview. The man honestly doesn't know a fact from a fantasy."

"You just can't stand it because he lets common people have just as much say as intellectuals like you," Molly said.

"Keenan, help me out, here," Lloyd said.

Fr. Keenan sighed visibly and paused. He tread carefully around political allegiances.

"Let's say, for the sake of argument, that a majority wants to scapegoat a minority for creating some problem," said Keenan, "even though the minority is no more to blame than anyone else. To do so, what logical fallacies are they likely to employ?"

"You know I hated Logic," Molly said. "Particularly that book on fallacy in argument. I passed your class even though I never read it," she said.

Anthony started to enumerate: "The *ad hominem* argument. The appeal to authority. Begging the question...."

"Yeah, those," Molly said, wrinkling her nose. She was not about to be deterred easily from an emotional line of reasoning. From Adrian's experience of her in classes over the years, he gathered she regarded this as a kind of moral cause in itself. Adrian would have spoken up in opposition, if Burgess had been at the table to side with him. As it was, Molly was the only woman in the group, and was all too willing to charge that a challenge to her amounted to sexism.

"Is there even anyone running against our congressman?" asked Thad.

"No," Anthony said. "Isn't that pathetic?"

"If people are happy, what's wrong with it?" Molly asked.

After lunch, Adrian volunteered his time for a couple of hours signing people in for a blood drive at the student center, then returned to Holy Name, where he got into his running gear and headed out to the road. He craved the exertion and the solitude. A fleeting interaction from earlier weighed on his mind. He'd been leaving the cafeteria, putting his tray on the conveyor belt, when one of the dishwashers accosted him about taking an apple with him out of the cafeteria, which was against food service rules.

"Thought no one would see you, didn't ya, smarty pants?" the woman said. Then she'd walked back to the kitchen, leaving him standing there with the apple in hand, feeling like Eve in the garden.

The woman's words stuck with him, ridiculously. All the students at Assisi took fruit out of the cafeteria—the rule against it was so unenforced, a person practically forgot it existed. Yet that epithet, "smarty pants," echoed in Adrian's thoughts. Why was Adrian wearing this shoe as if it fit? He tried to remember if he'd heard this taunt on the playground. Adrian in fact always had been a smarty pants—intellectual way beyond his life experience. He felt ill at ease, possessing keen perception, yet little confidence that it ever bore out, that consequences which seemed apparent would ever indeed prove true. Did he have such feelings because he, personally, was at odds with the world? Or is this how a twenty-four-year old was bound to feel?

He remembered a cocktail party Terry had taken him to in Omaha, given by Terry's co-worker at the D.A.'s office, Clint Davies, and Clint's lover, Rob. Adrian had been the object of general curiosity among the guests, and of knowing remarks about his *real* relationship with Terry ("friends, mm-hmm..."). But Rob, in particular, had been full of assurances—and very free with sharing them—that Adrian was in for a rude awakening if he thought for a minute he could be openly gay and practice law in Iowa. Clint was a lawyer and *he knew....* And as for *women!* Adrian could just forget about trusting straight women once they knew he was gay. If it hadn't been for Rob and Clint, Adrian might think Burgess' friends were totally imagining things when they thought gay men would be misogynistic. Where did this opinion of Rob's come from, that everywhere around them lay such a breach? Adrian had a miserable time at the party, and was relieved Terry agreed to call it a night early on. Rob's attitude— that Adrian was mistaken, things were not how they might seem to his naïve eyes, and Adrian should hide, should not go into life unguarded—seemed needless, but what did Adrian know? He was only a homosexual who'd never been on so much as a date with a man, right? He ruminated and ran, listening to his own footfalls on the warm asphalt of Highway 61. The sun was still high in the sky, and the autumn air flowed over Adrian's skin like a soothing balm, heavy with the scent of ripe durum wheat lying in swaths in the field beside the road. It seldom occurred to Adrian to pray *for* anything; this wasn't the way he'd been taught to pray as a child. But at certain times he thought: I'd like wisdom. *The counsel of years*, as the saying went. That would be nice.

-12-

Day of Reckoning

The houses of Fountain City, Wisconsin—although each in itself pedestrian, built of stucco or clapboard or brick—by their arrangement, on tiered streets down the side of a bluff as it dropped off to the river, formed a wondrous natural amphitheater. The families living there were afforded witness to the daily spectacle of the valley below, where grain barges and antique steamboats like the *Mississippi Belle* tread silently the ancient channel. The main highway into town followed the water's edge, and as Eileen approached Jefferson Street and turned inland, she shifted her car into low gear for the steep climb up the hill to Bloedow's Store and beyond it, to the cemetery. The graveyard was on the very highest elevation, behind Immaculate Conception Church, where the last cleared land gave way to wooded slope. Eileen stopped the car at the gated entrance, turning into the hillside and pulling the emergency brake hard to stay the wheels. She hadn't been here to tend the family graves in a long time. The groundskeeper had been as diligent as usual—even around the foundations of the headstones the verdant grass of the cemetery was trimmed short. It was getting late enough this Thursday afternoon that a few lightning bugs were flitting around, just inside the gate. Eileen popped the lid to her car trunk and fetched a wreath of silk flowers in its box. They were yellow roses, the color of the real ones her mother had grown in the garden, arranged with white stock and adorned with a big red bow. Eileen hoped that the last bouquet she'd brought had been taken away, frankly, and not left out here to look sun-bleached and pathetic, a testament to her long absence. She hiked up the slope to where the *Harran* and *O'Rourke* markers stood side by side over the graves of her grandparents and her family. Gazing at the stones, she noted the dates of death: '66 and '73 for her grandparents, '50, '69, and '84 for her father, sister and mother, respectively. Some tale was told in those numbers, about where the decades of her life had gone, but it was not one Eileen completely fathomed.

The graves were bare, and Eileen sunk the wire stand that came with her wreath into the ground between the headstones, then fastened the flowers in place at a slight angle. She found a Kleenex in her pocket and moistened it with saliva to clean a couple of bird droppings off the polished granite of her parents' stone. Helen's little marker, off to the side, had been made for a child; it bore an engraving of a lamb below Helen's name. Now it seemed incongruous to Eileen that this was her sister's stone, as if Helen ought to have aged with her and should no longer fit such a sentiment. Eileen looked around the spot where her family lay, at other people's gravestones and at the relatively sparse greenery in this section of the cemetery. In her mind she pictured what a couple of shrubs would do, and decided she'd ask the caretaker if she could plant a couple of upright yews as a backdrop to the family plot. She said a formal prayer, and after she finished—*may the souls of the faithful departed, through the mercy of God, rest in peace*—she made the sign of the cross. She picked up the empty box from the wreath and picked her way back down the steep hill to her car.

Eileen didn't actually remember the name of the caretaker, only that he and his wife ran the general store right there on Jefferson Street. "Howdy do?" the woman at the counter said, as Eileen entered the store.

"Fine, thank you," Eileen said. "I'm looking for the caretaker for the cemetery."

"You're looking at her," the woman responded.

"Oh, I thought your husband had that job."

"He did, until he died and had to be laid up there himself."

"I'm very sorry. I didn't know," Eileen said.

"No problem. You're not from here. You got family up there?"

"Yes. The names are Harran and O'Rourke."

"Oh, of course. You're the other daughter of Brigid Harran. Your father wasn't from here."

"No. He was from Milwaukee. But my mother buried him here in her family's plot."

"We don't have many outsiders here, so a person remembers the few we have. I guess most of 'em know they ain't too welcome in life, they ain't too welcome dead," she said, cackling. "They say this is a town you can be born and die in and still be considered an outsider, if you're not from one of the original settlers' families. Ain't it the truth. Now your grandfather, he was from Fountain City. They used to call him the Irishman. Almost everybody else was German, you know."

"My grandmother loved it here," Eileen offered.

"Yup, I knew her well. She was a nice woman. Baked lovely bread, she did."

"The best."

"Well, it is a lovely spot we have here. We're very proud of Eagle Bluff. Did you know it's the highest elevation on the whole river?"

"Oh, yes. Our grandfather told us that over and over. You could see it straight out the bathroom window, on the side of their house."

"Some of the young Gutknecht folk live in that place now. I suppose it's been years since you were in there," the woman said.

"About fifteen. I see they painted it a new color."

"Yup."

"About the cemetery," Eileen said. "I wanted to plant a couple of little yews behind my family's markers. Would that be okay? Can you tell me where the plot ends?"

"Oh!" the woman said, wearing a look of slight consternation. "I guess there's no reason why not," she said, reluctantly. "Let me get the map and check it."

"Looks like there's room on the plot, alright," the woman said when she returned. "It borders on an alley, so there's no obstruction of other graves to prevent it."

"There, then," Eileen said, and their business was concluded. "I'll be back to plant them in a week or so."

Eileen bid farewell and left the store. Standing on the sidewalk, she put her hand up to shield the sun from her eyes and gazed at Eagle Bluff, its crest cropping out from the trees above the town. It was a mighty grand sight, indeed.

*You are strangers and aliens no longer. No, you are fellow citizens of the saints and members of the household of God. You form a building which rises on the foundation of the apostles and prophets, with Christ Jesus himself as the capstone. Through him the whole structure is fitted together and takes shape as a holy temple in the Lord; in him you are being built into this temple, to become a dwelling place for God in the Spirit.** So Saint Paul wrote in his letter to the Ephesians. Today the words were read, on the feast day of St. Matthew the Apostle, from the lectern at Holy Name Seminary. Eileen tried to think of the words as being meant for her. She wished she could. *You are strangers and aliens no longer.* If a person came home to an empty house, to whom were they not a stranger? Eileen felt annoyed by the time the Liturgy of the Word had ended, and the Liturgy of the Eucharist began. Was it this way every Sunday, or for some particular reason today?

Her feelings of alienation had been too frequent in recent years. She would sit in a pew and look at the parishioners around her, thinking that the message of the scriptures or the homily was meant for them, and that she was merely intruding. The catechists of her childhood had taught her that anger was a near occasion of sin, and the thoughts attending it were peril to the state of grace of her soul. Yet how was she to resolve the feeling, when she didn't know the reason it arose? A small group of seminarians, two of them strumming guitars, sang a song at communion that echoed the words of the psalm from today's liturgy: *What marvels the Lord has worked for us! Those who are sowing in tears will sing when they reap. They go out, they go out, full of tears, carrying seed*

*Ephesians 2:19-22 *New American Bible.*

136

for the sowing: they come back, they come back, full of song, carrying their sheaves.

Big bouquets of wheat from the surrounding plain decorated the altar for the fall season, but rather than find them beautiful, Eileen felt the sight of them joined her other senses to mock her, in unison. Why did she feel so unredeemed, and so barren? The two young men in her pew stood to go to communion, and Eileen let them by, choosing not to receive the sacrament today. Why go through the motions, if she wasn't in the spirit?

She had been invited to stay for breakfast. Father Daimler had made a call earlier in the week to say that it was Vocations Sunday, and in its honor she and the nuns at the seminary were being asked to join the seminarians for a celebration. As the Mass ended and everyone moved toward the refectory, she could already feel herself concluding that this was an empty gesture, made to appease or deny the priests' guilt over privileges the Church reserved for men. She didn't know why she would think this, exactly. She usually felt more sympathy with the party line on the role of women in the Church than she did with the nuns who agitated for women's ordination. Couldn't they just leave tradition alone? But regardless, she was in a testy mood this morning.

Once they were seated, Fr. Daimler read from a pastoral letter on vocations, and some seminarians stood and shared their personal reflections. When attention turned to the nuns, Sr. Florence got up and went right for the heart of any controversy, assuring the room that she never saw the convent as a less dignified calling than the priesthood. The speech sounded a bit canned to Eileen, but then, it was probably one Florence was called upon to give every year. There was not much more ado; neither Sr. Stansilaus nor Sr. Bede spoke, and Fr. Moriarty

---

*Psalm 126 *The Psalms: A New Translation.*

closed with a few remarks of his own, before saying a blessing over the meal. Food arrived at the tables with the usual swiftness, and the room began to buzz with conversation.

"Florence tells me you're a teacher," Bede said, piling fried potatoes on her plate. "That's cool. I teach elementary school. Grade six. Just before the hormones kick in."

Bede was what anyone would describe as an odd-looking woman. Her shape was a lot of it. You'd hardly guess at first that she was only thirty. She was short, with enormous breasts and tiny short arms resting alongside them. She buttered her toast with such sleight of hand, one half expected to see her produce a dove twixt her finger and thumb when the knife came to rest, not this wedge of whole wheat bread. Her long black hair fell straight down her back.

"You teach science, isn't it?" she asked Eileen.

"Yes," Eileen said.

"I really like science. It's cool. I get to have the kids do dissections. Just little stuff, like worms. But they love it." She popped a morsel into her mouth with her fingers. "I belong to the Friends of Hixon Forest," Bede said, chewing, "so I take the kids out there two or three times a year. In the spring, for Earth Day. And we're going next month, to see the leaves. Have you ever seen the salamanders there, along the creek?"

"I certainly have," Eileen said. She wasn't sure Bede herself wasn't a sixth grader. Eileen did know salamanders, however, particularly the Hixon Forest salamanders. "I hope you aren't dissecting them!" she said.

"Oh, no. The naturalist there would never hear of letting us take anything alive out of the forest. But I have to stop the boys from digging them out of the mud. As soon as I don't have an eye on 'em, that's where I'll find 'em, on the banks of the creek."

"Bede is a...," Florence began. "What is it the kids call you?"

"A granola nun. It's what I became after college. In college, I was just a sanctuary rat," she said.

"Sister, please!" said Florence.

"What do you mean by that?" asked Eileen.

"One of those people who spent all their time studying in the Newman Center basement at the U, and hanging around the chapel practicing guitar music for Mass on Sunday. The other kids on campus called us sanctuary rats. We were the people without a social life. That was how I found *my* vocation!" She squinted her eyes closed and laughed a funny laugh through her upturned nose, like a rodent testing the breeze. "Father! I have something to say," she said, feigning a turn of her body toward the priests' table. Bede was a character, but she was well aware of it herself, and if anything, played it up. It seemed to work for her—she appeared to be a happy person, ultimately. Eileen looked up just then and saw Adrian across the room, waiting to catch her eye, and then bobbing his head once, in greeting. Eileen smiled back at him.

As the meal was breaking up, Alan Hennessey stopped by the nuns' table.

"Hi, Sisters," he said.

"Good to see you, Alan," Eileen said. "How's school going?"

"Very well! Aced my first Latin quiz," he beamed, giving a thumbs up.

"Good for you," she said.

He went off to chat with a couple of other sems, in giddy spirits.

The head prefect came and introduced himself, and Fr. Daimler extended his appreciation.

"Thanks so much for including me," Eileen said, and walked briskly along the back wall to the exit.

Mona St. John leaned across the lab bench and peered at Eileen through thick lenses smudged with fingerprints. Eileen was struggling with a vexing Erlenmeyer flask, which wouldn't release its grip on the rubber stopper and glass pipette Mona had stuck into it for a distillation in lab that day. All the other students had already cleaned up their stations and gone home. Mona was a puzzling combination of eagerness to please and need to be rescued, a pattern clear even three weeks into the school year.

"Miss Eileen, why does the water turn to steam and the salt stay a liquid? I don't understand."

"Because the sodium and chloride ions are charged, and have more affinity for each other than the water molecules, which merely have polarity. The energy from the flame isn't enough to drive them into a gaseous state. See?"

"But why does something end up sodium or chloride instead of hydrogen or oxygen?" Mona asked.

Eileen sorted through paradigms in her mind. Chemistry lab was supposed to be like offering doubting Thomas a chance to place his hand in the wounds of Christ—*see for yourself what I have told you is true.* Mona was on a different road from the other students, asking a different kind of question. Why was sodium sodium, and water water? Why fate? Perhaps Mona should be steered to the study of philosophy. She had the inclination, and it would get her out of the laboratory, where, with glassware and flames, she could be dangerous.

"I think I might want to be a scientist, like you, Miss Eileen," Mona said.

"Oh, no. I am not, I assure you, a scientist," Eileen told her.

"Then what are you?" asked Mona.

"I, uh...," Eileen foundered. "I'm the person looking after Ms. Haber's classroom while she's away."

"I never had Ms. Haber," Mona said. "I think this is your classroom. Might as well make yourself at home." Mona smiled sweetly, and carried her Bunsen burner back to the storage cabinet.

Eileen emerged from the benches of perennials at Valley Greenhouses with a yew under each arm and a pack of geraniums in each hand. By the time she got to the counter her fingers were about to buckle with fatigue.

"Find everything you need?" the cashier asked.

Eileen plopped the plants down and brushed the dirt on her hands onto the floor.

"More than I can carry, anyway!"

"Doing some landscaping?" he asked.

"Of a sort," Eileen said.

"Well, those two-gallon yews are a good buy. Everything's marked down to move before the end of the season."

"They're lovely, healthy-looking bushes," Eileen said. The cashier started ringing up the prices, and Eileen took out her checkbook and started writing a check. She looked at her watch for the date, and did a double-take at the time.

"Is it really 5:45, or is my watch wrong?" she asked the clerk.

"Yeah, that's what time it is. We close in fifteen minutes."

"How did it get to be so late?"

Somehow she'd lost an hour or more. She was doing errands after school, and didn't notice how much time had elapsed. They'd have expected her at the St. Francis Home by 4:30. She considered what time she'd arrive if she went now—too late for dinner, for sure. She really *must not* forget again, she scolded herself.

"That's $27.20, with tax," the man said.

Driving home, Eileen fretted that Adrian and Estelle would be wondering where she was. She hoped they wouldn't think she was avoiding them for some reason. The last time there, Adrian seemed happy to visit with Sophie and hardly said a word to her, right? What she remembered was that joke he made with Estelle, about her dying and her daughter coming to claim the body. Why had Adrian and Estelle both laughed, when it wasn't funny? It seemed beneath him, to make light of such things. But Estelle hadn't minded—she led him down that path in the first place. The problem was Eileen minded, and was irritated with him. Yet what need had this young man of her, at all? What need had Estelle, for that matter? Adrian was just a kid, she told herself. She shouldn't expect so much from him. And Mrs. Haney, well.... Estelle had never made any claims to being agreeable, had she?

Elsie Seaman added a special touch to her Saturday lunch with Eileen by picking a few pansies and a sprig of mint from her garden and putting them in a tiny finger vase on the table. Elsie sat, her usual chattiness reigned in. While Eileen downed her lunch readily, Elsie barely touched hers.

"I brought the boxes of your mother's things out of the closet and put them in the sitting room," Elsie said. "The light is best in there to see what we're doing."

"Your house has always seemed so much lighter than mother's," Eileen said, "although I know they're identical, architecturally."

"It's the crab apple that shades the front of your house, no doubt," Elsie said.

"Is the sitting room still the light yellow it used to be?" Eileen asked, peering around the door jam. "I haven't been in there in years."

"Yes, it is," said Elsie. "Far be it from me to paint."

Elsie showed Eileen to the sitting room and seated her on the sofa. "Let me bring the tea in on a tray, and we can get started," she said. In a moment she was back, and pulled her chair closer to the articles she had assembled.

"First these canning jars," said Elsie, picking up a few of them from where they sat beside two large cardboard boxes. "Will you ever have a use for them? They're nice quarts."

"If I ever put anything up again, I think there are dozens of these in my mother's basement. You should keep these, if you'll use them," said Eileen.

"Yes, I'll use them for something. Never throw out a good sealer, I say." She scooted the jars off to the side.

"Now these Pyrex baking dishes," Elsie proceeded. " I don't know how they ended up in my kitchen. Your mother used them all the time for cobbler. I tried to get them sparkling, but some of this crud has been baked on too many times."

"I could use those, I think," Eileen said, taking the dishes and placing them beside her on the sofa.

"I don't know if you still sew or not," Elsie said, as she opened the first box and peered in. "There are these patterns, and a lot of new zippers, and some buttons."

Eileen was struck by Elsie's deep respect for her mother's belongings. She hadn't used any of them in all these months since Brigid's death, had carefully stored them on a shelf instead. Her mother would never have fussed about Elsie's things this much.

"What about this?" Elsie said, holding up a pink cardigan sweater. "You don't recognize it? Your mother wore it on mornings when it was cool. She sent me home with it one day when the wind came up and we were digging the root vegetables in her garden."

Eileen shook her head.

"Well, no matter. I'll keep it, if you don't want it."

"Look at these...," Elsie said, lifting a pair of denim pants with an elastic waist from the box.

Not surprisingly, the things Elsie had collected here meant almost nothing to Eileen. As she entertained questions about how to apportion the effects stored in the boxes, Eileen was caught between indifference and bitterness. She didn't know what to say.

"What do you think of these old shoes?" Elsie asked, handling a pair of boots whose leather had gone rigid. "I guess they've got some wear left in them—I'm not sure by whom!" She laughed.

"You might consider the trash bin," Eileen encouraged her. Elsie tossed the shoes toward the hallway.

"Junk pile," she explained.

"What is this?" Eileen asked, picking a cornflower-colored wool blazer out of the bottom of the first box.

"Oh, I shouldn't have put that in there, really," Elsie said. "Your mother bought that at a thrift store and brought it to me just before she died. She liked the color, and said I should use it in a quilt sometime. I never have, I guess because it seemed wrong to cut it up."

Eileen held the garment up by its shoulder seams to look at it.

"It's pretty," she said. She stood up and slipped an arm into one sleeve. "Actually, I think I could wear this," she said to Elsie.

She pulled it the rest of the way on and looked about for a mirror.

"You certainly can, if you'd like," Elsie said.

Later that evening, Eileen mulled over the irony of her own life. She might be just as alone in death as her mother had been; perhaps even more so. To whom would her things pass? She'd probably be around to take care of things for Sister Anastasia and Sister Vincent Thomas when the time came, but who were the younger nuns who'd sweep up, after her own passing on? Recruitment to religious life wasn't exactly booming. She had an image of the women of the Fort Yates Altar Society poring through her junk, and clucking their tongues.

Eileen didn't make it out to Holy Name on Sunday morning, because she'd promised her principal at Beckett she'd attend Mass at the cathedral downtown, where many of the freshmen were being confirmed. After the service and a certain amount of well-wishing, the gathering at the cathedral broke up, and Eileen went home to change clothes. She was going to take advantage of a free afternoon to go get those yews she'd bought into the ground at Fountain City. Rain was expected for the next few days, so it was anyone's guess when the soil would be dry enough again to get them in.

Under a deeply overcast sky, Eileen made the drive up to Winona. A few drops hit the windshield as she was crossing the bridge to the east side of the river, and she worried that even today her plans might get rained out. She traveled the last few miles upstream, and as she coasted into Fountain City she watched Sunday services getting out at several churches, with families descending on the town's two restaurants for brunch, climbing into station wagons for trips to grandmother's. Little girls in lace and white patent leather and boys in clip-on ties were herded like a hen's brood out of Sunday school to their waiting parents. Eileen returned the waves from a few of them as she tooled up Jefferson Street to the heights overlooking the town. She thought the cemetery might have visitors, but the threat of rain had dissuaded anyone else who might have come. She parked and unloaded her supplies—the yew bushes, a spade, some mulch, a plastic five-gallon water jug, and other accouterments. Lugging this all up to the plot was going to be a bit of work.

Eileen toiled in solitude. Momentary breaks in the clouds eased the threat of a downpour somewhat. She selected a site for the first yew, just off to the side of Helen's stone, and behind it. The spade cut through the sod and lifted it out in a clean round plug. Eileen had foreseen the need for a gunnysack to haul this away, and maneuvered to open the bag and deposit the turf inside. She dug a hole, piling the dirt on some old copies of the *St. Paul Pioneer Press* she'd spread out for this purpose.

The day wore on. Eileen hardly noticed the town below her emptying out, the relative bustle dying down, resolving into a languid day of restful reading and mid-afternoon naps. The wind came up a bit as she was packing mulch with her hands around the little trunk of the yew bush. The color of the needles was deep green, and she remembered the ancient Irish yews—*taxus baccata fastigiata*—that rose, craggy and tall, around the foundation of the motherhouse in Eau Claire. Maybe some weekend soon she'd drive over there for a visit.

Out of the corner of her eye Eileen spied something creeping slowly across the grass, and looked toward it. A bit of fabric of some kind, printed in mauve and white and tan. She watched it leap and pause and make its way, wind-driven, past her toward the fence below. As it made its nearest approach, Eileen recognized it as a handkerchief of fading silk, probably dropped from someone's pocket at a grave site up the hill, who knows how long ago. Would it catch on the stakes of the cemetery fence, she wondered, or blow onward, maybe even to the storm drains of the town, or all the way to the river?

Eileen welled with tears at this fleeting, serendipitous sight. What about a lost silk handkerchief could be so sad? It was pretty, and must have been dear to someone at some point. But what tragedy was there, really, in its waste? Or in its owner's carelessness? How could she be suddenly so sentimental, when yesterday she'd been utterly dispassionate, while sorting Elsie's cache? Eileen finished the first yew and pinched a few straggling fronds, to tidy its appearance. She stood and surveyed the effect of her labors thus far. For a moment, the loss of her family felt strangely acute, and Eileen winced, wiping tears onto the long sleeves of her shirt. Her pain, it occurred to her, was not just at losing all of them, but at being lost to them—well, particularly lost to her mother—and thereafter, lost to herself. How did the dead do this—keep the living from having a life? Eileen dissolved momentarily, into grief.

In a minute or two she was fairly sodden, but she regained her grip and thought about the second yew, which still awaited her. She had a notion to plant it nearest the grave of her father, the man she never knew. Was it possible that she did have a memory of him? She searched, finding none. She remembered his death, because she remembered her mother's bereavement at his death. Eileen knew Brigid had taken comfort in Helen when Frank died. Helen would go sit on Brigid's lap, engaging her in chatter about her day at first grade. That picture was clear. Why did her mother not, the next time, take comfort in Eileen? Was *she* not something valued, something to live for? Her mother's refusal seemed to Eileen like rebellion against God, and against Eileen's persistence in living, when so much that was loved had been taken away. How was Eileen ever to please a mother who saw her existence as mockery from on high, a taunt for ever having held treasure in her grasp? Eileen couldn't endure the exile. She had found the convent, and Marquette, and her students, and eventually the reservation. She had found the volunteer fire department and advanced cardiac lifesaving. She had not, it seemed, ever found God, or a mother's love.

Eileen got busy planting the second yew bush. She felt the spade underfoot, separating the roots of the grass and wiggling past rocks in the subsoil. The turned earth teemed with the castings of earthworms, with clumped bulbs of onion grass and discombobulated millipedes shaken from their slumber. Could she feel sympathy for her mother? In Eileen's absence, Brigid could value her—there was so much evidence of that in the relationship Brigid had with Elsie, and the news she had shared with her friend over the years. But why only in Eileen's absence? Perhaps this was Brigid's bargain with their silent, inscrutable God. Eileen might be precious to her mother, as long as Brigid regarded her own love as a dangerous thing, to be cast out—to be expiated, if anything—whenever Eileen was in proximity. Oh! How had this family ever brought such a blight upon itself?

Packing her things in the car a half hour later, Eileen looked down the grade toward Immaculate Conception Church, which lifted its spire to the heavens. She decided to pay a visit there. It was her grandmother's church, a little Gothic chapel where Eileen had been taken as a child when visiting on summer vacation. Stepping in the door, she found the pastor of the parish in his clerics, putting away the lectionary for the day.

"Hello," he said. "Just visiting?"

"Ah...yes," Eileen said.

"I'm Father McClure," he said, extending a hand. Eileen took it and gave it a brief shake.

"On your way out?" she asked.

"Soon," he said. "Is there something I can help you with?"

"I feel like I want to make my confession," she told him. "If you have the time." This was why she'd come here, indeed.

"Sure. Come right back," he said. "Do you want to use the box, or to do it face-to-face?"

"Well, I guess the confessional would be pointless. You've already seen my face."

"Very well," he said.

In the sacristy, they took seats facing each other, and Eileen began.

"Bless me, Father, for I have sinned. It's been...a long time...since my last confession."

What came next? Eileen stumbled, and went blank. Fr. McClure smiled. What was she doing here?

"Feel free to depart from the script, if you'd like," he said. He seemed to be a kind man.

Eileen considered this, and searched for her own words.

"What I need to talk about, happened so long ago. I only fully realized it just now, after all these years." She paused.

"Yes?" he said.

"I was here today, in the graveyard, visiting my mother's grave, and...well, planting some bushes. I just realized.... I've always known that I left home, at fourteen, to escape my mother because she was depressed."

"Where did you go?" he asked.

"The convent," she said, almost sheepishly.

"I see," the priest said.

"I think I finally realized," said Eileen, "that what was wrong was not my going—*per se*—but the way I left. I left in order to need her less than she needed me. Which was not much, I'll tell you!" She laughed. "But, the terrible thing is," her eyes misted over now, and she turned her face away, "I've done everything else the same way. You probably know, to be a religious can be a way to be against the culture around you. For me it's been about nothing so much as rejecting people, and the lives they live. Wanting to disapprove of them, to denounce them, even—at the very least to deprive them of my presence. Like saying 'I am God's, not yours...so leave me alone.'"

Fr. McClure was silent for a minute.

"Who did I really want to deprive, if not my mother?" Eileen asked. "How have I managed to be so hateful? So 'self-sufficient'? And so superior? Hiding all the while behind that stupid veil!"

"You left the convent?" he asked her.

"Well, I'm in my first year of exclaustration," she said.

"And you left because you believed you were there for the wrong reasons," he said.

"I don't know....," she blurted. "I just left. I didn't know why I left, only that I had to get out. I was dying there."

"You'll have to decide if there's reason enough to return," he suggested. "I'm sure you did a lot of good for people, nevertheless."

Eileen stopped and considered.

"I suppose so. Of course."

"This *error*," he said, eventually. "You came here to confess it and to turn from it."

"Well, yes," she said. She was hardly a step ahead of herself today. She surprised herself with every next thought. What was she committing herself to, for heaven's sake?

He returned to the script, absolving her formally, telling her to say ten *Hail Marys*, and saying finally, "Go, Sister, and sin no more."

She stood, and he rose as well. She took his hands in hers. "Thank you," she said, and squeezed. He smiled and nodded.

Stepping out of the church, Eileen thought about the priest. He was probably younger than she. Eileen was humbled to have needed him in this way, so urgently, in a painful moment. And so grateful to have found him here at the church. Eileen stopped abruptly on the steps. *Adrian*, she thought. What had she done, in avoiding him? She needed to reconnect with him. That comment he'd made about Estelle's daughter hadn't been his fault. Eileen was merely galled by her own guilt, if anything, that she let her own mother die alone. How was Adrian to know she'd see no humor when Estelle groused about her daughter's neglect? She felt a rush of affection for him as she walked down the sidewalk and pulled out the keys to her Volkswagen.

-13-

To Love a Thing, First Set It Free

Adrian ran a squeegee over the soaped windows of the Chevette, clearing away several weeks' worth of grime. He'd stopped on the way to Northfield to fuel the car and took a few extra minutes to clear his view of the scenery. Interstates 90 and 35 might not afford much to see, but the landscape did wear its fullest fall color, and the cobalt morning sky made the blanched shocks of corn on the rolling hills stand out over the contented grazing herds of Charolais pastured along the highway. As Adrian drove the last stretch of Highway 3 from Faribault, he found himself thinking about people he was missing—Terry and David, mostly, and Anne. Anne was one of his classmates from first-year law, a would-be hippie with long blonde hair and pheasant-feather earrings who liked to discuss politics by the hour. Why on a trip to Carleton did he start pining for them? There was something inspiring about the academic environment there, and Adrian longed for the camaraderie he'd shared with them. Was there was more to his feelings than that? He wondered when he'd get to see Sr. Eileen again. Sunday at the sem, he'd turned around for just a moment and somehow missed her. She'd been talking to Fr. Daimler, and the next thing Adrian knew she was gone. On Thursday at the nursing home, she was simply a no-show.

Adrian's copy of *Medea* sat next to him on the car seat. Today was his second meeting with Professor Gundersen, and he'd finished reading the play the night before. Now he was armed with pages of handwritten notes and the text itself, on which he'd highlighted the conundrums he hadn't been able to decipher.

The sun had just risen above the east windows in Leighton Hall when Adrian sauntered into Gundersen's third-floor office. Gundersen was busy hanging a new map on the wall with a little ball-peen hammer and a box of brads.

"Hey, Adrian," Gundersen said. "Be right with you."

Professor Gundersen was not a hoary academic—he wasn't yet forty. His reputation had exploded at a young age because he was so talented. Carleton may have nabbed him, but he was periodically flown to New York by other institutions, where fragments of ancient text would be flown from overseas to meet him, and he would translate for the weekend before flying back to Minnesota for his Monday classes. The map he was hanging this morning was the product of just such a jaunt back east.

"I found this in a bookshop on Sheridan Square," he said. "I don't think they realized it's nineteenth century, by the price I paid for it."

Adrian pretended, even to himself, not to notice the contours of Gundersen's butt and shoulders as the man stood on tip toe to situate this *plan of the Etruscan city of Vulci* above a bookcase.

"Can you hand me that sculpture?" Gundersen asked, pointing to one of several objects on his desk that had been moved to make room for the map. Adrian handed him a Roman statue of a horse, rearing up on its hind legs, one front leg broken off at the knee.

"There's still room for this one," Gundersen said. "I'll have to find another place for the others, I guess." He climbed down and started pulling texts off the bookshelf, preparing to get down to business.

"So, last week you were telling me that you might go on to theology school for your diocese," he said. "You didn't really say what you'd do if you decide against it."

"Well, I've already done one year of law school. I'd probably go back and finish."

"You've never considered doing your doctorate in classics?"

"I never got much encouragement for that."

"Why not?" Gundersen wondered.

"The dearth of jobs, I suppose," Adrian said.

"If I thought that way, I'd be running Gundersen's Olds and Mercury right now," he said. "That's the family business back in Crookston."

"I'm not sure that your options and mine really bear comparison," Adrian said, smiling.

"We'll see about that," Gundersen said. "Don't be such a pessimist. Now, how are you and Medea getting along?"

"Okay, I guess. I think I understand most of these references to the mythic past. But sometimes I'm not sure if I'm deciphering events in Greek mythology that are fantastical, or just inventing them through bad translation. Like here...." Adrian opened his notebook. "*Light begotten of Zeus, check the cruel and murderous Fury, take her from this house plagued by spirits of vengeance.* Is the sense here that Medea is possessed by a punishing divinity?"

"Yeah, you've got it," Gundersen said. "Or perhaps more accurately for the Greeks, she's the divinity's unconscious agent. You know, if you're unsure, it's not really cheating to check a resource on Greek myth."

That was good to hear. Perhaps Adrian was less a fool than he feared.

"And here," Adrian said. "Line 120. *The minds of royalty are dangerous: since they often command and seldom obey, they are subject to violent changes of mood. It is better to be accustomed to living on terms of equality.* Is the sense of this that Medea is being heartless and dictatorial, or that Cleon is?'

"Perhaps Euripides means both; he refers to Medea in the immediate situation, but he relates Medea's ruthlessness to Cleon's cruelty, indicating that one feeds the other. See, the end of this speech—*excessive riches are no advantage for mortals; when a god is angry at a house, they make the ruin greater*—it foreshadows the losses Cleon will incur before the tragedy ends. So he is one of the dangerous, powerful ones, yet one who will suffer devastation, as well."

Birds chattered in the tree top just beyond the sill of Gundersen's office window, and in the distance a riding mower circled a plot of grass, tingeing the air with the smell of half-combusted fuel. Adrian was self-conscious about not looking too often at the hair rising above the webbed collar of Gundersen's shirt, or at his bare arms.

"Now, if you turn to compare line 426…," Gundersen continued.

Come Wednesday Adrian felt more distracted from the routines at the seminary. He had tried to call David and Terry twice each in the past couple of days, but never found either of them at home. A long run in the afternoon did not help him feel more focused—he merely obsessed the whole time about whether or not Anne would think he was strange if he were to call her up, out of the blue. He finally concluded that he probably shouldn't phone Anne just because his other friends couldn't be reached.

Father Moriarty seemed to be in a particularly dour mood when Adrian slipped into a back row seat for formation lecture that evening. The room didn't settle down until Moriarty had cleared his throat a second time and uttered a somewhat plaintive "Please, men." It was probably the sems' anxiety over midterm exams the next week that had them so restless. Moriarty started in on his lecture on obedience to God's will.

"The self-willed are characterized by the sin of pride," Moriarty said. "They believe they have no need of God, and no need to submit themselves to his will."

Self-willed took its place on the left side of the chalkboard. The sinister side, Adrian noted.

"Obedience to the Lord is characterized by humility—humility of spirit, humility of intellect, humility of body. We acknowledge our sinfulness and brokenness, and ask God to show us His way, through the teachings of the Holy Father and the magisterium of the Church."

I should really try to listen to this, Adrian thought, struggling not to dismiss Moriarty the moment he opened his mouth, or even sooner—the minute Moriarty affected the scowl he always wore, betraying his impatience and contempt. Adrian thought of his mother, glaring at him and Beth Ann for playing *itsy bitsy spider* with their fingers during church, although they did so silently, without singing the words. His mother's commonality with Fr. Moriarty certainly made it more difficult for Adrian to sit still for the rector's talks.

"The self-willed are arrogant and do not seek true knowledge, the knowledge of God's plan for man," Moriarty said.

Adrian thought of an early memory, not of being in church but of being at home, which was somehow emblematic of his relationship with his mother, and frequently came back to him. She had been cooking a stew on the top of the stove to take to a church supper, and Adrian had been standing on a chair next to her to watch as she chopped potatoes and carrots and put them into the pot. Adrian was three or four years old—it was before he went to school. He remembered her giving several shakes of salt and pepper into the stew before putting Adrian off the chair— "Get down, now," she'd said—and going to the bathroom mirror to fix her hair. Adrian had climbed back onto the chair, and Eleanor had come into the kitchen to find him shaking more pepper into the pot. He remembered her shouting, and swatting him on the bottom. And then her retelling, seemingly forever, how he had wanted to ruin her stew when she had no time to make another batch to take to the church. This episode came to mind whenever Adrian thought of his early years at home, before he'd gone to first grade and become a star pupil for Mrs. Hesch, and had risen in standing in the world. It was the memory of his mother looking at him on the chair by the stove and not seeing him, or seeing his true motives; instead being aware only of her own frustration, as if he were a witless animal, or nothing at all, save for an adverse circumstance in her world, like bad weather or slow traffic.

Moriarty was continuing to sketch what for him was apparently simple, this difference between self-will and God's will. Adrian ruefully cradled his chin on the heel of his hand and drummed his fingertips on the arch of his cheekbone. Sometimes these moments hadn't bothered him as much. He maintained a little hope, perhaps, that Moriarty would eventually recognize virtue in him, and would reflect this in some warmth, some praise or recognition. Any more, it seemed to Adrian that it would have to be *around*, and not through, this particular voice of the magisterium—the director of priestly formation at Holy Name—that he would find his own route to the priesthood. He should just accept it, already.

The notion seemed at once sad and a kind of relief. Moriarty was perhaps—no, surely—as flawed and broken as anyone else. Maybe his stridency came from the turbulent currents flowing under his own surface. Instead of just feeling angry, could Adrian step out of the shadows where blame was always being cast? Why did Adrian automatically assume that all of Moriarty's sackcloth and ashes were meant for him, personally? There in fact might be something new for Adrian to discover, sitting in this room.

Bob Holly sought Adrian out for night prayer when the talk had ended. They carried their breviaries back to Adrian's room.

"Does he get to you?" Adrian asked Bob.

"What do you mean?"

"You know. Does Moriarty get you down?"

Bob shrugged his shoulders.

"He's a little pessimistic," Bob said. "But I figure that's just him."

"Right," Adrian said.

They turned to the order of the evening office and began to recite the antiphon.

Later on, Adrian had insomnia. He got up with a slight headache, which wasn't helping him fall asleep, and he fumbled in the cabinet above his sink in the moonlight for a bottle of aspirin. Then he slipped on a pair of khakis, a pullover sweater and sandals, and stole down the back stairwell and out the door to the grounds. Crickets and bullfrogs chanted mightily in the crisp night air. If Adrian hadn't known the path through the woods so well, he might have stumbled down the slope to the river, but he walked here often. A fallen tree trunk served as a crude bench on the bank above the slough, and Adrian sat to gaze at the light reflecting across the water.

His mother was still on his mind. There was something about his being the youngest that seemed to amplify his mother's considerable impatience when it came to him. He'd been wrong in so many situations, for being childish, and being naïve to boot. As if Eleanor, having reared three previous children, expected not to have to repeat what she'd already taught one of them. In this regard—among others—she didn't live entirely in reality. Adrian had been able sometimes to joke with his Uncle Nance about this matter at family gatherings. Nance had been born last of Eleanor's siblings, and frequently got the same reproachful look Adrian got from her—as if he shouldn't have forgotten something he actually had no way of knowing.

"I don't know what sin I've committed," he said to Adrian, once. "But I'm supposed to remember it, and it shouldn't need to be named."

Adrian knew from his mother's comments the nature of Nance's transgression: Nance had been their father Jude's favorite, and remained so even though he left Minnesota, left the quarry for a desk job, even married a Protestant and quit going to church. Eleanor had never done the least profligate or scandalous thing, and what favor did she ever receive for it? Nance had no idea that this was what Eleanor resented.

Adrian was clueless, like this—he was born after the first chapters were written, and remained a bit confused all his life. His mother begrudgingly let him take up the French horn, but then she'd go to the lunchroom whenever the band played for halftime at school sporting events. Why such determination on her part to deny him? Someday, if Adrian had nieces and nephews, he might ask them if his mother ever explained her feelings toward him, and finally gain some insight. It couldn't all be about spoiling her stew.

Adrian nearly forgot this rumination had started with Fr. Moriarty's lecture tonight. He had his mother and Moriarty so thoroughly conflated, in his head. He seemed to feel responsible for the rift between him and his mother as much as that between him and Fr. Moriarty. He wondered if his mother even noticed it. He sometimes thought she'd married his father *because of* how little attention she was required to pay to him. Harvey's demands were unlikely to be very personal. (They were both English and Catholic, after all. What was there to discuss?) This state of affairs in his parents' marriage was pretty evident, and his father and mother seemed only to lack the imagination that it might be anything else. Sitting above the riverbed, with Holy Name at his back, Adrian felt alone, yet not nearly as doomed as usual. He sensed he was finally coming to terms with the past. Eventually he became aware of the mosquitoes biting him, and hiked briskly back to the seminary.

On Thursday morning, Adrian needed to chat with Fr. Moriarty about the upcoming liturgy for All Saints' Day. Bishop Simmons was expected to visit on that occasion, along with the chancellor and vicar of the diocese, and Adrian, as sacristan, was responsible for coordinating vestments for all of them. Some chasubles might have to be borrowed from the cathedral.

"Good morning," Father Moriarty said, when Adrian entered the rector's study. "I've been giving this celebration some thought. We have the option of wearing red or white for the Solemnity of All Saints. I think I'd like to use the white ones. Check the number we have on hand, will you, and also the length. Father Hanover is about 6'3", and needs an extra long or he looks comical. Have you had the cassocks dry-cleaned recently?"

"No, but I will," Adrian said.

"We haven't really had a chance to talk since you returned," Moriarty said. "How is it to be back?"

"Well…I feel I have a fresh eye for things, in some respects," Adrian said.

"That's good. You seem like you've matured in your year away," Moriarty said. "You seem more relaxed."

Adrian suppressed a giggle at this.

"Yes, Father," he said, giving Moriarty a nod before stepping into the hallway.

He reached David at the strangest of times—on a weekday, at mid-morning.

"Hey, what's up?" David said.

"Nothing special. I hadn't found you at home the last few evenings, so I took a crack at calling during the day."

"Well, I'm glad you reached me. How's Holy Name?"

"Not bad, actually," Adrian said.

"Come now. The truth."

"A lot of things are the same. But I don't know…a lot of the negatives don't seem to matter as much as they once did."

"Not even the big negative—Father meretricious, or, I mean—Moriarty?"

"It's funny. I just figured out he doesn't have to like me."

"That's good, since he's obviously never going to!"

"Isn't that the truth."

"Why the revelation now?" David said.

"I don't know. I'm slow to accept things," Adrian said. "It's like what my sister Carol told me once about acne."

"Acne?"

"Yes. She said not to worry about, I'd grow up and get over it. At the time, I thought she meant it would go away. I don't know why—it's not like hers completely cleared up. Finally I realized she meant I'd get over thinking it was so important. She never had any dates in high school because of it, and eventually, here she was a nursing supervisor in an ICU, and being rejected by a bunch of doofuses back in Ryder High School wasn't such a big deal."

"And Moriarty is a doofus."

"You put such a fine point on things, David. In a way...yes. Or, I'm not a kid any longer, and I can live with blemishes. They're not such a tragedy."

"Cool. It's about time," David said.

"As always, you're a paragon of empathy."

"*De nada*, dude. So, are you coming up to the Cities any time soon?"

"I still have to follow the rules, David. No free weekend until Thanksgiving."

"Oh, right. Self-denial. You groove on that, don't you? I keep forgetting."

"And how's *your* religion, these days?" Adrian asked.

"I'm tired of it. Maybe I'll become a fireman instead."

"Oh? What's bothering you?"

"The advancement committee. I have to write them an essay about my 'faith journey' and why I'm seeking ordination. It's such a hoop to jump through, it almost makes me start to ask, 'Yeah, why do I want ordination? What was I thinking?' Ted wants to kill me when I start talking like that."

"Aren't you sure you want it?"

"I don't know what my problem is. Putting the reasons on paper is intimidating. I guess it's committing myself to the idea."

"I can relate to that. If Moriarty isn't the obstacle for me, then what is?"

"Cel-i-ba-cy."

"You still don't really get me, do you?"

"Maybe not. But I'm telling you. Cel-i-ba-cy."

"How do we explain your problem, then?"

"Okay, okay. Score one for the Underwood."

"Thank you," Adrian said.

That afternoon, Adrian was studying in a window seat at the student center when a fine-boned pair of hands squeezed his shoulders.

"Hey there."

It was Burgess, leaning over him with a pack full of books on her back.

"Good to see you," she said.

"Hi!" Adrian said. "You look like you've been hitting it hard." He motioned to the weight of her pack.

"Tuesday/Thursday is my heavy class schedule," she said, "but I've got a two-hour break at lunch. Yay!" She plopped down next to him. "I'm starved. Have you eaten?"

"I was just thinking of going," he said.

"What do you say we get off campus and get something? Do you have time?"

"Yeah, sure. What did you have in mind?"

"Anything will do. I'd be happy with Burger King."

"I've never gone there. Is it just a few blocks?" he asked.

"Five or six, I guess. You're not a health food nut, are you? I have to confess, I love Burger King."

"No, just a creature of habit. I've always gone to the cafeteria."

"Then let a townie take you for a walk on the wild side," she said, getting up from the seat.

"Lead on," he answered.

At Burger King, they carried their trays into the dining room and sat looking out at the jungle gym, where pre-schoolers swarmed and their mothers called for them to take bites of their burgers and sips of their pop.

"Were you a put-me-down child or a pick-me-up child?" Burgess asked.

"A what?" Adrian asked.

"Look at the little boy in the red sweatshirt. He's a pick-me-up child. See, he keeps looking to his mother to pick him up, even though she expects him to run and play."

"Yeah, I think you're right," Adrian observed. "That makes him a pick-me-up child?"

"I have this theory that we're all either put-me-down children or pick-me-up children. And it follows us all through life. I was a put-me-down child. My mother never got it. She still doesn't. 'Put me down, I want to go to Europe.' She wants to know 'Why would you want to do that?'"

"I'm not sure this would stand up to scientific scrutiny," he said.

"Probably not. But I think it could explain a lot," she said, stuffing shreds of lettuce back into her burger. "So which would you be?"

"What's your guess?"

"I'd say a put-me-down child, definitely."

"No question," he agreed. "Is that obvious?"

"I've gathered as much from your comments in class."

"What comments?"

"Any of them. You never accept anything on authority—which is good. But it's not the attitude of a 'mommy, pick me up' child."

"Hmm," he said, and smiled.

"What?" she asked.

"I was just thinking of a conversation I had once with Bill Nelson. He was the head prefect in my class at the sem. I really liked him, but I remember the exact moment when I realized how different we were."

"When was that?" she asked.

"We were standing in the stairwell at Holy Name, and we were talking about Sr. Bart's class on the New Testament. He was really troubled because Bart said in class that the historical Jesus is not shown by biblical criticism to have thought of himself as God. And Bill said, 'If my parents knew they were teaching me this, they'd probably want me to come home.' Meanwhile I was thinking that that was one of the most thrilling days of my life, learning that the Church didn't require a literal reading of even the New Testament."

"Sure. There you have a classic 'pick-me-up/put-me-down' divergence in thinking," Burgess declared. "Some people want security, and others want freedom."

"You've got the divergence part right," Adrian said. "Bill went to Mount St. Mary's for theology school, the most conservative place in the country. I could barely fathom it."

"I'm telling you, it's a theory with great explanatory power," Burgess said. "Don't underestimate it."

"Could you go have a talk with Father Moriarty for me? Tell him I'm just a put-me-down child, I can't help it if I question authority."

"Okay. I'll try," Burgess said. "That is, if women are allowed past the door of the seminary."

"You're allowed on the first floor," Adrian said.

"You're kidding! Nowhere else?"

"No, I'm not kidding."

"Jesus."

"Stricter than Jesus, actually. Jesus let Mary Magdalene, Joanna, and Susannah travel with the twelve throughout Galilee."

"I don't know why that reminds me, but can you explain something to me?"

"I'll try," said Adrian.

"Explain *Humanae Vitae*."

"Sympathetically?"

"How ever."

"Well, it was a 1968 encyclical...."

"I know that much."

"And it unexpectedly took the position that using birth control was a sin. It reverted to Thomistic moral theory, which is based on the idea of Natural Law. Natural Law Theory is a teleological theory, or in other words, it holds that the will of God can be inferred from observing the natural end, or purpose—*telos*, in Greek—to which things are directed. So it concluded that copulation without the possibility of conception is counter to the natural purpose of the act, and counter to the will of God."

"Aren't sterile people, or women after menopause, or women menstruating equally unable to conceive?"

"I guess the idea is that those are circumstances God created; He's allowed to frustrate his own ends. And we can't."

"Is this where the Church got its teaching about homosexuality? Two men or two women can't conceive?"

"There's also Lot's wife turning into a pillar of salt. But basically, yes."

"Doesn't God make homosexuals, they same way he makes menses and menopause?"

"Don't ask me to explain it."

"They really think conception is the only important purpose in sex? What about it's interpersonal meaning? That counts for nothing?"

"You have to realize that the whole idea of companionate marriage is a relatively recent innovation."

"And not a worthy one?"

"When I am pope, trust me—the whole thing will get revisited."

After Shakespeare class, Adrian walked with Jenkins back to his office, to borrow a book for the thesis he was writing.

"Are you done for the afternoon?" Jenkins asked, handing him the book from a shelf.

"Yeah, I am. Why?"

"I'm trying to round someone up to help me load a rototiller. I had to bring it in to the Coast-to-Coast for repairs, and it's ready. But the old man who owns the shop says his help got off work early, and he's too frail to help me load it. All my work-study students are gone for the day. I could come back for it Saturday, but I live quite a few miles out. I'd like to get it today if I could."

"Sure, if you can drop me back at campus afterward. I have my bicycle here."

"No problem. I'd really appreciate it," said Ernie. "Let me just get my keys and turn out the lights."

"Where do you live?" Adrian asked, as they headed down the back stairs to the parking lot.

"Out near Money Creek, actually."

"On a farm?"

"Yes. My friend raises dairy cows, so it's a working farm."

"By friend you mean...your lover?" Adrian asked.

"Well, yes," Jenkins said, stammering slightly.

"How long has he done that?"

"He used to teach philosophy. He bagged it about ten years ago and bought this farm. He worked on a dairy farm in high school, and liked it, so he found a way to make the switch. He gets up at four in the morning to milk, and he's done by eight and in for breakfast. Then he's often free until the four o'clock milking. There's always the crop work to do, and haying season, but he reserves a lot of time to read. He couldn't deal very well with the politics of teaching. He says this is his ideal life."

"Sounds like it is," Adrian said.

They reached the truck and climbed in. Jenkins looked over at Adrian for a moment, then shook his head before starting the ignition.

"What?" Adrian asked.

"Nothing. I usually never come out to students. I'm not sure what came over me. And a seminarian, to boot!"

"I suppose it's because I asked you. Do you think it's a problem, your telling me?"

"It could be. I might lose my job, actually. It's what drove Doug out of teaching."

"Doug is...."

"My partner."

"He got into trouble?"

"Mostly just the threat of trouble. He finally couldn't live with it any more. Now he makes no bones about it with anyone. To a fault, I'd say. He's perfectly blunt about it, and lets the other farmers down at the feed store just deal with it. I'm not sure how he pulls it off, but he does. We're quite different in that way."

Adrian looked at Jenkins's cardigan sweater and loafers, and surmised that this was just the beginning of that story.

"Could you really lose your job?"

"Theoretically. It's actually only happened once here, with a priest who had sex with a student and got shipped off for 'treatment.' But I was officially unofficially warned about it."

"By whom? The president?"

"Her surrogate."

"Wow. That's serious," Adrian said.

"Well, you of all people should know about the ways of the Church. I don't know if I'm safer being with Doug, or more vulnerable. Common sense would say I'm less a threat if I'm happily married, but then, the magisterium says the only good gay is a celibate gay, so who knows. Of course it can't even be acknowledged at Assisi that we exist."

"We?" Adrian said.

"Oh, no," Jenkins protested. "I'm not about to come out on anyone else's behalf. They'll have to take their own risks."

"No, it's not that. I thought maybe you figured...." And now, Adrian stammered.

"Oh," Jenkins said. They had arrived at the store, and Jenkins turned off the engine. "Look, I'll pay you for helping out. I'm taking up your time."

"No need," Adrian said, firmly. "I'm happy to help."

Jenkins settled his repair bill, and he and Adrian hoisted the tiller into the truck bed.

"Who gardens?" Adrian asked.

"It's mostly me. Doug farms the forage crops, and I grow vegetables. I just brought in the squash and tomatoes, so it's time to spread the compost and till."

"Sounds pretty idyllic."

"I never thought I'd say this, but we're both very happy out there," Jenkins said.

It was strange to view Ernie in this light—no longer just an academic, but a person with a life away from Assisi. Adrian didn't know why he'd been privileged with a glimpse of it. Adrian gazed at Ernie, slightly surprised. Jenkins pulled up in front of Marian Hall to drop Adrian off.

"You know, speaking of good gays and bad gays...," said Ernie.

"We were?" said Adrian.

"Stay away from Father Tyler."

"I shouldn't run any errands with him?"

"Definitely not. The man is truly evil. I don't know why *he's* never been sent away. There's got to be something unholy that goes on between him and the bishop. Not sex, of course, but power. It's the only way to explain why he's still around."

"I'll follow the advice," said Adrian.

"Good," said Ernie. "Well...see you in class."

Adrian watched Ernie lift one finger from the steering wheel in a farmer's wave and drive off. Adrian walked to the bike rack next to the building. His own instincts had warned him off Fr.

Tyler years ago, but Ernie didn't know that. His protectiveness toward Adrian was sweet, and fatherly.

Adrian shoved off from the asphalt and lifted his far leg over the seat of his bike. The sun was low in the western sky and the clouds on the horizon were tinged with red along with blue and white. He would be just in time to meet Eileen for dinner hour at the nursing home.

-14-

Not an Island

Eileen hardly knew what to do with herself the past few days—and that was a good thing. An affliction that had always permeated her life, of indeterminate origin, was finally pinned to a specific cause. Now it remained in the past, captive of its own time, a hostage of memory where once it had been its warden. In the present, in the space it left vacant, there was suddenly air and light. Eileen could see her forlorn state in junior high school, and her increasingly lonely sojourn through the years, yet imagine a future open to possibility, not mired in a certainty of despair. Initially at one with the vagrant handkerchief passing through the cemetery, now she felt only murmurs of regret for its decease.

Eileen did what was immediately possible, which was throw herself into work on the house, making it look like someone owned it and lived there. She repaired the mortar between the foundation stones, re-hung the gaping rain gutters, replaced the shattered glass on the porch light. She sometimes sang while she worked, catches of songs she'd forgotten she knew, rounds from grade school choral programs, and from Girl Scout camp: *To catch rats as cats can, catch as cats catch them, only cats' children can catch to match them.* It was a silly nonsense song that she and Helen had sung, to their mother's eventual torment. Rather than stay at school in the afternoons and complete lesson plans,

Eileen came home as soon as possible to work on projects until the sun went down. Indoor work could wait until after dark.

At the St. Francis Home on Thursday, Adrian had grinned to see Eileen, even before she'd said hello to him. Eileen hadn't needed to explain herself, only to show up and resume where they'd left off. Life was such a surprise, at times. Adrian was full of excitement about any number of things—a plan to go build houses in Appalachia over spring break with the campus social justice group; the prospect of going to see *The Trojan Women* performed at the Guthrie Theater over Thanksgiving; a liturgy planned at Holy Name for the Solemnity of All Saints. He appeared to be unaware of her foolish twists and turns, and that was just as well. She was content that he was happy to see her again.

On Saturday Eileen had a date to help Elsie dig her parsnips and potatoes in the garden. Elsie could ill manage the trips up and down the cellar steps to put them in storage. Eileen brought wooden crates up from Elsie's basement to the yard, and pulled a stocking cap over her head to stay the wind blowing in from the east.

"Oh, the carrots!" Elsie said, as if she'd forgotten even about planting them. Perhaps she had, in fact. They were as plump and colossal as the claims in any seed catalog, growing under aromatic whorls of vivid green leaves next to a row of four o'clocks, now limp and blackened by the frost. Eileen fetched spadefuls of sandy soil at one end of the garden and shook them over the carrots Elsie piled into a crate.

"Your mother planted those golden nugget carrots," she said. "I thought they were a waste of space. All that top and just a tiny round root. But you could stew them whole, like a new potato."

The parsnips filled three crates, the potatoes five and counting. Eileen lumbered to the cellar with the fifth, and when she returned, she found Elsie hunched over a little, with both hands grasping the handle of her spade.

"Time for a break," Elsie announced.

In Elsie's house, Eileen lifted the lid of the cookie jar, a fat monk holding a scroll saying "thou shalt not." Eileen was sentimental about this old piece. As a girl Eileen loved to go into Elsie's house partly because of the cookies in that jar, although she'd never been allowed in the house without her mother, even if invited. Now she wondered why. Did her mother fear she and Helen would be an imposition? Elsie baked continually for her own family, fat molasses cookies and fork-marked peanut butter cookies, chocolate oatmeal drops and butter spritzes. Eileen remembered watching Elsie replenish the jar on occasion from tins in the pantry, amazed that there was no end to abundance here.

Eileen was thinking for some reason about her mother sewing Helen's first communion dress, and trying it on her in stages. Helen had been rapturous in that white lace A-line gown and veil. Come her turn, Eileen wore the same dress, borrowed.

"You know what?" she said to Elsie, who was lathering her hands at the kitchen sink.

"What."

"Remember the summer of Helen's first communion?"

"Certainly," said Elsie, whose thoughts were in the past more often than not.

"I wish mother had made me my own communion dress, instead of putting me in Helen's."

"I suppose she thought that would be a waste of lace, since she was living on the pension by then," Elsie said.

"Exactly," Eileen said. "But I'd have been happy with cotton voile, if only it were my own."

Elsie looked halfway in her direction. "Yes, I know that," she said.

Eileen took a pecan sandie out of Elsie's jar and put the lid back in place. There was a moment of silence, and Eileen wondered if Elsie would say more on the subject. She wasn't sure what she wanted Elsie to say. Just something.

"You're going to take the last crate of vegetables home for yourself, now, aren't you?" Elsie said. "We'll put in some of everything. Do you have one of those new crock-pots? It would be worth it for a working person like you, that's for sure."

Eileen thought back to Sr. Vincent Thomas, who insisted Eileen take with her the crock-pot she'd bought for their house in Fort Yates.

"I have one," Eileen said.

"Good," said Elsie. "I pulled the onions last month, and they're tied in bunches from the rafters, down there. Bring one of those up, too."

"Yes, ma'am," Eileen replied, although she was weary of the cellar stairs herself.

Eileen was in her own cellar when the phone rang. It was Cindy, calling from the nursing home.

"I thought you might like to know, Estelle was sent to the hospital last night. It's probably a bladder infection. She's prone to those, being in the wheelchair like she is. I expect they'll treat it and she'll be back in a few days. But if you're on campus during the week, she's right there at St. Joseph Hospital, so you might drop by with a book, if you want."

"Thanks so much for calling," Eileen said.

"Well, that's all," Cindy said, and hung up.

Eileen thought about how to reach Adrian. Could she simply call Holy Name? She would see him if she were there for Mass tomorrow, but maybe he'd like to plan to visit over the weekend, given his schedule. She found a phone directory in the hall desk, and looked under "Catholic Church" in the yellow pages. There was a listing for Holy Name. It was almost ten minutes before the seminarian who answered the phone came back and said, "He'll pick up in the booth."

And then in a minute Adrian said, "Hello?"

"It's me. Eileen."

"Hey. What's up?"

"Cindy just called to say that Mrs. Haney went into the hospital last night, maybe for bladder problems. She thought we might want to visit and take her a book or something."

"Is it serious?"

"I didn't get that idea. Apparently it's happened before. She's prone to them, since she doesn't ambulate."

"Today is not good. I could go tomorrow, after Mass."

"I'll wait out front, okay?"

"Till tomorrow, then."

At St. Joseph Medical Center, the woman at the patient information desk scrawled a complicated series of digits and letters on a scrap of paper and handed it to them.

"Fourth floor," she said. "Take those elevators."

When they arrived, the geriatric medicine wing seemed noisy, and the nurses were dashing in and out of sight, from the supply closet to the chart rack and back to patient rooms.

"32B is infiltrating. Can you call the i.v. team?" a nurse asked the ward clerk.

"There is no i.v. team. It's Sunday, remember."

"Of course. I forgot. You'll have to page the resident, then."

"Soon as I get off the phone with pulmonary," the clerk promised. "I'm on hold right now."

As a background to the rushing staff, a low continuous moan came from one of the patient rooms, and up the hall, screams of anger over some procedure.

"Go away! *Go away*, I say. Let me die. Oh please, God, let me die. Put that catheter up your own God-damned pee hole! Oh, Jesus."

"Can I help you?" the ward clerk asked, with surreal calm.

"We're looking for a friend," Eileen said. "Mrs. Estelle Haney."

"Well, you found her. You hear all that commotion?"

"Nooo...," Eileen uttered.

"None other. She's not able to have visitors just now. Maybe in a half hour or so. She usually calms herself down. Although this time I think she might be a bit delirious. I'm not sure she knows where she is, or why. You might have to make it brief."

Eileen and Adrian took a seat in a waiting area near the elevators.

After a few minutes, Cindy stepped off the elevator, looking remarkably civilian in an olive pantsuit and pale yellow blouse.

"Cindy!" Adrian said, when he spied her.

She turned and came over to where they were seated.

"How do things look today?" she asked. "Have you been in to see her? Has the doctor been here yet?"

"Things are volatile, from appearances," Eileen said. "No, we haven't been in to see her."

"She tends to get very cranky when she's ill. I probably should have warned you. Yesterday she did let me into her room—but then, I don't give her much opportunity to object. She's used to me seeing her sick."

"They said to wait until some procedure is finished," Eileen said.

"Okay. I'll wait with you here."

But Cindy was not good at waiting. Within a few minutes, she had padded down the hall to the nursing station and determined exactly what was being done.

"It's low urinary output," she informed Adrian and Eileen. Then she went up the hall to Mrs. Haney's room. She stood in the doorway for a minute, and before long insinuated herself into the matter. "Let me tape that for you," Eileen heard Cindy say, before her voice became muffled by the room. And then in a moment, the single word, "Stelly!" was decipherable in the hubbub.

The commotion in Estelle's room did not subside with the addition of Cindy, and in fact, the pitch seemed to climb. Finally, there arose a voice shouting, "I said, leave my hands free!" and then there was a crash of glass against the floor.

"Well, that's sure to convince us!" said another female voice. "Get a pair of wrist restraints. Has someone called the psychiatrist?"

Cindy came out of the room, a wet streak diagonally across her face and shoulder, looking a bit stunned.

"She threw her flowers at me. I brought her those flowers, yesterday. I guess she really wants to be left alone."

"Come on," Adrian said, placing a hand on Cindy's shoulder. "Let's go to the cafeteria and have some coffee."

"Okay," she said. For once, Cindy looked ready to be led.

As the elevator descended in quiet, Cindy unexpectedly lost her composure.

"There, now," Adrian said, pulling her shoulder against his chest.

"I'm sorry," Cindy said. "I can never get past the door with Estelle. I don't know why I don't just give up and stop caring."

Eileen felt strangely paralyzed for a moment. The elevator chimed, and the door opened on the cafeteria.

After they got their coffee, Adrian began to entertain them with stories about his year volunteering at the hospital.

"You never told me about that," Eileen said.

"Or me, either," said Cindy.

Adrian shrugged his shoulders. "The seminary is big on the corporal works of mercy. Sems even go visit prisoners at the jail. It's one way I've always been in sync with the place."

"Sounds like you got in there and got your hands dirty," Cindy said.

"I helped the aides and orderlies do the scut jobs, basically. There was this aide named Linda, who was really bad-tempered. One night she and I were it, as far as non-licensed staff went, and we were trying to get all the incontinent patients dry before shift change, because that was her responsibility. There was this old woman, Hildegarde, who spoke only Norwegian, because she didn't care to speak English—not because she didn't know any. She would swear at all of us in Norwegian until we said, 'We can't understand you,' and then she'd swear at us in English. She was waiting in her chair to be put back into bed, and when I looked in on her, I thought she'd fallen asleep in her chair, she was so slumped. I told Linda so. Then when Linda walked into her room, I heard a scream, and Linda rushed out, urine streaming down her whole body, including her face. Hildegarde had been hiding a full bedpan, and laying in wait for her. All Linda said was, 'I...am...going...home...now.' And she left me there by myself to clean up Hildegarde and finish the others."

Cindy took comfort in this story, it seemed, able to laugh at a horror worse than her own.

"That girl could have been fired," Cindy said.

"The supervisor took pity, I guess. And after that, whenever Linda was cranky, the other aides and nurses had this joke. They'd say, 'Is that a *pissy* mood you're in, Linda?' And everyone would crack up."

"Including Linda?" Eileen asked.

"Including Linda."

Mona St. John was sitting alone in the library at Beckett High School when Eileen came up the hallway with her bag to start the week. Eileen was used to being the early bird, meeting the dawn in the echoing caverns of the school along with the superintendent, who arrived to unlock the building and brew a pot of coffee in his office before any traffic stirred in the neighborhood. Mona held a book to her bowed head and read through glasses barely at rest on the tip of her nose. She sat moving her lips just slightly, quite mesmerized by her subject, which Eileen now recognized was the freshman Spanish book, *Curros y Chocolate.*

"Good morning, Mona," Eileen said.

"Oh!" Mona said, nervously putting a finger on the page and closing the book against her chest. "Good morning."

"It's alright, Mona. It's only Spanish."

"Oh. Yes," she said.

"You're here early."

"It's my new resolution," said Mona.

"Resolution?"

"My father had another heart attack, and my mother is going to early morning Mass at church every day during the week. She wanted me to go with her, but I said I would make my own resolution. I would come to school early every day and study so I can get a scholarship for college. That way my father will know I am taken care of, and he won't have to worry."

"Do you have brothers and sisters?" Eileen asked.

"Yes, lots."

"How many?"

"Lots," Mona said. "But I'm third from youngest. After me there's just Henry and the twins. I guess that makes me fourth from last, actually."

"And your father worries about who will provide if something should happen."

"A lot."

"An admirable plan, you have, then," Eileen said.

"Thank you, Miss Eileen."

"Have your brothers and sisters gone to college?"

"No. They didn't want to go. But me, I've always said I was going. It's been Dad's promise since I was little that I could go, because he knew I wanted to."

"Do you know where you want to go?"

"No. I don't know that much about colleges. I know they have them in Minnesota. And some are in Wisconsin. Some I could never go to, though."

"Why not?"

"They're for people smarter than me!" Mona said.

"You should wait and see," Eileen advised her. "How did you get the idea to go to college, if none of your family went?"

"There was this one time on *Charlie's Angels* when.... Do you know Kate Jackson? She is talking to one of the other angels, and they're trying to catch this guy, and she says—because she figured out where he was staying with his girlfriend—'I didn't go to four years of college for nothing!'"

"That was it?" Eileen asked. "Because one of Charlie's Angels had gone to college?"

"She was pretty. And her hair was dark like mine," Mona explained.

"Was that the first time you heard someone say they'd been to college?"

"Anyone cool I could think of. Besides my teachers. And like, Rosalyn Carter or someone."

"Did you like Rosalyn Carter?"

"Sure. And I liked Amy."

"I'm almost sure Amy Carter is in college, now," Eileen said.

"I knew she would go. She was a bookworm. And she was the president's daughter."

"A lot of people go to college who aren't the president's daughter, Mona."

"If they're smart enough, right?"

"And if they make up their mind. A lot of people don't go just because they didn't make up their mind."

"I hope I can learn chemistry, Miss Eileen. I might want to be a doctor. Or maybe a science teacher. I don't know yet."

"It looks like first you have to learn *un poco Español*."

"*Si, señora*," Mona said, and laughed.

"Well, I'll leave you to it. See you in seventh period."

Every time Eileen had seen Sister Florence, she noted how sculpted and thick Florence's head of hair was, emerging from the sides of her veil. It was quite surprising when she looked in the mirror at the Beauty Barn on Tuesday afternoon and realized that the woman in the chair back-to-back with her own, emerging from under the tempestuous toweling-off administered by *Hello my name is...Raylene*, was none other than the diocesan comptroller herself. Eileen giggled involuntarily. "Sister Florence!" she said.

"Who is...? Eileen O'Rourke? Is that you?"

"Yes, it's me."

"Well, fancy meeting here!"

"Yes, fancy that."

"I keep thinking we're going to invite you for dinner, but something is always happening. I've been travelling so much lately. How are you?"

"Good! And you?"

"Very well."

"I would have thought a look as refined as yours came from a ritzier place than the Beauty Barn," Eileen said.

"Shhh, now. You'll embarrass me. Or insult Raylene."

"Don't worry," Raylene offered. "I don't need credit here. With hair like this, the barber down the street could use his clippers and she'd come out looking like dynamite."

"Is that something I want to look like? Dynamite?" Florence asked, skeptically.

"You do, Sister. You are. Dynamite, or whatever word the kids have come up with lately," said Raylene.

"I guess it's a compliment," Florence said, with a roll of her eyes and a slight tone of renunciation, as befitted a nun.

"Get used to it," Raylene said, snapping her gum.

"What are we doing today?" Eileen's stylist asked her.

"Just an inch off, everywhere but the bangs."

Soon the sound of scissors was all that punctuated the quiet.

"Eileen," Florence said, "there's a retreat coming up in November, at the Augustinian House in Racine. I didn't know if you might be interested. I have a couple of friends at Assisi who are making it with me. We'd be pleased to have you along, if you'd like."

"Gosh. I guess that might be possible," Eileen said. "I'll have to think about it."

"The deadline for registration is November 15, I believe."

"Then I'll let you know before then."

By Thursday when school let out, Eileen recognized she was feeling anxious. She had just an hour until she had to be at the nursing home, and the contingencies therein loomed in her thoughts: she had to drop some resource manuals at the school library and stop on the way home to put gas in the car. Hopefully she'd get to the house in time to take the coupons from Sunday's paper over to Elsie, and would find Elsie at home. But what if she didn't? Would it matter? As Eileen greeted Sr. Adele in the library and deposited the manuals on a table, she realized she might be feeling a *good* anxious. Cindy had left a message yesterday that Mrs. Haney was back from the hospital, and her infection seemed to be resolving. Eileen was happy to be going, to see

Estelle on the mend, and to natter with their seminarian for a while.

The nurse on "C" wing today was not a familiar face. She looked up at Eileen and Adrian when they walked onto the ward, and her first words were jovial, almost a whoop.

"Hello! You the volunteers? Quite a day you've picked. But God bless you, we can use you. Half the regular staff is tied up trying to accommodate the new arrival."

"Half the staff?" Eileen asked. "Must be no ordinary admission."

"You can say that again!" the nurse said. "Only a handful of people in the world have what he has. *Myositis Ossificans Progressiva*. It's made his whole body stiff as a board, or all of his striated muscle, at least. Nothing's normal on him but his internal organs, his eyelids and his lips."

"He's coming to live on 'C' wing?" said Adrian.

"Nope. That's half the hullabaloo. Even though he can't move a stitch, they're putting him on over on 'A,' on account of his mind being normal as it is. None of those ladies over there has known a time when there was a man on the ward. And what a demanding one he's going to be. 'Nurse, I wanna smoke!' and staff has got to come hold the cigarette in his mouth while he puffs. They're going to have to set some limits with him."

Just then Cindy came through the double doors from the other ward.

"Sheesh, that man has a mouth on him," she said. "I hope that's not how he expects to get his way around here. I haven't been called...well, *that* word...since...I don't know when. High school." She dropped a handful of wrappers from medical supplies into the garbage. "Hi, kids."

"Hello," Eileen said. "Hectic day today?"

"That's an understatement."

"Well, let us get busy with some of these trays, then," Adrian said, walking to one of the carts and opening a door.

"Actually...," said Cindy, "come here a minute." She motioned toward the hallway, and Eileen and Adrian followed her. "We can manage here alright," she whispered. "Why don't you two get on over to Estelle's room. She's just back from the hospital, and hasn't had much attention today, with everything going on. I think she could use some company. We'll handle the feedings."

Adrian and Eileen took her suggestion, and headed over to "A" wing.

"I'm sure I look a mess," Estelle said when they entered her room. "I missed my weekend appointment with the hairdresser, and now I have to wait until this Saturday."

"That's the last thing you should be worrying about," Adrian said.

"You know, I haven't read that last book you brought me, yet. You'll have to leave it another week."

"Of course I will. You've been sick," he said.

"All the same, doesn't mean I have to be helpless," said Estelle.

"I understand you were quite ill," Eileen said.

"Oh, pshhh," she protested.

"They were exaggerating, obviously," Adrian said, giving Eileen a wink.

Estelle drooped more than usual, and moved with deliberation as she accommodated the guests in her room. She picked a newspaper up from one of the chairs beside the bed, and seemed unsure about what to do with it. She folded it smaller and smaller, and finally handed it to Adrian. He found a place to file it on top of her bureau.

"Is everything in order here since you got back?" Adrian asked.

"I'm not quite sure," Estelle said, looking at him. "I can't think of anything missing, but everything seems out of place, or something."

"I'm sure you'll have it all straightened out again in a couple of days," he said.

"Do you have a good appetite?" Eileen asked.

Estelle seemed not to hear the question.

"Can you help me with these?" she said, handing Eileen an envelope with a cellophane window, which she'd been unable to tear. Inside were dozens of return address labels sent to her by the lung association.

"Do you have letters to send?" Eileen asked.

Estelle just waved her hands, as if she'd already lost patience for the subject.

"So much junk mail," she said. "It keeps coming here for years after people have died. I had a whole bag waiting for me, and I was only gone a few days. Why I open it, I don't know. They make it look important, when it isn't."

"Feel like getting out of here?" Adrian asked.

"Out of here?" Estelle asked.

"Out to the courtyard, perhaps? It's been very sunny today."

"You'll have to get the nurse to unlock the door. If one of them can spare a minute."

They were enjoying the breeze under the arborvitae when the nurse's aide came to the door and motioned to Adrian.

"Can you help me for a minute?" she asked. "Vernon has his call light on, and I'm not about to go in there alone. He asked the nurse on the last shift if she'd scratch his privates for him."

"Sure thing. Say no more," Adrian said, getting up to go with her.

When Adrian had disappeared through the door, Estelle said, "Some of these young girls ain't got a lick of sense. What business is it of mine, after all, what the old man says to them?"

Eileen laughed. "None, it would seem," she said.

A couple of nuthatches were perched on the bird feeder in the upright yew, making as short work as possible of the millet inside.

"You know," said Estelle, after a few minutes, "I don't have a lot more of these left in me."

She looked at Eileen, and Eileen could take no issue with the ninety-six-year-old. The two of them continued to watch the birds, in such silence that the ruffling of feathers and the fall of seeds onto the pachysandra covering the ground were the only sounds Eileen could hear.

"It's the tail end of Indian summer, isn't it?" Eileen said. "The sun won't be this warm again until April."

"Thanks for bringing me out to sit in it," said Estelle.
"It's my pleasure, Stelly."

Eileen didn't turn in at eleven. Laundry was a half-day project, and she started it at nine o'clock at night. She was, like Estelle, somewhat discomposed, but not for the same reasons. The cause was hard to put a finger on. Finally, between taking the towels out of the tub and putting in the first load of bright colors, Eileen thought of something: It was none of the material effects in her life that seemed out of place, not the newspapers by her bed or piles of unopened mail, but rather a feeling that she'd lost any certainty about how to spend her time. She'd devoted her life wholesale to the needs of others, surely, but that was always in predictable ways. Today she'd had an exchange with Adrian that stuck in her mind for the rest of the day. They'd been under the portico again at St. Francis, and parting for the evening. What had he said? Something so simple, yet a gesture that clutched her. "I'll call you," he'd said, over his shoulder, as he walked off toward the bicycle rack. That was all.

What was she dealing with? She wanted him to call, and knew she'd find herself listening for the jangle of the phone from other rooms of the house for the next several days, not quite knowing why. For a minute, she nearly labeled the hold this had on her as the grip of a romantic wish—the suggested promise of a "date" of some kind—and in doing so, dismissing it as irrelevant. But that would have been too easy, a quick vindication where in fact she was unlikely to achieve any such thing. Would he call because of his need, or hers? Or not out of need at all— just for company? It seemed that a feeling of happiness over having him in her life was hard to bear. She found herself thinking a couple of times this week about the possibility he might choose not to enter religious life, as if that should make any real difference to her. What she actually wanted, if she ever got honest with herself, was a fellow traveler, someone on the journey with her, and more than anyone in ages, she wanted to find one in Adrian. Why was this so hard to admit? It seemed at odds with what everyone expected of a professed religious, of course. Yet her feeling seemed to go beyond that, to tap some core of shame over needing too much. The promise of a particular bond between her and Adrian seemed to depend on their mutual celibacy. She was supposed to embrace the paradox that to remain truly open to others she had relinquish her wishes to choose a particular person. *Yeah, well,* she thought. Right now living on paradox seemed a lot like living on irony; she didn't feel up to it. Her feelings were not aligned with what she had been taught, or had always held to be true. She wanted Adrian to choose religious life as a way of choosing her—hardly an altruistic motive. She wanted to capture him, not relinquish him; to carry him with her through life, like some Charlie McCarthy in a trunk. There was a disturbing image. Why would it come to mind? Was it sort of a self-reproach? She had some far-off memory of herself and Helen sitting with their mother on the couch, watching Edgar Bergen on *Do You Trust Your Wife*. More clearly than ever, Eileen missed Helen, felt how empty life had been, these twenty-three years since her death. She longed to sit cross-legged with Helen on the bed upstairs, to clasp her hands and giggle mindlessly at whatever Helen giggled at. Even before it occurred to her what they were, streaming down her face, she blotted tears onto one of the cotton anklets she'd been attempting to match in her laundry basket. The smell of bleach and detergent was comforting, and she kept the fabric pressed against her face.

On Friday, Eileen stopped by the library at Assisi to copy some articles Professor Brannigan had put on the reserve list. She'd been having a struggle with her decision to take this ethics course, now that the term was well underway. Brannigan had recently had them reading Ernest Becker, who described Christianity as a system of "cultural heroism" that people used to deny the basic fact of human mortality. Such a line of thinking was vaguely Freudian, and Eileen wondered what Brannigan intended by giving it such a prominent position in his course, if not declaring himself its champion outright. She could always count on Catholic school to confront her with the most non-Catholic of philosophies.

The next thing she knew, Brannigan himself was striding up the sidewalk toward her, and she felt almost guilty, caught as it were in the middle of thoughts about him.

"Sister!" he said. "I've got you scavenging in the library for review articles?"

"How did you know?" she asked.

"You should enjoy the articles. There are a couple of pieces on death, one by Becker and another by Kübler-Ross," he said.

"That Becker fellow," Eileen couldn't help saying.

"What about him?"

"He quite a relativist."

"I guess you could say that," Branningan said.

"Is there any reason to think him otherwise?" she asked.

"I wouldn't say it's his main point, that's all."

"If every system of belief is just as good as any other, what point is there?"

"I think there's still a point," Brannigan said, grinning. Eileen shook her head, as if to clear her ears.

"Philosophers!" she said. "You like to mess with people's minds."

"I'll stop bothering you, then, and see you in class," he said as he walked away.

She chuckled at him, despite being ill at ease. At the door to the library, she turned to watch Brannigan walk across the quad. She thought of how often she had seen him on campus in the company of that odd English professor, Dr. Jenkins, and she wondered about their friendship. She supposed Jenkins was a homosexual, and that Brannigan might be as well. On the pope's American trip in '79, John Paul II had made it clear that homosexuals could remain faithful simply by remaining celibate, and Eileen marked an internal sense of relief that men like this, by adhering to such a rule, could remain in the good graces of the Church. The papal trip that year had been such a great success. Hadn't even *TIME* magazine anointed the pope a hero, back then? Brannigan's intellectual ideas, however, might really get him into trouble.

In the library, Eileen scribbled the reserve numbers on a slip of paper for the girl at the research desk.

"Be right back," the girl said to Eileen, sunnily, flipping her pigtails over her shirt collar and reckoning where the anthropology titles might be shelved.

-15-

The Shit List

Kevin Meade was in Adrian's room, puzzling over the meaning of various objects he found there. He examined the knick knacks on the shelves, read the spines of books, even lifted the lids on the rattan trunks and peered into them surreptitiously, as Adrian tried to study and the two of them chatted. He was incredulous when he picked up a family picture from a cousin's wedding, with Adrian wearing a knit leisure suit.

"So, did you really, like, groove on these contrasting patch pockets?" he asked.

"No, not really," Adrian said.

"I guess your family hasn't had a more recent picture taken."

"Nope," Adrian said. "I guess not."

The passing of clothing styles did not evoke in Adrian typical feelings of embarrassment. He might no longer own that suit, or the outlandish silk shirt he wore to his eighth grade graduation, but he kept the photographs of himself wearing them both out on his shelf, next to the last birthday card his Grandpa Jude had sent him, and his valedictory trophies.

"Do you still have this hanging around?" Kevin asked. "You could wear it some day, if they ever start having seventies dress-up parties."

"No, I don't have it," Adrian said. "I think it went to the St. Vincent de Paul in Fort Dodge."

"This is so uncool, someday it will be cool again," said Kevin.

"It's probably just as well I jettisoned the thing. We could both be in clerics by the time that look returns."

"Don't remind me," Kevin said, putting the photo back on the shelf.

"Does the idea of wearing clerics bother you?" Adrian asked. He sat at his desk, his Shakespeare open in front of him.

"A little, I guess. Doesn't it bother you?"

"The uniform?"

"The loss of individuality."

"That kind of individuality, at least, never weighed very heavy on me. I sort of look forward to clerics. I've always felt I never really belonged to anything. So I say, give me my membership card. I'll take it."

"You sound like you're sure the seminary was your idea," Kevin said.

"As opposed to...my parents' idea? Oh, definitely. Even my mother would rather have grandchildren than a priest in the family, I think."

"I wish I could say that. My parents have been so gung-ho on this since I was little, I'm not sure what is really me."

"That's pretty common for guys here. It seems like it's either that, or the other extreme."

"What other extreme?"

"Quite a few guys are converts. Or zealots, born of lapsed Catholic parents. That sort of thing."

"Is that you?"

"No, it's not. I left out a third category."

"What's that?"

"Guys who are terrified of sex."

Kevin shook his head. "You surprise me sometimes, Underwood."

"I'll take that as a compliment," Adrian said. "However you meant it."

On Halloween night, Adrian passed the freshman sems in the stairwell, all in a group.

"You want to come out with us? We're going to the Ground Round for beers," said Keith Fischer.

Adrian had to get up early the next morning to get the sanctuary ready for the celebration of All Saints' Day.

"I think I'll have to pass on that. You guys have a good time," he said, and they pressed on.

Adrian heard nothing that night to indicate a night of revelry. He turned in early and slept straight through till morning. He thought little of it when, on his way into chapel for morning prayer, he noticed Fr. Moriarty looking taciturn in a *tête à tête* with Fr. Daimler outside the assistant's office. Only at breakfast would he understand the rector's extreme displeasure this morning. The freshmen had all broken curfew the night before.

When the bell rang for mealtime and the sems assembled in the refectory, Fr. Moriarty erupted with his anger.

"I was hoping this morning to share a spirit of joy as we prepared to celebrate the solemnity of the saints of the Church," he said. "I was appalled to find that a number of you chose to celebrate the spirit of a pagan holiday instead, and forget the everyday rules of our life together, never mind any special heed to the importance of today's celebration to the Church. Fortunately, we have this morning to reconsider our priorities before the bishop and our guests from the chancery arrive. I hope everyone is in a more sober mood by that time."

The seminarians poked lamely at the fare on their plates when it was dished up. It took a strong set of nerves to be hungry, even if you were among the innocent. Fortunately the celebration later that morning followed a script. Fr. Herman had been rehearsing a brass quartet of sophomore and junior seminarians, and the bishop and his retinue processed into the sanctuary to the auspicious sounds of *Fanfare for the Common Man*. None of the guests invited for the occasion were the wiser throughout the service, or the festivities that followed. As the last visitors were ushered from the building, Fr. Moriarty made himself scarce. Adrian was among the small group that lingered on the steps of Holy Name, wishing the straggling guests well and putting a seal on the day. Eileen was leaning against the rail at the bottom of the steps as Adrian bid farewell to the aged Monsignor from St. Thomas More parish.

"Hey," she said to Adrian. "How are you? That was a lovely service."

"Was it? I wouldn't know, exactly. It wasn't too easy for any of us."

"What's wrong?"

"It's just Father Moriarty. He's pissed off because the freshmen went out to celebrate Halloween, and didn't come in by curfew."

"And that's a serious infraction?"

"Today it is, anyway. I think he was a little insecure about the bishop coming. But it's not as if anyone puked in the stairwell or anything."

"I should hope not!" Eileen said.

"I only mean that, relative to freshmen anywhere else, he doesn't know how lucky he's got it."

"What did he say?"

"It's not so much what he said, as the anger with which he said it. And the pouting afterward."

"Are you free now?" she asked. "We could go for a walk, maybe."

"Yeah, I'm on my own time until dinner. Let's get off the grounds," he said.

"Okay by me," she answered.

As Adrian fetched his jacket, he realized how much he'd come to rely on Eileen as some kind of anchor. Sure, in certain ways she was like his mother, but in others she unmistakably *was not*. Perhaps that was the point.

Late that evening, Adrian was sitting on his bed, trying to make his way through Euripides' *Ion* before his trip up to Carleton in the morning. What had been a murmur of voices in the room next door, inhabited by Alan Hennessey, grew louder, and eventually Adrian could make out most of what was being said.

190

Alan and Keith Fischer were in animated discussion about the rebuke they'd been given for breaking curfew.

"So you might not become head prefect! So what?" Keith said. "Do you really want to be his patsy, anyway? We're all in the same boat. He can't write off an entire class. And he won't have any choice, if we all stick together."

"Jon and Peter will say they weren't drinking. I sure would, if I were them."

"Drinking isn't against the rules. Breaking curfew is. And we all broke curfew together."

"But they wanted to go back in time for curfew. They said so. They'll tell him that."

"They've got legs, don't they? They didn't leave any earlier than we did," Keith said. "We all broke curfew together. Case closed."

"I can't believe we've got a Latin quiz first thing tomorrow," Alan said. "I haven't even cracked the book."

"So get to work, dude," said Keith.

"You're so calm. I'm just sure! Like I could concentrate to study right now."

"You act like someone who's never been in trouble before in his life."

"I am," Alan said.

"Welcome to humanity, then. You'll survive it."

"What have you ever been in trouble for?"

"Just the usual stuff," said Keith. "Drinking, staying out all night with my friends. Once the highway patrol came to our school because me and my friend Myron painted the name of our principal on the highway with a buck-toothed idiot face next to it. It was pretty artistic, actually."

Alan's response to this was muffled, and Adrian couldn't hear it.

"You guys all act so virginal," Keith could be heard to say.

"That's probably on account of us being virgins," Alan said. "What were you expecting, at a seminary?"

Touché, Alan, Adrian thought.

Water started coursing through the pipes in the wall. Alan must have been washing at his sink, or filling his electric teapot to make tea. Adrian could no longer follow the conversation, and he lost himself again in Euripides' play, reading about the ecstasy of Ion over the rising of the sun.

When Adrian returned to La Crosse from his trip to Northfield, a handful of sems were gathered in the rec room at Holy Name, shooting pool and listening to *Jonathan Livingston Seagull* on the stereo. Bob and Peter were cleaning up pretty well in a game against Kent and Keith.

"Hey, Adrian," said Paul Nice, who was standing on the sidelines for the moment. "Want to join me in taking on the winners?"

"Um. Sure," Adrian said.

"Peter, when are you planning to study for tomorrow's test in Logic?" said Kent, who had already survived the perils of Fr. Keenan's class. "Tonight is rosary after dinner, isn't it?"

"Hey, going to rosary is optional," Keith reminded him.

"I've never seen Pete opt out of it before," Kent said.

"Maybe it's time I let up, then," said Peter.

"Whoa!" said Bob. "What's the occasion?"

"He probably figured out the point of devotionals is contemplation, not scoring points with Moriarty," said Keith.

"I don't think that's why he was doing it, in the first place," said Paul Nice.

"Actually, I tink it was," Peter said, quietly, in accented English.

There was a strange moment of silence. Then Bob started to giggle, despite every effort not to. Eventually Kent joined him. Soon all of the guys were broken up—even Paul. There was nothing like having Moriarty fuming mad at all of them, it seemed, to put a few things into perspective.

"Seriously," said Keith. "Do you think devotion is what makes a good priest, in the first place?"

"I think it's holiness," said Peter.

"What is *holiness*, anyway?" Kent wondered.

"It means turning over your will," said Peter.

"If that's it, I'd put it rather low on the list," Kent said.

"Me, too," said Bob.

"Really?" Peter asked.

"Really," they chimed.

"What about you, Adrian?" Keith asked.

"I'd say it's ministry," Adrian said.

"And how do you define *that*, while we're at it?" asked Kent.

Adrian thought of the window that he loved most in the sanctuary, with its inscription about the badge of weeping and of tears. Was grief the principal emotion one ministered to, or just the one that most readily came to mind? He pondered for a moment.

"I think of ministry as being there, to consecrate people's emotions—whether joy or pain—by sharing in them, on behalf of the community," he said.

The sems looked at him, knowing they'd have to think about that for a while. Adrian could play a role other than court jester, after all.

"I wouldn't have expected that definition from you," said Paul, contrarily. "Seems to me that you're pretty aloof."

Mr. Head Perfect! Adrian thought, and rolled his eyes the slightest bit. *It's easy for some golden boy like you to be gregarious, while the rest of us are on tenterhooks.* Still, he worried that Paul's words were true, or at least had been up until now.

"How important do you suppose a guy's pool game is to being a priest?" said Keith.

"Bingo!" said Kent. "Bingo's the only game that matters in the priesthood." He swilled a bottle of pop and twirled his pool cue. "Set me up nice now, Bob. My shot is next."

The second floor hallway had fallen silent by eleven o'clock, when Adrian went down to place a call to Terry.

"Hey, little bud, what's up with you?" Terry said.

"Not a whole lot. Just hanging out with the lads."

"I guess that means one thing with you and another with me, doesn't it?" said Terry.

"And personally you'd prefer your way, I'm sure...."

"Don't get me wrong. I'm not knocking your being there. A man's got to do what a man's got to do, I say. How's it going? You okay?"

"Yeah, I'm fine," said Adrian. "Good, actually. No real complaints."

"So things are working out? Twenty-eighth Street isn't the same without you. The Doberman at the place with the blue vinyl siding isn't half as excited now that you're gone. He's lost all his spirit."

"Well, it's good to know I'm missed."

"Most definitely," said Terry.

"Right now I sort of feel like I'm fitting in here."

"You mean, you don't hate it?"

"Right. I don't hate it. I've been thinking I just might last."

"Well, bless you, child."

"Really?"

"Really."

"What's the news from Lake Oh-ma-gawd?" Adrian asked.

"Let's see. *Another Norwegian bachelor farmer was laid to rest down at the First Lutheran Church today. The ladies of the auxiliary said they had to make two roaster pans full of hamburger hot dish to feed all the other bachelor farmers who came to pay their respects.*"

"You're not joshing, are you?"

"No, I'm not. Someone did die. Did you ever meet Clark? He was an old friend of Clint and Rob's. You probably didn't. He wasn't at the party at their place. He'd already been in and out of the hospital with pneumonia a couple of times by then."

"Have you ever known anyone before who died of, you know...."

"Of AIDS? Not anyone I've known this well. Just a couple of guys I knew by first name, from the bar."

"I'm sorry," Adrian said.

"It's okay. Really," Terry said. There was a pause, and then a new subject. "Do you think you might ever visit Omaha?"

"Sure I will," said Adrian. "I was hoping to come between Christmas and New Years, in fact."

"Great. I won't be going anywhere that week. I'll just be doing the usual two days up in Yankton—midnight Mass and Christmas dinner with the folks, then back to Omaha. Do you want to stay here with me?"

"I hadn't thought ahead that far," Adrian said.

"I guess I shouldn't impose myself," said Terry. "You may have other friends you want to stay with."

"It's not that. I just hadn't given it thought. Thanks for the offer. Really."

"It'd be my pleasure," Terry said.

Adrian swung by Eileen's house on Tuesday afternoon. She said she'd be out painting the soffit, and indeed there she stood, on a ladder with a pail and a brush.

"Can I help with that?" he asked, sauntering across the lawn.

"There's only one ladder," she said. "But you'll give me an excuse to take a break. Keeping my arms over my head like this is killing me."

She sat her tools on the highest step and climbed down.

"If there's a clean spot on this rag, I'll mop my brow!" she said, and eventually found one. "So, have things settled down over at the seminary?"

"A bit. Moriarty hasn't come out of hiding yet, but the whole thing has brought the seminarians closer together. There's nothing like a common enemy to create a united purpose, right? Who said that?"

"I don't remember, I'm sure."

"It's very true, whoever it was."

"Isn't the common enemy supposed to be the devil?" she asked.

"I don't know about that. We'd have to decide first whether or not we believe he exists."

"Oh, don't even say that!"

"Why? That's upsetting?" he asked.

"Of course it is. Why did I learn the catechism if someone's just going to come along and change it? You modernists!"

"Because the catechism isn't for adults?" Adrian ventured.

"Stop that talk, and come inside," she said. "I'll put on some tea."

Adrian peered from the kitchen into the hall as Eileen rummaged in the dish drainer for a tea ball. There were spackling repairs waiting to be painted on the walls, and newsprint down on the tile floor.

"Do you know Sister Florence very well?" Eileen asked.

"I can't say we're friends," Adrian said. "She's been around Holy Name ever since I came there, but mostly I see her at chapel. Why?"

"She invited me to go on a retreat next month, and I have to give her an answer soon—the application deadline is coming up."

"At the Augustinian house?"

"Yes, it is. Do you know it?"

"Vaguely," he said. "They're supposed to be...well, more Augustinian than Thomistic. I was never sure that was a good thing."

"I've been trying to talk myself into going. I don't know why Florence intimidates me so much," Eileen said. "I guess because she's so successful at being a nun. Makes me feel weak. I should just get over it, I suppose."

"I know what you mean," he said.

"You do, don't you?" she stated, pouring the water and bobbing the tea ball in the pot.

"We could start a club, couldn't we? Sort of a support group for ambivalent vocations."

"I wonder who else we might get to join," she asked.

"Well, it won't be Sister Florence," he said.

"No," she agreed. "Not Sister Florence."

After Jenkins's class on Thursday, Adrian dawdled as the other students filed out of the room.

"Hey, Underwood," Jenkins said. "What's up?"

"Not too much."

"Is there anything you need out at Valley View Mall?" Jenkins asked.

"I've hardly ever been there. Why?"

"I'm making a trip out there, to get a new battery for my watch. I thought you might like to come along."

"Sure," Adrian said. "When are you going?"

196

"As soon as I put my notes in my file and lock up. Want to come with me past my office?"

In the car, Ernie turned down the classical music station on the radio. "I thought you might appreciate a trip out into the world," he said. "The way I imagine it, the seminary must be pretty isolated. There's a good music store at the mall. You must get to buy records, at least."

"We have pretty free rein when it comes to that. I should develop some taste in music."

"What do you like? I'm a big fan of opera, of course. I usually take a group of students up to see the Minnesota Opera in the cities once a year, with Lloyd Hecht."

"I've never been," said Adrian.

"You should come this year, then," Ernie said. "We usually see a comic opera. The tragic operas tend to be harder for twenty-year-olds to take seriously."

"Does Doug like opera?" Adrian asked.

"Not really. And besides, I couldn't bring him, with students on the trip."

"That must be hard, having to keep him hidden."

"We socialize with some of the other professors. It's not really an issue for a lot of people. But there aren't any other gay couples. That's something I miss."

Ernie parked near an entrance, and the two of them went in to search for a jewelry store. While the salesperson installed his battery, Ernie inquired about the store's cut crystal. Adrian found himself wondering what kind of house Ernie and his mate kept on their dairy farm. As if reading Adrian's mind, Ernie said, "Maybe you could come out to the farm for dinner sometime. I'd like for you to meet Doug, and see the place."

"That would be nice," said Adrian.

"It would be a first for us."

The first student to visit the farm? The first one to meet Doug? Adrian wasn't sure what this meant.

"Let me know when's a good time," said Adrian.

On November 7, there was no news in the La Crosse Tribune about the Roman Catholic Church. In the Minneapolis Star-Tribune, there was just a small item—*Pope Chastises Bishop*—in the religion section. But the news that day that Archbishop Raymond Hunthausen had been relieved of his duties as archbishop of the Diocese of Seattle coursed through Assisi College like electricity. The campus press picked up the news from the Catholic News Service, and Lloyd Hecht telegraphed it to all the liberal arts faculty. By noon, discussion of the event crackled at the lunch table.

"It's stunning!" said Jim Coughlin. "I think it's unprecedented in modern history. And after Vatican II! Imagine the audacity of the man."

"What difference does Vatican II make?" asked Molly Powichroski.

"Every commentator who wrote about the accomplishments of the Second Vatican Council," said Lloyd Hecht, "pointed to the principle of collegiality among bishops as its greatest achievement. Gone were the days, supposedly, of a single man dictating truth to everyone. The very theology of divine revelation became one of revelation through many, and the bishop of Rome was defined as the first among equals. Now John Paul II doesn't like Hunthausen's anti-nuclear stance, or his liberalism, and he takes it upon himself to remove him. I never thought he'd take things this far. He's truly turning back the clock."

"You can say that again," said Coughlin.

"Does he have the authority to do this?" asked Verna Luckritz.

"He didn't, and that didn't suit him, so he invented it," said Lloyd. "Or shall we say, he went all the way back to the fourth century to find some precedent for it."

"And no one can really stop him," said Coughlin.

Dr. Shelbe was shaking his head, in grim silence.

"He'll die, eventually," said Brother Phillip. "But not soon. Not until he's elevated a generation of bishops and cardinals who think just like him. It shouldn't set us back more than say, fifty or sixty years."

"He could die any time," said Thad Benson.

"Are you kidding?" said Coughlin. "He probably issued that decision and then went skiing in the Alps. He'll live until the next century."

Anthony Wahlgren was doing the arithmetic. "I think you're right," he said. "That's a sobering thought."

"But isn't Hunthausen kind of a nut, anyway?" Molly asked.

"What does it matter?" said Lloyd. "It's the principle of the thing. Hunthausen is simply anti-nuclear. And he belongs to *Pax Christi*. John Paul II and Cardinal Ratzinger, the prefect of the Congregation for the Doctrine of the Faith, are so anti-Communist, they don't want it diluted by any liberal talk of pacifism. As if Hunthausen were going to infect all the episcopate with his dangerous ideas. What paranoiacs. For men so opposed to totalitarianism, they're awfully afraid of intellectual freedom."

"Maybe it's just that Hunthausen is rebellious," said Thad. "Doesn't he have girls serving as altar boys, or something?"

"Don't kid yourself that this is about altar girls," said Coughlin. "There have to be thirty or forty bishops in the U.S. allowing that practice, and they're not being relieved of their authority. This has got to be about something else."

"As much as it seems ironic that men afraid of totalitarian government should act so dictatorially, I think it's the case here," said Brother Phillip. "Ratzinger's youth was dominated by the Nazis, you know, before he went into the seminary, and it's shaped his whole point of view. I think he believes opposition to absolute evil has to be absolutely pure, and that justifies whatever intellectual tyranny he carries out within the Church."

"We don't really know, of course," said Verna. "But that's how it is with an institution that's not democratic. No one has a constituency to answer to. We're just left with our fantasies of what it's all about."

"First Reagan got elected, and I thought I'd have to become a Canadian," Coughlin said. "Now this pope! What do I do, become an Episcopalian? I'll have no home. I'm about to become a spiritual refugee."

Adrian went past Father Keenan's office later that afternoon.

"Hello!" Keenan said, when he spied Adrian in the anteroom. "Have you come to look through my books? Glad to see you here, at last."

"I missed you—we all missed you—at lunch today," Adrian said. "There was a lot of discussion about the Hunthausen situation."

"Oh, yes," Keenan said, shaking his head. "It's very unfortunate."

"What do you think of it? People were pretty upset, in the cafeteria."

Keenan turned toward the window and was silent for a moment. He took off his glasses and wiped his brow before replacing them. "You know I don't like to be alarmist," he said, finally. "But there's a cold wind blowing." He sat down at his desk and traced the outlines of his blotter gently with his hands. "We have reason to worry, I think, about what will become of academic freedom."

"Brother Phillip has this theory, about Cardinal Ratzinger's Nazi-dominated past, that Ratzinger believes liberals will be soft on opposition to totalitarianism, so liberals have to be silenced in the Church."

"I don't know it's source," said Keenan, "but I wish that 'silenced' were an exaggeration. How do we avoid the word? Kung, and Schillebeeckx, and Curran. What word is there for them, but silenced? And now this—a bishop stripped of his authority. Indeed."

Adrian's stomach fluttered as he listened to Keenan's assessment. If liberals were debarred from the Church, where did that leave Adrian? What had happened to the Church of Father Neimeier, the Church of his childhood parish?

"It makes me feel I might have been mistaken," Adrian said.

"Mistaken about Rome?" Keenan asked.

"Mistaken about the Church."

"Well, don't give up on the *Church* yet. The Church is more than Ratzinger and the pope."

"We've been telling ourselves that a lot lately, haven't we?" said Adrian.

"People have to be more vigorous in reminding themselves of it. But it remains the truth."

"Thanks for your optimism," Adrian said. "I think I need some, right about now."

"You're a good man, Underwood," said Keenan. "Don't lose heart."

Adrian furrowed his brow deeply, and felt tears starting to well. He looked away from the priest, pretending interest in the titles on his shelf. He touched the spine on a volume of *Philosophical Investigations*, by Wittgenstein.

"Thank you for believing that," Adrian said.

"There are a lot of people devoted to the truth," said Keenan. "And different individuals equally devoted to the truth can disagree. The individual conscience is still bedrock. But I'm not telling you anything you don't already know. You've studied your moral theory as well as I."

"We were having this talk the other day—a group of the other sems and I—about what makes someone a good priest," said Adrian. He sniffled, not so concerned now that Keenan might hear. "It's funny. No one even mentioned devotion to the truth."

"Then I'm not doing my job very well, am I?" said Keenan.

"You do a great job, Father. You're just one man."

"With an increasingly irrelevant task."

"Now, don't *you* go being a pessimist!" Adrian said.

"Sorry. I forgot myself, for a moment...." He stood up from his desk. "So!" he said, clapping his hands. "Now that *aggiornamento* has fallen out of fashion, can I interest you in reading about it? I have this copy of Karl Rahner's *Foundations of Christian Faith*...."

Adrian sat in the dark chapel at Holy Name in the hour before dinner, watching the sun, low in the sky outside, ignite the red and yellow-green and sapphire glass of the windows. The inscriptions there, in frosted glass letters outlined by blackened lead, blazed like the white center of a furnace: they looked truly like the thoughts of God rendered in English for the supplicant here to take them in. Many were the days Adrian had been that supplicant, yearning for the voice of the Almighty, hopeful that the words would be words of encouragement for him. Today what struck him was the presence of the light outside, and the darkness of the space in here, so cool and silent one felt entombed. He thought of other moments—happy ones, when a congregation somewhere had filled a sacred space like this with song and celebration, Sunday mornings when matrons in hats and suited fathers glowed not only in their finest clothes but also with their best intentions, and children, chastened with awe, looked with infant eyes on the golden fixtures of their church, the chalices and monstrances and reliquaries of a religion, and felt like the citizens of a wealthy kingdom. Where had that cele-bration been? Somewhere in Adrian's past, in the soft impres-sionable mind of a Catholic child marking the holy days of the year with his native tribe. Dr. Coughlin's words at lunch that day came back to Adrian, along with the image Coughlin had evoked, of his likely expatriation. A life in exile would hardly be a mod-ern invention. It had a certain lineage—a noble one, even. But was it, for anyone, the fulfillment of a dream? In the hallway out-side, the bell rang for dinner, and distant footsteps hastened at its call. By the time dinner was over, the sun would have slipped behind the hills and the chapel would be dark. Adrian felt reluc-tant to leave his meditation, but knew he should rise and join his peers at the meal. At the end of the pew, he paused to genuflect and move his fingers, as always, through the sign of the cross.

-16-

To Speak Its Name

The flea market at the La Crosse Fairgrounds on Saturday mornings drew purveyors of everything from local honey to eight-week-old puppies. Adrian had suggested they go to take it in, "just for the experience." Eileen was generally not one to browse merchandise, but she'd agreed to the trip, hoping to find some houseplants there to brighten her kitchen before the start of winter. When she and Adrian arrived, there were tables covering a lot as big as a baseball field, and Eileen peered over the rows of dealers for signs of garden wares for sale—for hanging baskets, ornamental windmills or wishing wells, arbors or *etageres*. She knew she would lack the patience to survey every table on the lot.

"Look at this," Adrian said, plunging into a mishmash of objects at the first vendor. He held up an architectural ornament rescued from an old building, an Atlas in plaster ready to shoulder the weight of some roof truss. "Isn't he great?"

"He's handsome," she said. Adrian lifted him high above his head, to get the right angle.

"Too bad I don't own an old house," Adrian said. He put the piece back on the table and scanned for other treasure. Eileen realized she was in danger of getting dragged through more of the goods for sale here than she'd planned. A few tables down, Adrian took a serious interest in a pair of pant stretchers that he found in a box of old linens.

"Would you actually use those?" Eileen asked.

"You might not know it, but I do own several pairs of jeans," he said.

"Well, if you could use them, there's a set my mother had at the house. I could give them to you."

"Really?" he asked.

"I'd have to find them," she said. "They're probably in the attic. But sure."

Adrian smiled and returned the pair in his hands to the box.

"It's nice to get out into the country," Eileen said. "There won't be many more weekends they can have something like this in the open air."

"Next Friday, I'm going out to Money Creek to have dinner with one of my professors, on his dairy farm," Adrian said. "He said we'll gather some wood and build the first fire of the season in the fireplace."

"Which professor is that?" she asked.

"I don't know if you've met him. It's my Shakespeare professor. Ernie Jenkins."

"Yes, I have," she said. "He seemed to me a little"—she stumbled, here—"eccentric, or something."

"He's gay. Could that be it?" said Adrian.

"Well...yes. Isn't it a little unseemly, for him to have you to his house?"

"Professor Jenkins is very settled down with someone. I don't think there's anything improper about the invitation," Adrian said.

Eileen was not terribly reassured by this prospect. Should she be? So Jenkins had a lover, and must keep it hidden from the college—or worse yet, didn't bother to. She had known homosexuals for years, in Milwaukee, and even on the reservation. The Church's teaching about them was a little hard for them to follow, perhaps, but still—it was the Church's teaching, wasn't it? Why didn't it give Adrian more pause?

"What?" she said.

"I said, Moriarty would probably view it as simply being on the wrong side of morality, but I don't view morality as being quite so dichotomous as he does."

"Does Moriarty know where you're going on Friday?"

"No. It's a night when the sems are all at liberty. No one has to sign out."

"And that doesn't trouble you?" she said.

"I suppose that's Moriarty's problem with me, in general. I don't regard his views as all that authoritative. I'd have to disregard my own experience about half the time, and I don't have a great talent for that."

"I guess our generation gap is showing, here. The way I was taught there was no dichotomous or not dichotomous, or choosing which one fit you. There was just 'do as you were told.' Did you learn those terms in moral theology?"

"Yes, I did. From a priest, mind you."

"It's almost like two different Churches," she said.

"That's too bad," Adrian said, "even if it's true. I can hardly imagine going back to being Catholic the way I understood it in grade school or high school. Catholicism never really interested me, until I started reading someone who looked at it critically. Who looked at it as more than just an inheritance."

Adrian was spinning these thoughts effortlessly, as if his intellect gave him great security on what seemed like a dangerous precipice. Adrian saw a woman struggling to carry a bulky chair to a station wagon backed up to the lot, and he dashed over to lend a hand. Eileen stood and watched, wondering what exactly she was going to do with him. Scold him? No. Cajole him, perhaps, or humor him. Give in to him? Anything except dispense with him. She was more alive in recent weeks than she had felt in years—felt the way she had when hiking with her sister Helen, and Helen, abandoning caution, had waded knee-deep into Bluff Slough to catch a water snake—with no concern as to whether or not their mother would think it was a good idea. If Adrian remained in Eileen's life, one thing was certain: it would be nothing like having a dummy in a trunk, or a doll on a shelf, and she would desire it, nonetheless.

The attic smelled like mothballs and old wood. After grumbling at the shaky stairs and eventually finding the pull for the light switch, Eileen climbed onto the plank floor and stood to her full height. It always amazed her that an adult could stand up in this space. Perhaps because her mother had almost never come up here. Eileen shook her head to see the amount of stuff piled under the rafters. She would have to hire help when the time came to clear it out. Why had she ever told Adrian she'd look for those pant stretchers? She'd underestimated what a chore it would be.

At one end of the attic, near the vent in the gable, there was a chair, and Eileen dragged a likely box over to it. She took a rag and wiped the dust off the carton before she opened it. This was not going to be the right one. Nothing here but laundry supplies. She tried another that was marked "basement" as well. That proved to be completely inaccurate, which Eileen might have known, since the word was in her mother's handwriting, not her own. The basement must have been the original destination for the box rather than its origin, because the items in it were her father's personal things. Eileen sifted through them, out of curiosity. Most of what was in the box she didn't actually recognize; she inferred that a box of men's things in the house must have belonged to him. There were shoes and trousers and belts. Oddly, in a bundle of long-sleeved shirts and pajamas, there was one article of women's clothing—a silky piece of lingerie. What was it doing there? It was a nightgown, about three-quarter length, and decorated very simply with scallops at the front. Eileen thought for a minute, before realizing that her mother must have retired it here with her father's clothes once he'd died, regarding it as equally useless now. She felt an aching feeling about her father's death then, and a twinge of sympathy for her mother. In the bottom of the box were his razor and shaving brush, and an old container of shaving soap. Eileen considered taking these impractical things down and putting them on the bathroom shelf alongside her toiletries. To what end, she didn't exactly know. To make the museum complete, perhaps.

School was out of session on Thursday and Friday, on account of the state teachers' convention. Eileen was at a loss for what to do with herself. She spent a few hours in the library on Thursday morning, and when she came home the house was still so cool the frozen loaves of bread dough she'd taken out the night before had scarcely begun to rise in their pans. Eileen checked the thermostat, and turned the heat in the house up a bit.

A letter from Teresa lay where Eileen had read it this morning, on the table in a shuffle of other mail and the soiled plates from breakfast. It had been intruding into Eileen's thoughts ever since she opened it. She didn't know what had ever made her feel as uneasy as this. By late afternoon, she gave up waiting for the hour to go to the nursing home, and called Holy Name. When the seminarian handling the phones told her that Adrian was out, she left a message for him to call her as soon as possible. Eileen picked the letter up again, reading to see if there were some alternate meaning in it that she had missed. She was still staring at it when the phone rang.

"Eileen?" It was Adrian, already.

"Hello."

"What's up? I got a message saying it was urgent that I call."

"It's okay," she said. "I was just hoping we could talk. Are you busy right now?"

"Not with anything important. Shall I come over?"

"If it wouldn't be too much trouble."

"Not at all," he said.

It was raining as Adrian drove up in his old gray Chevette. Eileen pulled on a hooded sweatshirt, got an umbrella out of the hall closet, and went out to meet him. The windshield wipers were beating a cadence as she peered through the driver's window at Adrian. He rolled it down part way.

"Do you mind if we just drive somewhere?" she asked.

"Fine with me," he said. She ran around to the passenger's door and climbed in. "Any place in particular?" he asked.

"No. I just want to be moving," she said. He drove up the block and turned onto South Avenue.

"So what's up?" he asked.

"I feel like such a fool," she told him. "I don't know how I could have been so clueless."

"About what?"

"Where do I start?" she said. "When I first got back to La Crosse I decided I was going to look up this old friend of mine, from the Bonaventures. I didn't really think anything of it, that she hadn't written back in so long. I thought she was just busy with other things." Eileen paused. Adrian drove, and looked at her a couple of times, waiting for her to continue. "I finally got a letter back from her today," she said. "My letter took almost two months to get to her, because I sent it to the order, and they had to track her down. She's left the convent—for years now. The letter was forwarded from the last address the Bonaventures had for her, on to where she currently is, in Chicago. So much has happened, and I didn't even know about it. I lost touch with her five years ago."

"You're upset that she left the convent?" Adrian asked.

"No," she said. "I mean, yes. But that's not all. She says.... Where is it? Let me read it to you." She pulled the letter from the pocket where she stuffed it on her way out of the house. "*Shirley and I have been together for three years, now, and we're quite happy in our new house here in Downer's Grove. It would be great if you could come to visit sometime. We just finished repainting the guest room, and look forward to someone inaugurating it before long.* Don't you see?" she said. "It sounds like she's living with a lesbian."

"It sounds like *she's* a lesbian," Adrian said. "Are you very surprised?"

"No, it's.... It's that...I loved her so much. We were so inseparable, all through those early years, and then when we roomed together at Marquette. We were so affectionate with each other. Do you suppose it's my fault?"

"Is what your fault? Her being a lesbian?"

"I don't know. Yes. I think that's what I mean. I guess I'm not making any sense. This is just so unnerving." Eileen leaned her head against the side window, and made squiggles in the condensation with her finger.

"Hadn't it ever occurred to you before?" Adrian asked, at length.

"No, it hadn't. Well, maybe. When I think of it, there were some things she said before she left Eau Claire. But I couldn't see it at the time."

"Is it you that you're worried about?" Adrian asked.

"No! Of course not," Eileen gasped. "Not really. Maybe. Oh, God, this is awful."

"What is awful?" Adrian had driven past the end of town, and continued on Route 61 in the direction of Dubuque. Their destination did not matter, at the moment. They were obviously going to skip their shift at the St. Francis Home tonight.

"We were so young when we went to Eau Claire. We used to sit on her bed every night in her room, and I would brush her hair before we went to sleep. I thought she was so beautiful, and…. What if she misunderstood my intentions? What if I…."

"Were leading her on?" he asked.

"Ugh," she said. "I can't really talk about this. I probably shouldn't have even told you about it." She could think of nothing to change the subject to, so they rode for a few minutes in silence.

"You were what—fourteen, fifteen?" he asked. "I don't think that's the way it works, Eileen. A lot of people have all kinds of attractions at that age." Eileen merely nodded in response to what Adrian said, still at a loss for words.

"I sort of had a friend like that, except at a younger age," he said. "I was in first grade when we met. He was Lutheran, and lived outside of town, so we never met until we started grade school together. We had this immediate fascination with each other. I was always dying to get to school in the morning to see him. Then, at the end of first grade, his family moved away to Cedar Rapids. I was really wild about him. His name was Robert—Robert Bergstrom."

Eileen finally began to relax. Her neck ached from the tension of the day, but the catch in her throat was finally gone. Adrian kept driving south, and the rain kept coming down in sheets. She had no idea where they were, or where they'd end up. She didn't care. She curled her feet up under her and lay her head on the headrest. Adrian kept talking, although Eileen stared out the window. He must have sensed that his storytelling was a comfort.

"His family only came to visit once, after they moved away," Adrian said. "I remember, it was on a Sunday, and my mother made scalloped potatoes with ham. It's funny, the things that come back to you. But the important part I remember is what Robert and I did. He'd learned this game from a friend where he'd moved, and he was going to teach it to me. But any place we went in our house, he said he couldn't tell me about it, because the grown-ups might overhear us. It was a *dirty* game, he whispered. Finally, we climbed into the back coat closet by the stairs and shut the door. He said the rules of the game were to go through the alphabet and think of the dirtiest word we knew starting with that letter. So we crouched there, together in the dark, below the coats hanging over our heads, and he started. I'm not sure I remember what we said. I think he said 'ass,' and I said 'boobie,' and then probably it went 'cock' and 'damn.' Then it was his turn, and he couldn't think of anything for the letter 'e,' and I was waiting, knowing I had 'f,' and finally I blurted out 'F is for fucker.' And he howled in my face, and opened the door, and ran downstairs to the basement. When I ran down after him, he said, 'Did you say what I think you said? And I said 'What did you think I said?' And he said, 'If it's what I think, it's really, really dirty, boy!'" Adrian was quiet for a few seconds. "God, I don't know when was the last time I thought of that!" he said. Eileen chuckled slightly.

"Did you ever see him again?" she asked.

"Just once. It was that year I worked in the farm supply store after high school, and he came in looking for a tractor part or something. He stood there at the counter and said to me, 'You don't know who I am, do you?' And I said, 'You're Robert.' And we both grinned ear to ear."

"Did you talk about the time he came to visit?" she asked.

"About playing the game? No. I wanted to. But I didn't."

"Why not?"

"I don't know," he said. "I don't actually know. A big part of me wanted to."

Eileen shifted in her seat, wanting to be able to look at Adrian. He smiled at her for an instant, and then looked back at the road. The sky was getting very dark now, as the day waned. In a minute, Adrian no longer seemed to be present. She wondered if he regretted having told the story.

"Are you okay?" she asked.

"Yeah, I'm fine," he said. "I just figured out something that's been bugging me for months." He pursed his lips a bit, and drove on in silence. Eileen realized he wasn't going to share what that might be.

Letter from Rome

"Did I ask him if he remembered playing the game? No. I don't know why I didn't. I wanted to. A big part of me wanted to."

Once he'd uttered the words, other thoughts went through Adrian's head in rapid succession. The memory of standing across the counter from the adult Robert, who was handsome as shit by then, and wanting to explode with joy at having him just walk into the store like that and recognize Adrian, and also at having Robert remember—Adrian could tell by the look on his face that Robert remembered, too—that coat-closet moment so long ago. What inhibited Adrian, then, from speaking up? They were standing in broad daylight in the Cenex dealership in Ryder, with some of Adrian's fellow employees looking on. They were not in a dark, insulated space this time, and Adrian felt so conspicuous he thought he might cause a ruckus just by standing there, silent and ecstatic. Before he could summon the name of the co-worker who'd been standing next to him (Dan? or Don?) something else came to mind, something that went off in his head like the ignition of gasoline: *Don't stay up too late, gentlemen.* He remembered the words from his dream last summer, the words Father Moriarty spoke as he exited the Halloran Lounge and left Adrian lying there with Father Sweeney. *Don't stay up too late, gentlemen.* What did it mean? Not the obvious. Or maybe it did mean the obvious. Staying up was staying in the moment, letting the excitement build to where there was no turning away, and no turning back. The other seminarians might believe that

213

jerking off was wrong, and then experience the consummations in their dreams as actually "legal," but for Adrian it wasn't the practice of masturbation he scrupled to avoid so much as thoughts that might truly excite him. *Don't stay up too long.* Why not? He'd felt guilty for years about his sexual dreams, but the clarity of this one had stayed with him for months. If he thought about the image in the dream, of himself lying there with Father Sweeney, and tried to stay with it, he could barely force himself. When he pictured kissing the priest, what came to mind eventually was kissing Terry, and then he knew, unmistakably, the meaning of Father Moriarty's words. Don't let it go too far, don't let him come on you, or come in you. Coming out was sure to lead to someone coming somewhere—wasn't it obviously what one desired?—which lead to getting infected, and then to AIDS. Which wasn't necessarily true, of course, but that was the meaning of the words in the dream. *Don't stay up too long.* Goddamn— that was doubtless the meaning. Don't risk death by lethal injection. Learning last year that Terry had the virus might have set Adrian back years in his coming to terms with sex.

In a flash, he was lying beside Terry again in that tent at Wind Cave State Park, and feeling not just his grief at losing so quickly what he had finally found, but also feeling his intense desire for the man, for this marvelous other, so stubbled and dewy next to him, so glowing and fragile all at once. He remembered the smell of the cypress trees and the damp clay, and of Terry's sleeping bag bunched up against Adrian's pillow, where Adrian lay very still all night even though he was fairly bursting with the urge to breach the space that separated the two of them.

Right now, Eileen was resting next to Adrian, her head down. Possibly she was asleep. He thought it might be best if he turned the car around, and took them both home. A sign at the side of the road marked the turn-off for Sinsinawa. How had they come that far? He'd better make haste back to La Crosse. He might end up breaking curfew with a nun, and have to explain that to the rector. Eileen did not stir as Adrian watched for traffic, slowed the car, and pulled it into a three-point turn.

On Friday night Adrian followed the Root River west toward Houston, then took tiny Route 76 up to Money Creek. He could see the farmhouse as he turned off the main road, clearly sitting on the edge of the plain by the tree line, above the creek. It was a small Queen Anne, a pastiche of yellows and white, fancy by farm standards and obviously built by one of the early wealthy families in this township. The dairy barn was off to the west of the house, slightly over the edge of the hill, painted white and shingled in deep mineral green. A track of dust followed Adrian along the gravel road, advertising his arrival to anybody within a mile or two. Sure enough, as Adrian pulled into the yard Ernie was standing on the porch waiting to greet him, a dishtowel over his left shoulder.

"Come on in, Adrian. Doug is just coming up from the evening milking in the barn. He ran a little late today. He's been doctoring a cow that has mastitis." Ernie opened the screen door for him and they walked into the foyer, which had an oak staircase leading up to the second floor. There were framed forebears hanging from a picture rail by thin black cables on two walls. Underfoot, a thick oriental runner led past the parlor toward the dining room, and Adrian could see the bright light of the kitchen beyond.

"Give me a second to take some towels down to Doug," Ernie said, fishing a set out of a closet off the hallway. "We've remodeled the cellar door, so Doug can come in with his coveralls and shower in the basement before he comes up. No need to have cow manure in the front hall, anymore." Ernie opened a door that led to the basement and descended the stairs. While he waited for Ernie to return, Adrian peered into the large formal rooms. There were Victorian oak furnishings against dark-colored walls, and framed Audubon prints lit by amber-hued lights.

At dinner, they sat to one end of the big table in the dining room, Adrian at the head and Ernie and Doug flanking him.

Doug was a square-headed hulk of man, probably six-four at least and well past two hundred pounds. His hands were a larger order of magnitude than human, dwarfing the cutlery and his dinner plate, and his hair grew in long brown curls past his collar. He laughed easily.

"When Ernie told me it was a student coming, I figured I must have finally cleaned up my act enough to be presentable," Doug said.

"You know it isn't you...," said Ernie.

"I'd better watch myself, I could be slipping—become so mellow I'm no danger to impressionable minds."

"Doug likes to think of himself as too nonconformist to have survived in academia," Ernie explained, "when the truth I think is that he just likes it better dealing with the cows every day."

"It's true," said Doug. "Cows have no pretense. If they need to break wind, they break wind. They don't say, 'Hmm. What's that smell wafting over here from the Olesons' yard? Must be that Simmental of theirs....'"

"I shudder to think," Ernie said, "what that is supposed to be telling us."

"You know very well. All those priests and brothers running around, professing shock that a man has sexual yearnings for another man. Give me a break. Who do they think they're kidding, besides themselves?"

"Now Doug, they aren't all gay," said Ernie.

"Well, the silence of those that are, given what gets said in the pulpits year after year, I think is reprehensible."

"Doug would like nothing better than for me to leave teaching," Ernie said. "And do what, I ask? I'm afraid I don't love cows the way he does."

"It's true," said Doug. "I hate it that he teaches for them, and because of it feels he has to hide all the time. It's no way for a grown man to live."

"It's not as easy for everyone as it is for you," Ernie said to his lover. "You could chuck it all and not miss it."

"You can say that again. Last time I set foot in a Catholic Church was when they buried my dissertation adviser, Brother Blaise. And I don't miss it. No offense," he said to Adrian.

216

"Now, don't go getting into that," said Ernie. "I didn't mean 'miss the Church,' I meant 'miss teaching.' Our guest didn't come all the way out here to debate religion."

"I'm not sure how you still consider yourself a Catholic," Doug said. "You don't believe one quarter of what they're teaching."

"Because," said Ernie, raising an index finger, "I still believe that when the priest holds up the host and says '*hoc est enim corpus meum*,' that really becomes the body of Jesus up there, and it isn't just 'hocus pocus.' That's how I call myself a Catholic."

"I guess you believe that, too," Doug said to Adrian, "or you wouldn't be in the seminary."

"Yes, I believe that, too," Adrian said.

"See," said Doug, "I don't have trouble when you say that. When Ernie says it, all I hear is that on some level he's thinking, 'If God can change bread into Jesus, he can change me into a heterosexual,' and that's why he doesn't quit the church over their stance on gays. It's probably quite irrational of me. I think anything else would be easier—he could even be a Republican. But because it's religion, it just feels impossible to deal with."

"I'm simply less of a rabble-rouser than Douglas. I always have been," said Ernie. "Call me boring, if you will."

"Excuse me," said Adrian. "Can you tell me where the bathroom is?"

"There's one right there under the stairs," said Doug.

"Thanks," Adrian said.

"I made a squash pie for dessert," said Ernie. "Why don't I dish it, in the meantime? With or without ice cream?"

"With," Adrian said.

"For me, too," Doug requested.

On Sunday morning, Adrian woke up to rapping on his door.

"Phone call!" someone was saying.

"Be right there," Adrian responded. He stumbled out of bed and reached for his bathrobe. November mornings had grown chilly, and thankfully someone had put a space heater in the phone booth on the second floor. Adrian took a seat on the stool and picked up the phone.

"Man, is this about enough, or what?" said the voice on the other end. It was David, calling from Minneapolis.

"Is what enough?" said Adrian.

"You haven't read the news yet, I guess."

"What news? Where?"

"I'm sitting in the library at school. I just picked up this week's *National Catholic Reporter*. Did you see what Ratzinger has done now?"

"What is it?"

"As far as I can tell, he just turned Catholic teaching on homosexuality back about...well, I don't know how many centuries. Maybe to someplace it's never even been before. You tell me— you're the moral theologian."

"He's issued some statement?"

"It's a *Letter to the Bishops of the Catholic Church on the Pastoral Care of Homosexual Persons*. It was issued by the Congregation for the Doctrine of the Faith, October 30. And published in *NCR*'s November 14 issue."

"Shit," said Adrian. "I wonder why no one at school mentioned it Friday."

"Because they're straight, and it's no skin off their backs," said David. "They won't even notice the change it represents. But it's pretty clear to me, that little ledge you've been able to sit on till now has just been blasted away."

"Is the letter there? Read it to me," said Adrian.

"It's long...you'll have to look it up yourself. But here's the crux of it." David read aloud, rapidly: *Explicit treatment of this problem was given in the congregation's Declaration on Certain Questions Concerning Sexual Ethics, of December 29, 1976. That document addressed the duty of trying to understand the homosexual condition and noted that culpability for homosexual acts should only be judged with prudence. At the same time, the congregation took note of the distinction commonly drawn between the homosexual condition or tendency and individual homosexual actions. These actions were described as deprived of their essential and indispensable finality, as being intrinsically disordered and able in no case to be approved of. In the discussion which followed the publication of the declaration, however, an overly benign interpretation was given to the homosexual condition itself, some going so*

218

far as to call it neutral, or even good. Although the particular inclination of the homosexual person is not a sin, it is a more or less strong tendency ordered toward an intrinsic moral evil, and thus the inclination itself must be seen as an objective disorder.

"What?" said Adrian. "There's no basis for that in Natural Law Theory! What is he doing, making this shit up as he goes along?"

"You tell me," David said.

"Fuck," Adrian said.

"That's what I thought. I just wanted to check it out. What are you going to do?"

"I don't know. I have to read the whole letter."

"Well, call me when you have. I think it's time you transferred up here."

"Yeah, I'll call you," said Adrian.

Adrian suffered through Lauds and Mass and breakfast, then hopped on his bike and headed for campus. Someone was reading the library's issue of *NCR* when he first arrived, and Adrian paced until the paper was free. At last he snatched the issue from the rack and sat down at a table to scan for the article. It started on page eighteen. He found the passage David had quoted to him, and looked for any further explanation of Ratzinger's assertion about homosexuality being an "objective disorder," but he found none. What could account for this sudden assault? *Humanae Vitae* had disappointed most Catholics, by taking the stance that heterosexual acts not open to procreation were a sin. But did it say the inclination toward non-marital sex, or the inclination toward sex when procreation was not a possibility, was an objective moral disorder? No. Something beyond Natural Law Theology was at work here, and Adrian couldn't help but think that homosexuals were being made a scapegoat. As humane and reasoned as Cardinal Ratzinger professed to be, his logic was not logic at all. Adrian read further: *What, then, are homosexual persons to do who seek to follow the Lord? Fundamentally, they are called to enact the will of God in their life by joining whatever sufferings and difficulties they experience in virtue of their condition to the sacrifice of the Lord's cross.*

Jesus Christ. The marvelous thing about running an institution where suffering *literally was Godliness* was that you could cause people suffering and always, but always, push the blame onto God and His will. It was a brilliant scheme, and utterly simple. It was a wonder the Jews hadn't hit upon it centuries earlier, no wonder that the Hellenists immediately appropriated it, that the Romans made it the religion of an empire. It so ably served the needs of rulers, and assuaged the sorrows of the ruled.

Adrian thought these thoughts, not so much rapidly as ruminatively, sitting in the sunny window of the library that morning with the paper. They were on his mind later, when he lay sprawled on a bench on the quad; and again as he ate his solitary lunch at the whole foods co-op on Jackson Street. He was angry, and anger made him intensely intellectual; it gave him access to all the manifold theories and arguments and trivial facts he had packed into his mind in five years' time. It made him able to recount the entire history of moral theology up through the twentieth century—which he did several times in those next couple of hours—as if he had crammed for the final just the night before. Anger had always been the source of whatever brilliance Adrian summoned from within himself—anger, or spite, or indignation. He'd been taught these were the makings of a Deadly Sin, but to him they seemed almost a gift of the Holy Spirit, the charism he'd been granted, to advance the Kingdom of God. Anger, if anything, made him clear-sighted and bold.

"Father?" Adrian asked.

"Come in! My young logician," said Fr. Keenan.

"This is not a happy visit, I'm afraid."

"What troubles you?" Keenan asked. "Sit down. Put your feet up!"

Adrian plopped onto Keenan's decrepit red sofa.

"It's sort of a sensitive issue," Adrian said. "Mind if we shut the door?"

Keenan shut it, then sat down in a chair opposite the couch, rather than the one behind his desk.

"Did you happen to read a letter issued by Cardinal Ratzinger's office a couple of weeks ago?" Adrian asked.

"On the pastoral care of homosexuals...it was just in the paper this week," Keenan said.

"Yeah, that's the one. I just read it at the library today. Well...I'm one of the homosexual persons in question," said Adrian.

Fr. Keenan's mouth formed a restrained smile, and he nodded. "You have some feelings about the congregation's letter, I assume," Keenan said.

"I'll say!" Adrian blurted. "It's so...I don't know what. Punitive, or something."

"He's found himself another whipping boy, I fear," said Keenan.

"It sure feels that way. I mean, walk me through the moral theology here. If heterosexuals have conjugal relations without being open to procreation, it's contrary to natural law, and a sin. But if homosexuals so much as harbor the *desire* to have conjugal relations without procreating, we're intrinsically morally evil. They're two different standards. So it's not about who's violating natural law, it's about saying 'You people are the evil ones. You're not like us. *We* struggle to make our actions moral, but you people are just plain *bad*.' Why would he say such a thing, except out of bigotry? He ends up with this paranoid view of homosexuals, as if we're not moral. Sure, he cloaks his statements in a lot of protestations about homosexuals being equal children of God, but then he indulges in this gratuitous censure of our very difference. I don't see where he gets off, claiming not only piety, but also rigorous concern for the truth! His claim of *charity* toward gays is like...some sort of kiss from Judas." Adrian felt his anger boiling as he talked, and a vise grip in the muscles at his temples. He put a hand up to massage them.

"Do you drink sherry?" asked Keenan.

"What?" blurted Adrian.

"I have a bottle of cream sherry a former student just brought me. I thought I'd have some. Can I pour you a spot?"

"Yeah, I guess," said Adrian.

Keenan got up to retrieve the bottle out of his coat closet, and took a couple of tumblers from a little shelf by his desk. "I don't have any proper glasses. You'll have to excuse these." He poured and gave one to Adrian. "There's probably nothing to toast right now, so let's just drink."

Fr. Keenan sat leaning back in his chair, looking at the ceiling of his office, and sipped from his glass.

"Tell me," the priest said, "what led you to enter the seminary."

"You mean other than misapprehension?" Adrian cracked.

"Yes, other than misapprehension."

"I suppose I should have some list of reasons I can give you. I'm afraid anything I say will sound stupid, like some kid."

"Like what?"

"Like, 'I thought I belonged. I thought this was my family.'" And then, "I thought this was what I was meant to do."

"Maybe it was," said Keenan.

"But the priesthood is partly about preaching. How could I ever preach what this Church teaches? If there were room for some divergence of opinion, yes, but…that value in the Church seems to have been lost." He looked at Keenan. "Something's wrong here. A person isn't supposed to be wistful about the good old days at the age of twenty-four. It was a great misfortune to be born in the middle of Vatican II."

Keenan was silent for a long time.

"Tell me what you're thinking," Adrian said, at length.

"I was thinking about what it was like when I was your age. Paul Tillich had just published the first volume of *Systematic Theology*. Before we knew it, John XXIII became pope, and the second Vatican Council was convened. They were such heartening times." Keenan did not have to say what they both felt—that present times were such disheartening ones.

"It must have been exciting," said Adrian.

"Oh, it was. By the time the second council was completed, I had finished my doctorate in Paris and was teaching at Catholic University. The Sulpicians were in the thick of things, very much in the main stream. I couldn't have been happier to be making my life in the Church."

"And now?" said Adrian.

"I was just thinking about how different it is for you. My moment was so full of hope. But whatever that day was, it's come and gone," he said. "For you, this is your moment. You're deciding what to dedicate your life to. You have to ask yourself what is worth it. I can't say that if I were in your shoes I would still choose the priesthood."

"Really?" Adrian said, a bit incredulous.

"I do still choose the priesthood, of course—every morning when I get out of bed I choose it—but I'm an old man, who's had his opportunities. What do you think the chances are that I'm going to leave now, just when it's time to collect on the pension plan? Allow me my little worldly concerns. But you? Your situation is entirely different. A priest at the novitiate gave me a very wise piece of advice when I was considering the Sulpicians. He said a religious order is like a spouse; you want to choose it carefully, and to know when taking your vows that the marriage is the right one. I knew with the Sulpicians that I was going to be happy. Happy enough, anyway."

"A practical man, your counselor," said Adrian.

"Yes, and a kind one," said Keenan. "So I'm telling you, know what marriage is right for your life. The *big* pension plan, the only one that matters, is waiting for everyone who's faithful to a true vocation."

"You mean...heaven?" said Adrian. "Father, you're getting a little corny on me."

"Corny. Sentimental. Whatever," Keenan said. "Indulge me. I'm old enough to have earned it."

"Okay," said Adrian. He finished his sherry and put down the glass, which Keenan filled again without his asking. Adrian considered a protest, but too late. "What about Ratzinger?" he asked.

"What about him?" said Keenan.

"If I didn't know better, I'd say you just intimated to me that marrying a man might be my Christian vocation."

"I guess I did, didn't I?"

"You could be next on the Cardinal's list to be reprimanded."

"Fortunately, I lack the stature to publish my opinions," said Keenan. "I'll slip by undetected. Unless, of course, you go writing to Rome."

"Don't worry, Father, your heresy is safe with me," Adrian said. "If you were me, and it hadn't been the priesthood, what would it have been? Would you have found someone?"

"I might have."

"A woman?" said Adrian.

"No, actually," Keenan said.

"No kidding?"

"Why would I be kidding?"

"I don't know. I just never suspected, that's all."

"Well, I'm not sure I'd have been up for the censure. I'm a different person, and it was a different era. Not to mention, whether anyone would have had me. But you? Here's my personal theory about the Holy Spirit: It can only work through you if you make yourself happy. Otherwise, good works are just empty actions. The life of the Spirit is a life of joy."

"You're very subversive, you know that?" said Adrian.

"Thank you," said Keenan. "Jesus was subversive. I am honored by the comparison."

"This sherry is going to make me drunk," Adrian observed.

"Good, then," said Keenan. "To a measure of drunkenness." And with that, he raised his glass.

That night at Evening Prayer, Kent Sisely delivered the reading, from the Book of James, to mark the memorial of Albert the Great, one of the doctors of the Church: "Wisdom from above is first of all innocent. It is also peaceable, lenient, docile, rich in sympathy and the kindly deeds that are its fruits, impartial and sincere," read Kent. "The harvest of justice is sown in peace for those who cultivate peace."[*] Fr. Herman led the group in singing the first verse of "Faith of Our Fathers, Living Still." The seminarians joined in heartily, welcoming the familiar sentiments of a traditional hymn, and bringing evening prayer to a close. *We will be true to thee 'til death,* rang the final syllables of the descant, swirling round the walls of the clerestory.

---

[*]James 3:17-18 *NAB.*

-18-

Hiatus

Eileen couldn't imagine who was letting the phone ring so many times. She first heard it when she turned off the water in the shower, and it persisted as she toweled herself off and twisted her hair into a turban above her head. Finally she reached the phone and picked up the handset.

"Leen?" the voice said. She hadn't heard herself called that in years. It startled her.

"Who's calling?" she asked.

"It's me. Elsie."

"Oh," said Eileen. "I didn't recognize you."

"I hope I didn't wake you up. I figured it was safe to call, since you already took the Sunday paper in. I suppose you were in the shower," said Elsie.

"You're quite the little private eye, you know that?"

"Yes, I suppose so," said Elsie. "I notice things. Say, I was wondering if you have plans for Thanksgiving dinner."

"Actually, I hadn't thought about it much. I don't have plans."

"Say you'll join us, then. Jack and Arlene will be up, and I'm sure they'd be glad to see you."

"Sure, Elsie," said Eileen. She probably hadn't seen Jack Seaman in twenty years, maybe not since his wedding to Arlene, which had taken place in the tiny church over in Baraboo, where Arlene grew up. Eileen had attended it with her mother, and could still remember watching in amazement the long train of the wedding dress as it trailed the tiny Arlene when her father marched her to the altar. It seemed like something that had happened in a different lifetime, now. Only in the context of a friendship like the one between the O'Rourkes and the Seamans could a twenty-year hiatus like this be taken in stride, as if it implied no real abandonment of kinship. Sure, Eileen could spend the holiday with Jack and Arlene. No one else had claims on her. "Tell me what I can bring," she said.

"The bird is already ordered from Quillin's Market. Why don't you bring pie. That's what your mother always brought."

"Um, sure," Eileen found herself promising.

Eileen pondered for a moment whether or not she could engage Adrian to lend her a hand. If all else failed, she could buy a pie or two at the bakery.

"The only tablecloth I have that's big enough is a bit shabby," Elsie said. "I wondered if you might have any. Of course we could buy a paper one, but I never think they're as special as cloth."

"I'll look, Elsie," said Eileen.

"Okay. That's all I wanted for now," Elsie said, and got off the phone.

Eileen sank into the chair next to the telephone and took the towel off her head. The weight of her own arms seemed oppressive, and her feet, leaden. She'd been trying for several days now to adjust to the news from Teresa, to accept somehow the strange configuration the world had taken. Whether she liked it or not, it was upon her, and there was no point debating whether she could abide it. Last Thursday night Adrian had bundled her home, like some Red Cross worker bringing her to shelter, and she had gone straight up to bed and slept through till Friday morning. It reminded her a bit of the time she'd struck a deer on a dark road while coming back from Eau Claire: in the shock thereafter, she could only collect her wits, assess the damage she'd suffered and caused, and try to think what to do next. On Friday Adrian had made a special call to ask how she was and to see if she were coming to Mass on Sunday at Holy Name. She had begged off, feeling somehow too disconcerted to face that large a public. He had come over for coffee then, on Saturday, and had behaved too normally, not only as though nothing out of the ordinary had transpired, but in fact as if he felt more familiar with Eileen than ever, and could suddenly putter in her kitchen fixing sandwiches, guessing what cupboards held the luncheon plates or which drawer held the flatware, while she herself was feeling lost and paralyzed, even in her own environment. She didn't know how to respond to Teresa's letter. It remained on the table, tossed on top of its envelope, a mess she needed to tidy. But she couldn't just file it away with other correspondence.

Why did she feel apprehensive, if she didn't believe she'd done anything wrong? She felt vaguely guilty. Adrian's story about his childhood friend, Robert, hadn't made her censorious of him. She was mortified instead over what she'd told Adrian of her intimacies with Teresa. It didn't make a lot of sense, if she thought logically. Could it be that she had never done *anything* in her life that was simply loving and righteous? She was used to feelings of guilt about her withdrawal from people, about her propensity to be unloving, but never before had she worried about her *love* for Teresa. Until this week it was something she might have viewed as her finest hour. What was it now? The wet towel was growing cold in her lap, and she got up to hang it over the bar in the bathroom. If she was going to make it to Mass at the cathedral, she'd better get herself ready.

As Eileen unlocked the side door at the school on Monday morning, Mona St. John was coming up the sidewalk.

"The early bird, as usual!" Eileen called to her.

"I don't know, Sister," said Mona, arriving at the door. "I think maybe I should have gone into church with my mother for Mass this morning."

"Is something wrong?" Eileen asked.

"My dad. He's worse. They say his heart's failing. I don't understand the difference between heart failure and a heart attack, except one's slow and one's fast. This is the slow kind. He coughs all the time, and he can't breathe very well."

"Is he in the hospital?"

"No, he's just taking pills and staying home from work."

"Did your mother want you to stay with her?"

"She said it was up to me. But all she says, day and night, is 'pray for your father.' I don't *like* praying. I want to be able to do something. Is that bad?"

"I think it's a way to keep your sanity," Eileen said. "No, it's not bad."

"Whenever I do pray, I just want to say 'damn you, God.' Now, that I know is bad. I'd be better off spending my time on work."

"Saint Benedict says that to work is to pray," said Eileen. They were walking up the hallway of Beckett High School toward the library, and the classrooms, smelling of floor polish and fresh chalkboard cleaner, were all dark and silent as they passed. Mona stopped at the door to the Spanish room, and switched on the light.

"If you do your work out of love," Eileen said, "then I think God understands your actions."

"Thanks, Sister," Mona said, sliding into a desk and opening her Spanish book. "That helps."

"I hope he gets better," Eileen said. She proceeded down the hall to the chemistry lab.

"There's something I haven't talked with you about," said Adrian, standing on a chair and taping a garland of brown and gold honeycomb tissue over a window. He and Eileen were putting up decorations at the St. Francis Home in preparation for Thanksgiving.

"What is that?" Eileen asked.

"These two latest moves by the pope really have me flabber-gasted," Adrian said.

"Which moves?"

"Haven't you heard about the Hunthausen controversy out in Seattle?"

"Oh, yes," she said. "Some sort of rogue bishop who was given a reprimand, wasn't he?"

"Well, that's the way Ratzinger would put it, I suppose. It wasn't a reprimand. They relieved him of the duties of his office."

"Is that true? I wasn't paying much attention."

"Campus was buzzing with the news. I'm surprised you didn't discuss it in your class with Brannigan."

"People may have talked about it before the lecture. I tend to shy away from those discussions."

"Doesn't it burn you that the pope would do that sort of thing?"

"I don't know. I'm really just a lay person. I imagine the pope has reasons that I don't understand."

"And you always accept whatever he does? Isn't there a line beyond which you'd say he was wrong?"

"Well, I don't know. Maybe," she said. She furrowed her brow. Certainly in the history of the papacy, there were plenty of examples of error. But questioning the pope seemed to require such an expenditure of collateral. Was the dispute worth the fuss involved?

"And then to add to it there was the letter from Ratzinger about homosexuality," said Adrian. "It made for a pretty bad week, all in all."

"What was the letter about?" asked Eileen.

Adrian rolled his eyes. "I don't know if you want to get me started," he said. "He calls homosexuality an intrinsic evil."

"Maybe that's something I should read," she said.

"It was in the *National Catholic Reporter* on Friday."

"I don't always get around to those things. I'm not sure how much they matter, in the long run. I haven't even read the last couple of encyclicals yet—it seems I'm always busy with something else."

Adrian was silent, frowning at a die-cut turkey he was trying to punch from the card in his hands.

"These are such conservative times," he said, finally.

"I figure the political affairs of the Church aren't what's central to faith, anyway," Eileen said. "The beatitudes counsel us to let go of temporal concerns, don't they?"

"Yes," said Adrian. "Blessed are the persecuted, blessed are the meek, blessed are the peacemakers. I know that's what the gospel says. I guess I have trouble looking forward to justice coming in the eschatological future, when the pope is saying all one should look forward to is burning in hell. It starts to wear a person down, if you know what I mean."

"I don't think he's threatening Bishop Hunthausen with hell, exactly."

"When he speaks of error, and evil, and pain of excommunication, he's hitting pretty hard, I think. What else is he implying?"

Well, Eileen wasn't sure. She could feel Adrian pulling her off her usual orbit, although it didn't seem—as at times with others—like argument for argument's sake. It felt like someone pressing to be heard. Eileen struggled, however, for comforting words.

"I'm sure it will all be all right," she said. Adrian did not look at her, but instead kept rolling loops of cellophane tape and putting them on the back of the turkey cut-out.

The next week flew by. Eileen was busy grading mid-term papers and helping students complete their chemistry labs after school. The academic year had a certain rhythm, and the pace quickened going into the Thanksgiving holiday. When the kids came back from break there would be just a few short weeks before Christmas, with band and chorus practice and Advent services vying for attention with classroom studies. Eileen liked to enter the season with all of her classes a little ahead of schedule, to compensate.

It was Tuesday when she realized she wouldn't see Adrian at the nursing home this week. They hadn't any contact since last week, and she'd been behaving as if they'd see each other on Thursday. By the time she called the seminary, he'd already gone home to spend Thanksgiving with his family.

On Thanksgiving morning, Eileen made a trip to the nursing home with some pumpkin cookies she had picked up at the bakery.

"Here without your sidekick, I see," said Cindy.

"Yes, Adrian is away on break. I didn't think I'd see you here today."

"One of the head nurses covers every holiday. Thanksgiving is my turn. I don't mind. It's not like I have a family to cook for, anyway."

"Oh. I didn't know. I assumed you were married."

"I'm a widow, actually. Never had any kids. Don died before we could have any."

"Parents?" Eileen asked. "Siblings?"

"I have a brother in Palm Springs. Sometimes I fly out there for Christmas. But Thanksgiving is just a quiet day."

Eileen thought of inviting Cindy to Elsie's, but knew the day shift would end too late for dinner.

"I brought a tray of cookies for the staff, and a couple for the patients," Eileen said. "I'll just leave one at the nursing station."

Over on "A" wing Estelle Haney was playing LPs on the stereo in the dayroom.

"I didn't know you liked music, Estelle," said Eileen.

"Usually I don't," said Estelle, "but I was in the mood to dance."

"Estelle!" Sophie admonished.

"Well, can't a woman in a wheelchair be in the mood to dance? It's a holiday."

"Any special reason? Or just Thanksgiving?"

"Don't you know, I've been waiting for the least excuse to cut the rug? Don't go telling Cindy, though. She'll have them double my medication."

"What medication?"

Estelle pretended she hadn't heard. "Too bad our young man isn't here," she said.

"I'm sure he'll be back next week," said Eileen.

"I don't think he'll be with us much longer, though."

"What do you mean?"

"Did you see the long face he wore last time? When they're that unhappy, they're not long for Holy Name. Mark my words."

"Oh, no," said Eileen. "He was just discouraged, over some bad news that day."

231

"Well, I've seen them come and go. I can tell you which ones stay on and which ones don't. I tell you, he's too miserable, that one."

"Well let's hope not," Eileen said. "Let's hope that when he leaves us, it's for the major sem."

"He's a bit of a looker, too," said Estelle. "That can only tip the odds against his staying."

"Shh, now. Don't even talk that way."

"Well, I'm a practical woman, if nothing else. That one last year—the Sorenson boy? Now, no one was begging him not to take his vows, I'll tell you that."

"You are full of the devil," said Eileen.

"Why do you suppose I haven't died yet? I'm too ornery for anything to kill me. So don't try to make me a pious woman. It would finish me off tomorrow, I tell you."

"Don't worry, Estelle," said Eileen. "I wouldn't attempt it."

"Good!" said Estelle.

"Eileen O'Rourke!" said Jack. "What has it been—decades? You haven't changed a bit now, have you?"

Jack Seaman had changed. He'd added maybe sixty pounds and gone bald. And he was friendlier than Eileen remembered.

All of the Seamans were gathered in Elsie's kitchen, Jack and Arlene dishing the accompaniments to the turkey into serving bowls, Elsie cooking the drippings from the roaster pan into a roux.

"Dinner won't be a few minutes," said Elsie. "Jack, can you see if Eileen wants to wet her whistle?"

"Nothing for me, thanks," said Eileen.

"Arlene, can you believe it?" said Jack. "The last time we saw her, she wasn't even professed—were you? You were still in that little white veil."

"I was a novice," she said. "What a memory."

"How could I forget? You were the only person I knew who went to the convent. None of us ever thought you'd stay, you know."

"Really?" she asked.

"That's not true," said Elsie.

232

"None of the boys did, anyway. We thought for sure you must want...well, a regular life. To get married. Like we did."

"He was about to say something else," said Arlene. "They thought you'd be thinking with your hormones, like they were."

"Now, hon, give us more credit than that. But you know what I mean. We thought you two were just regular girls. It crushed Bobby Steinke's hopes, when you went off to Eau Claire."

"Oh, please," said Eileen. "Now that is a tall tale."

"Not so! You can just ask him," said Jack.

"Where is he now? No longer little Bobby Steinke, I guess."

"He's a lawyer. Up in the Twin Cities, isn't he, Ma?"

"One of those suburbs," Elsie answered.

"His whole life could have been different, except for you," said Jack.

"Mine, too, apparently," said Eileen.

"Of course," Elsie said, "but let's not think about that. Eileen is where God wants her."

"You think so?" said Jack.

"Currently, that seems to be half in and half out," said Eileen. "Maybe God can't make up his mind."

"Well, it's allowed you to be here with us, so I'm sure He knows what He's doing," said Elsie, pouring the gravy into its boat. "Dinner is ready. Let's eat."

Arlene put the last of the serving dishes on the table and scooted her chair into place. "I wish you wouldn't talk that way, Elsie," she said. "I hate the idea that everything that happens in life is God's plan. If I believed that, I might as well think God meant for *me* to be a nun. He never gave me any children, after all."

"No one ever said that," Elsie protested.

"Still, if you follow that line of thinking. It holds a lot more attraction, I suppose, for someone who's had a happy life."

"You've had a happy life, haven't you?" asked Jack.

"Don't take it that way, now," Arlene said. "You know what I mean."

"I'm with you," said Eileen. "I don't think it's God's particular plan that I have no living relatives, for instance."

"Exactly," said Arlene.

"You moderns," said Elsie. "What would your priest say to you?"

"That's funny," Eileen said. "That's just what I say to Adrian about his ideas."

"Who's Adrian?" asked Jack.

"My young seminarian friend. From Holy Name," said Eileen. She turned to Elsie. "Now don't tell me you haven't noticed him at the house, Elsie," she said.

"I didn't think it was any of my business," Elsie said. "He's the redheaded one?"

"Unh-huh," she said.

"Well, that's nice," said Elsie. "I guess."

"He's become a real friend."

"And you say he's even more modern than you? Well, he's hardly out of grade school. I suppose that accounts for it."

"And I'm hardly out of college," said Eileen.

"No, come to think of it," said Elsie, "I think of you as a grown woman, now that your mother is gone. Funny how that is."

"I suppose that makes sense," said Eileen.

"For my part," said Elsie, "I'm thankful you've been back, and that I'm around to enjoy you. I don't take another year of living for granted. Especially since your mother passed."

"We're thankful to have you, too, Mother," said Arlene.

Estelle refrained from saying "I told you so" when Adrian did not show up at the nursing home the following Thursday. He must be back from his break, but he hadn't called to say he was going to miss today. When the shift was done, Eileen drove downtown, parked her car at an open meter, and popped into the Woolworth's. She needed to find something to send to Sister Vincent Thomas and Sister Anastasia for Christmas. She stopped briefly to look at figurines and candles and stationery. In the back of the store she found herself in an aisle filled with pet supplies, fish, and birds. The birds looked lovely to Eileen. She stood before their cages for twenty minutes, cooing and chirping, before she realized these were not a suitable present for anyone she knew. Perhaps she would come down after Christmas and buy one for herself. She had never owned a bird. She'd never even thought of owning a bird. But it didn't mean she couldn't. A cat or a dog—that would be impossible. But a bird was something she could picture having.

What was she doing here, anyway? Not going home to her empty house, for one thing. She tried to tell herself that Adrian's absence today didn't bother her, but she knew that wasn't true. She feared Estelle was onto something, despite her wise-cracking demeanor. What were Eileen's worst fears? An image, almost dream-like, sprang into her thoughts in odd, clear detail. She pictured Adrian among some chanting throng of protesters, fists raised, angry. When had she ever seen such a mob? Maybe on television in the '60s. She must be associating him with the radicals of that era, thinking that this is what he would become: disaffected, unruly, full of contempt for tradition and for those who went along with it—for herself, and people like her.

Maybe there was a perfectly good reason he'd missed today. Maybe he had to study for an exam. Maybe he had a flat tire. She felt worried now that she might do the wrong thing, but no alternatives occurred to her, other than simply to wait.

Eileen had decided to say yes to Sr. Florence about going on the retreat. Now the day was around the corner, and Eileen began to make preparations. She consented to ride to Racine with Florence, although the prospect made her somewhat nervous. They would have to leave as soon as school got out next Friday, and Florence would pick her up outside Beckett. Eileen considered where to leave her car parked, how she'd get to school Friday morning if she left it at home, and where to store her bag during the school day. None of these were significant problems, but she didn't settle on their solution until she had obsessed for two or three days. She became so apprehensive in the week before the retreat, she hardly thought about her Thursday shift at the nursing home, or the impact it would have on her if Adrian failed to show again.

When he was absent another time, Estelle made no issue of it. She just launched into a little performance, teasing Sophie about sending out holiday cards to everyone in her address book, whether or not she could remember if they were still alive. Cindy, however, was annoyed with Adrian.

"I might have known he had more worldly things on his mind than the priesthood, or coming here to care for the sick."

"Why do you say that?" asked Eileen.

"You heard him last time. All that liberal talk. I don't think he rightly belonged at Holy Name. I mean, there must be some better place for him," Cindy said, pulling fresh linens off the linen cart in the hallway. "The Church can do without that kind of thinking."

Eileen looked after Cindy in surprise, as Cindy disappeared into Margaret's room. Eileen went home early, and repacked her bag one last time before bed.

"I've noticed you in the large group," the woman said, scooting her lunch tray onto the table beside Eileen at the retreat. "I thought your comments about that passage from St. Augustine were really interesting."

"Mine?" said Eileen. "Oh, I said nothing, really. I just wanted to remind people of that prayer. I've always found it lovely."

"Well, it was so apt. And I had forgotten the part about the deafness and the blindness. What were those lines again?"

Eileen recited them.

Too late have I loved you, O beauty of ancient days, yet ever new! You were within, and I abroad, and there I searched for you. You called, and shouted, and burst my deafness. You flashed and shone, and scattered my blindness. You breathed odors and I drew in breath—and I pant for you. I tasted, and I hunger and thirst.

"Wow. You must have memorized a lot of poetry as a child."

"Because I remember those lines?" said Eileen.

"Yeah. I could never recall anything like that."

"We memorized poetry when I was in school. And my mother knew lots of poems. She'd just start reciting one, in the middle of whatever she was doing, if something reminded her of it."

"How wonderful," the woman said. "I'm Catherine, by the way."

"Nice to meet you," said Eileen. She looked more closely at the woman, who had short blond hair and a pug nose, not quite sufficient to keep her enormous spectacles on her face.

"I live in Milwaukee," said Catherine. "I work for a community housing project, renovating old houses for homeless people. Most of them used to live in mental hospitals."

"That sounds very interesting," said Eileen. "Do you do the renovation yourself?"

"I'm the director, so I sit in an office a lot. But two days a week, I supervise a construction crew."

"That's wonderful. I've been trying to do a little renovation myself, except on a smaller scale," said Eileen. "I came home this year to fix my mother's house up so I can sell it. She died a couple of years ago."

"Oh, I see. So you don't work with Sr. Florence?"

"Oh, no. I'm on leave from my order this year."

"What's the work you'll be going back to?"

"I wish I knew."

Another look now, this one suffused with sympathy.

"Well, we can always use another advocate at House the Homeless. You should think about it. Seriously."

"Oh, I couldn't."

"Why not? Certainly you have to do something, if you don't go back to where you were before. Will you be in La Crosse beyond this year?"

"I'm just filling in for a year."

"See, then," Catherine said, as if something very obvious had been demonstrated.

Eileen did not trust this woman's impetuousness. What did she know of Eileen, except that Eileen could quote St. Augustine and use power tools?

"Well, it's a nice offer, really," said Eileen.

The centerpiece of the Augustinian retreat was a period of silence from noon until midnight on Saturday, followed by confession. They called it the *sacrament of reconciliation* on the program, of course, according to current fashion. Eileen wasn't sure which she felt less prepared for, confessing or reconciling. Just a few weeks ago, something about her vices—about her pride— seemed clear to her, and now it was all a muddle again. Perhaps in twelve hours' silence, something would make itself known once more.

Father Bob was a portly giant, towering and barrel-chested, and rustic in his black Augustinian habit and sandals. He sat next to her, oddly, when she took her seat in the sacristy, and he handed her one end of his stole. There was no choice tonight but to confess face-to-face, and he abandoned the rite from the outset.

"Bless you, Eileen," he said, conveying that he knew her from the past day's activities. He closed his eyes and said a prayer. "Father, open our eyes that we may see your goodness."

Eileen welcomed the freedom to speak what she was truly thinking.

"I last made a *good* confession a month or two ago," she said. "Good, in that I knew with some clarity what I wanted to mend about my ways. But since then, I know less and less for certain. Nothing seems clear—what I thought was the right path, seems perhaps reckless and willful. What I took to be vice could turn out to be virtue. God is so damned hard to figure, you know! Did I say that? Listen to me."

"Shhh," said Fr. Bob. "God survives our efforts to damn Him."

Then he was silent. They sat in the dark room for some time. Eileen felt conscious of her own heartbeat, racing at first, then calming into a regular cadence.

"I think it may be part of our human condition," said Fr. Bob, finally, "that we find it hard to picture the existence of the holy without taking something to be the unholy. Sometimes that unholy is in others, and sometimes it is in ourselves. But to do so is part of our humanity, not our divinity. God is more loving than we are, I think. He is less mindful of virtue and vice than we are."

Who was doing the confessing, here? thought Eileen. At the moment, she couldn't tell if Fr. Bob's words were actually part of the sacrament or not. Once she stopped to consider them, however, she was immensely grateful—they felt like the hand of God reaching into the night, to cradle her, like a small animal in arms. Fr. Bob eventually leaned his head against hers and put an arm around her. She found herself thinking that whatever the boundaries of the sacrament, this was a minister doing God's work.

As Wisconsin winters went, this one had a late start, and there was no snow on the ground. As Florence and Eileen drove back to La Crosse, a freezing rain was falling, and pretty soon they could only creep along the highway. Florence, obviously frightened by the conditions, was no longer her usual talkative self. She quickly accepted Eileen's offer to take over the driving at Milwaukee, and began praying the rosary silently to herself in the passenger's seat.

"Do you want to stop and take a room?" Eileen asked, at one point.

"Oh, no," said Florence, her voice quavering. "As long as you can see fit to drive, I'll be okay."

"I have pretty good traction under forty-five, and the other traffic does, too," said Eileen. "I think we'll make it back."

Florence nodded, and kept praying.

Eileen's mind wandered, to the upcoming final exams she would need to grade, and the coming Christmas break. She thought of asking Florence what her plans were for the holiday, but she didn't want to interrupt Florence's rosary-saying. Holy Name must be all but deserted by Christmas. It would be a good time to have Florence and Bede and Stanislaus over, if they could come. The gesture was overdue.

After a while, she began contemplating her life back in Fort Yates—something she'd seldom done since leaving it. Fr. Bob was probably right, as Fr. McClure had been, up in Fountain City. She couldn't view her years there simply in terms of what she had done wrong, or what she had done selfishly. Somewhere in her anger at her mother and her anger at the Bonaventures, she had also laid the foundations of a worthy life, hadn't she? She couldn't honestly toss the whole thing away and call it a mistake. There were things about it she missed dearly—the smells of sage and juniper on the wind, for instance; the bustle and color of pow-wow season; the joshing she took from the ladies about how she coveted their Indian babies, whenever she showed up for a baby shower at the tribal hall. She missed Vincent Thomas and Anastasia, too, but not in the same way. They had less need of her, ultimately, than the students she helped with science and math, or the adults she tutored through EMS training so they could work alongside her on the ambulance crew. She was starting to think of the possibility of going back.

Right before the turn-off to Sparta, the car in front of them braked aggressively. Eileen tried to see what the danger might be. Then she spied it—an oncoming car out of control on a curve, and sliding down into the bar pit toward them. It would probably lodge at the bottom, and not bounce in front of her, since its speed was not that great. But the occupants would land with quite a jolt. Eileen slowed to a stop and pulled to the side of the road.

"Do you have a first aid kit in here?" she asked Florence.

"Oh! My! I don't know," said the nun. "Are you going to get out?"

"Of course I'm going to get out," said Eileen. "That bump was pretty hard. They might have hit their heads." She peered into her mirror at the scene, which was behind them now. Someone was getting out of the driver's side, indeed holding his head. "Who knows if they were wearing seat belts."

"I think there might be something in the trunk," said Florence.

"Let me look," said Eileen, pulling the keys from the ignition. "In the meantime, get in my overnight bag in the back seat and find my flannel nightgown, just in case."

"For bandages?" said Florence.

"Yes, for bandgages," said Eileen, swinging her legs out the door and tentatively testing the traction underfoot. She skated off to pop the trunk of the sedan.

Arrangements

Where does a person take his sadness? When anger is all spent, when bravery is exhausted, and all that's left to do is submit and feel one's grief, what place of refuge does a person seek?

Adrian spent his Thanksgiving break running in the streets and byways of his hometown, contemplating the weight of recent events and longing for the simplicities of his childhood there. On his way back to La Crosse he stopped in the town of Austin and visited Queen of Angels, one of the churches his grandfather had built. The sanctuary was still, except for the flicker of votives in the dark. Adrian knelt for a minute to pray in one of the rear pews. On his way out, he lingered in the doorway, running a hand over the smooth stone, hoping he might actually feel Jude's tenderness in the curves of the carved pilasters. When Adrian got back to Holy Name, he sat for a long afternoon in the chapel, beneath the badge of weeping and of tears. Refuge? There were places to go to be alone that were obvious enough. But Adrian was not sure whom he might find to share his heartache with him. He struggled with the possibility that no such person existed, but also with his own disinclination to go in search of any. He was all for taking in another person's pain, and ill-adept at admitting to his own. He found himself wondering which of the seminarians who'd left during his tenure might have been gay, but he came up with no definite answers. Surely some of them must have been. But ex-seminarians tended to disappear, never to be heard from again. They did not have a support group.

"So, did you break the news to your parents when you were home for Thanksgiving?" asked David.

"What news?"

"That you're leaving Holy Name. That you and the seminary are kaput," David said. "What news did you think I meant?"

"I hadn't really made up my mind by that time. And I didn't want to say anything until I was certain where I'd be going," said Adrian. "I thought maybe you meant did I tell them I'm gay."

"No, I knew you weren't ready for that."

"As I see it, the news won't necessarily be far behind."

"Really? You think they're ready to absorb that, too?"

"I think if I'm going to be honest about why the seminary isn't for me, it's going to come out."

"Either that, or your mother will start fixing you up with debutantes."

"We don't have debutantes, David. It's Iowa."

"Well, okay. With the Pork Princess, then."

"Maybe I just want the trauma to be over."

"Man, one week it's 'Carol's marrying a Presbyterian,' the next week it's 'Adrian's marrying a seminarian,'" said David. "Do you think they're ready for that kind of leap?"

"Well, Mom always acts like she's going to blow a gasket, but she did that when Charlie decided he was going to marry at nineteen and drop out of college. She gathered her indignation for all of two days, and then it was over."

"Do you think it'll be that easy?"

"Well, the outward show, anyway. And then she'll be thinking about how to recover her pride, or how to wear her martyrdom. But as far as the relationship between us? There isn't really much of a relationship *between* us, frankly."

"What about your dad?"

"Well, I worry about Dad more. I guess I care more what he thinks."

"You've never disappointed him before."

"Right. He's the easygoing one. 'Sure, major in Greek and philosophy. You're the smart one. I trust your judgment.' I'm not so sure what he'll trust, after this."

"Are you planning to tell them right away? I mean, shouldn't you get established back at Creighton, first."

"Assuming I go back to Creighton."

"Well, I wouldn't dare hope you'd come over to the dark side, and come to Union. I've put that forth often enough."

"Yes, you have. Fact is, I can't see myself taking my ball and playing somewhere else. It isn't going to work that way for me."

"You keep telling me that—an alienated Catholic isn't automatically a Protestant."

"This time, will you believe me?" Adrian said.

It had been three weeks since David had called about the Ratzinger letter, and Adrian had talked to Fr. Keenan. The seminarians around him continued to plod along, but Adrian's mind was soon made up. Something was clear that before had always been ambiguous. Adrian *would not* carry out the teaching function of the priesthood in a Church that taught that he himself was evil. Whatever grief was to come of this, he was prepared to bear it, because clarity came at such a premium for him. Clarity, he knew, would carry him through whatever trouble he confronted from here on out.

"Hey, kid, what's up?" said Charlie, fairly alarmed to be called when travelling out of town. "What's wrong?"

"Relax," said Adrian. "Mom told me you were staying at the Holiday Inn. I knew you were planning to be in Dubuque for the college holiday tournament because you said so at Thanksgiving, remember? I thought I might drive down and we could have dinner together."

"Really? It's quite a drive, isn't it?"

"Did you have other plans? I thought you were going to be there alone."

"No, no other plans. That would be great. What time do you think you'd get here?"

"Why don't I meet you at 6:30."

"Okay. You know the north bypass? Heading west, there's a Bonanza steakhouse. Let's say we meet there."

"Cool. 6:30 then."

Darkness had already fallen when Adrian pulled into the parking lot at the restaurant. He didn't see Charlie in line, so he placed an order and carried his tray into the dining room. As Adrian approached Charlie's table, his brother grinned. "So what's up?"

"Who says anything has to be up? Can't I call my brother up for a visit when he's nearby?"

"La Crosse, Winona, Rochester—those are nearby. Dubuque—now, that's a haul. You obviously wanted to talk to me with Mom and Dad and Cynthia all out of the way."

"You're too damned smart, you know that?" said Adrian. "Why do we let you get away with your 'uneducated farmer' shtick? Just because you left college...."

"You didn't come here to call me up short on that again," said Charlie. "You going to spill the beans soon, or wait until the waitress brings me my medium-rare?"

"We can start," Adrian said. "I know you were anxious about telling Mom and Dad when you and Cindy decided to get married."

"Uh-huh," said Charlie.

"Well, I've decided to leave the seminary again. For good this time."

"They should find that a relief," said Charlie. "No one's invested in it like you. They'll be happy you've settled the issue. God knows, you've got plenty of smarts. Will you go back and finish law school?"

"Yeah," said Adrian, "I'm pretty sure of that. But here's the deal. If I'm not going to be celibate—I'm gay."

Charlie cocked an eye at Adrian, and broke slowly into a little grin.

"Well, that," he said, "is a horse of a different color."

The waitress arrived with their platters.

"Sour cream? Butter? Anthing else I can get you gentlemen?" she asked.

"No, that's fine," said Adrian.

"Okey-doke," she said.

After a minute, Charlie was still pouring A-1 sauce patiently into a pool next to his steak.

"You don't seem very surprised," said Adrian.

"That's because I'm not," said Charlie. "I could have told you that when you were four years old."

"Really?"

"Mom would have a fit if anyone brought it up, but I remember it being discussed—ever since the time you cried over Santa not bringing you an easy-bake oven for Christmas."

"Oh, God," said Adrian. "You remember that?"

"Of course I remember it. All of the cousins remember. How could we forget?"

"How embarrassing," said Adrian.

"Don't sweat it. It's okay. Really."

Adrian watched Charlie slicing steak and putting it into his mouth.

"You really mean that, don't you? As far as you're concerned, I mean."

"Yeah, I mean it. Like I said, I've always figured as much. And I'm a lot more comfortable with you out in the open with it, than hiding it in the seminary."

"That's not why I was there, you know."

"Yeah, I know. But still, a person can't help but think maybe...."

"Shit. Here I thought you'd be disgusted if you knew."

"What's to be disgusted by? I've always made it clear that if anyone in the family was going to balance Mom's hysterical attitudes about sex, it was me."

"I guess you did," said Adrian. "Thanks."

"Weren't nothing. Believe me," Charlie said. "So, you're going to tell them soon?"

"I think so," said Adrian. "How do you think they'll react?"

"I'd say, Dad—give him about twenty minutes to adjust. Mom—give her twenty years."

"Why do you say that? Don't you think Dad will take it hard, like Mom?"

"Well, it isn't like he's the model of purity himself, you know. He might even get a kick out of how worked up the old lady gets over it."

"What do you mean?" Adrian asked. "What are you saying?"

"Don't tell me you don't know. You have to have known. He hardly hides it."

"Know what?" Adrian asked. He was clueless.

"Oh, don't tell me you've come all the way down here, and *I'm* the one with the bombshell," said Charlie.

"Know what?" Adrian repeated.

"Know about Dad and Madeleine."

But Adrian knew the name, even before Charlie had formed the "M." He *had* always known. How he had kept it from himself, when it was plainly there in front of him, he didn't know. For his mother, realities she didn't approve of simply didn't exist: Harvey was glad to have a jewel such as her, and that was that. Did Adrian take after her, in self-deception? There were the pool balls. There had always been the pool balls.

"You know, Charlie," he said, finally. "I did know."

"Yeah, well, why act shocked, then?"

"I mean, I knew, but somehow never let myself add it up. Whenever I'd go downstairs at night to start the water softener, before we closed the store and Dad and Maddy would stay to count the till, the pool balls were in one position on the pool table down there. And then late at night, when we went to turn it off again, they would have been moved. But Maddy was always saying...."

"'I don't play pool, boys. I never cared for it.' Yeah. I guess she thought she was covering her tracks. And all the while, she was just pointing them out."

"When did you figure it out? And how did you live with the secret?

248

"I figured it out when I saw the pool balls. And there were a lot of other signs—like the hidden stash of condoms in the office that wasn't for sale, but kept disappearing."

"Oh, stop! I don't want to know," said Adrian, wrinkling his nose.

"I don't know how I 'lived with the secret,' as far as that goes. It's his cheating, not mine. Why would I feel responsible?"

"I don't know—I would have."

"Maybe that's why you never let yourself know. I figure that's what it is with the girls—they both preferred Dad. Maybe it's harder for all of you to face knowing he could step out on her. You already feel guilty for not liking her."

"And you truly preferred her to Dad?"

"Yeah, I did. I know I razz her a lot, but the bottom line is, I feel closer to her than to him. I just always have."

Charlie kept blithely shoveling food in his hatch, like none of this was about to shake their family very much. Maybe because it wasn't. Adrian made an attempt to start eating his own meal, but he'd lost whatever appetite he'd had.

"When did we stop talking?" Adrian asked.

"You and me?" said Charlie. "We never talked."

"Now, come on," said Adrian. "Really."

"When you were such a goody two-shoes, I guess."

"When was that?"

"Like when you ratted on me to Dad about smoking at the lake, just so you could be his favorite."

"Jesus. What was I, eleven?"

"Ten."

"And you still hold that against me? I was a little kid."

"Yeah, well, I kept waiting for you to stop."

"When did I ever rat on you again?"

"I mean, stop being a goody two-shoes."

"Well, my coming out should put that issue to rest."

"You want to go to a basketball game?" said Charlie. "It's Luther at Loras tonight."

"I hate basketball," said Adrian.

"Yeah, so humor me. Go anyway."

"Okay, okay. You got a second ticket?"

"No, but these things never sell out. It's Iowa men's basketball. If it were women's...that's a different story."

The roundtable was assembling when Adrian arrived in the lunchroom on Monday. Lloyd Hecht and Jim Coughlin were already in debate about something with Fr. Keenan.

"I don't know if you'd call it worship of the sun, exactly, but the aboriginals in Ireland built a structure at Newgrange that allows the sun to shine into the back of the cairn only at sunrise on the winter solstice, and that dates back to 3,300 B.C.," said Fr. Keenan. "So I'd say the pagan origins of Christmas go back at least that far."

"It's not just a guess, then, that they venerated the solstice," said Coughlin.

"No, nothing approximate about it," said Keenan.

"Hi, Adrian," said Lloyd. "Father was just giving us a little lesson on the rituals of the holiday, from holly and ivy to pomegranates. He thinks if they were good enough for the pagans and the Romans, they're good enough for us."

"Good for him," said Adrian. "It's always best to have the benefit of history."

"I don't know where the other students are today," said Coughlin. "You don't suppose they're already gearing up for finals?"

"Of course they are," said Lloyd. "They don't have it down cold, like Adrian, here."

"I don't have anything down cold," said Adrian. "But I'm only taking two classes, and one's an independent study."

"Right," said Coughlin. "Flood was telling me he talked you into that. I wish I could get some of my students to take advantage of Carleton like that. How's it going?"

"It's been really good."

"Are you taking another with him next semester?"

"Actually, I won't be on campus next semester at all," said Adrian.

"What will you be doing?" asked Lloyd.

"I've decided to leave Holy Name."

"Does Moriarty know that, yet?" said Lloyd.

"No," said Adrian. "I suppose I shouldn't be telling all of you. But since Jim asked."

"So," said Lloyd, "you've finally discerned your calling, and Holy Name isn't it?"

"I finally discerned something," said Adrian. "I think it was the Ratzinger Halloween letter that did it."

"I read that letter," said Lloyd. "It really annoyed me."

"What's that?" asked Coughlin.

"The letter on homosexuals," said Lloyd. "It was really nasty."

"*I* thought so," said Adrian. "It went beyond a turn toward the conservative. I don't think I can represent those people."

"Well, I'm glad it's spurred you to take a stand," Lloyd said. "I'm surprised you haven't read it, Jim. It reminded me of reading the *Bowers v. Hardwick* decision this summer, where Justice White wrote that none of the established constitutional rights to liberty in family relationships, marriage, or procreation *bear any resemblance* to a right to private consensual homosexual relations between adults. You really haven't been thinking about gay civil rights as an issue of social justice, Jim, and you should. It's right up your alley."

"You think so!" Coughlin joked, uncomfortably.

"Yes, I do," said Lloyd.

"Aren't there some basic questions of morality?" said Coughlin.

"I don't think homosexual identity in itself is a moral issue," said Lloyd.

Lloyd Hecht was probably the most effeminate, squeaky-voiced heterosexual man on campus, but that didn't deter him at all from staking out a liberal position in this matter. He was either oblivious that anyone would doubt his masculinity, or else so secure he simply didn't care. Coughlin, on the other hand, might very well switch the subject to the Minnesota Vikings as soon as he was able. That didn't prove necessary, as Molly Powichroski arrived at the table, diverting their attention.

"Hey, guys. Have you bought tickets to come hear the *Messiah*? Two performances, next weekend!" She coaxed Jim Coughlin and Fr. Keenan to take a flyer from her hands.

"I've already bought mine, Molly," said Adrian.

On Wednesday afternoon, Adrian took Burgess Lichter to shop for Christmas presents at the antique malls up in Winona. Burgess had finagled a semester in Portugal as she'd hoped, and felt something special was in order to console her mother over her going away. Burgess hadn't been able to find anything at the mall on third street, the one within walking distance of her apartment.

As Adrian and Burgess entered Memory Lane Antiques, the shop was bustling with holiday traffic. The usual coffeepots by the door had been replaced by urns of steaming cider and plates of gingerbread men.

"Anything special you're looking for today?" asked the shopkeeper, who stood behind the counter, wearing a long calico dress with a bonnet and apron.

"No, we're just looking, said Burgess.

"Well, you'll know it when you see it," said the woman.

Adrian and Burgess surveyed the aisles of the old mercantile that housed the store. Burgess was the kind of shopper who made salespeople nervous—she touched things, dusted them off, squeezed them, smelled them, sometimes tried them on. She put vintage hats on Adrian's head to estimate their size.

"What are you, a seven and a half?" she asked. "An eight? Who'd have thought! My father is a seven."

Burgess took a fancy to a black ostrich boa, and wore it thereafter, booth to booth, as they took in the goods for sale. Adrian wasn't sure if she intended to buy it, or only to use it as an accessory while they shopped, and then return it to where she'd found it. Next she discovered a black bowler and made Adrian put it on.

"Will you have anyone to plunder antique shops with you in Omaha?" she asked.

"No, not for a while, at least," he said. "Yes, I'm going to miss you, if that's what you mean."

"Who knows where I'll be—after Lisbon. I might get a fellow-ship in Chicago. Maybe I can come see you in Omaha. There must be some cheap airfares."

"You could find more exciting places to vacation, I'm sure," Adrian said.

"But there are no antiques like Midwestern antiques. Come on—look at these prices. Omaha is worth checking out."

She suddenly spied something halfway across the store, and started toward it.

"Would you look at that," Burgess said. "Roseville, Monti-cello."

On the shelf of a display case in the back of the store sat a stout vase in earthen tones of soft green, ochre, and cornflower blue. It flared at the base, where graceful handles arched up to clasp it at the middle.

"This is it," Burgess said. "I'm buying this for my mother."

Adrian checked the price. $42. An absolute steal.

On these ever-shortening days, the seminary chapel was dark by late afternoon and cold by the time of evening prayer—the furnace was never fired up for a twenty-minute night service. Nevertheless, when Fr. Moriarty rose to speak he wiped perspiration from his face with his palm.

"Today I had the experience of leaving our community and venturing into the world," he said. "I had to attend a meeting of the diocesan rural life conference up in Eau Claire. It made me appreciate all the more our little universe here at Holy Name—one I seldom have reason to leave."

He went on to detail the trials he'd had reading the highway map, negotiating busy traffic, and stopping to fill his fuel tank at a gas station. He described his enormous anxiety, being exposed in such a way to a world not in his own grasp.

"It made me thankful I could return here, where there is peace," he said.

Adrian looked around at the other seminarians. He wondered if any of them could relate to the feelings Fr. Moriarty described. No one seemed to—their faces all wore blank stares. Moriarty referred now to Jesus saying that a prophet was not welcome in his own land. He didn't seem to appreciate that no one in the room was with him.

"We must always remember that the Church is the light of hope in the darkness of the world," Moriarty said.

Adrian noticed something unusual then, about the rector's dress. As Moriarty paced across the altar addressing the seminarians, the hem of his clerical jacket drooped in the back. Adrian could see that the stitching in the jacket's hem had come undone in one spot, allowing the hem to fall. Adrian felt a trickle of fear, realizing Moriarty was unaware of the problem. The defect in the jacket was no big deal, but if someone pointed it out, Adrian thought, the already shaken man would completely lose his composure.

Given this picture, Adrian finally glimpsed something that maybe should have been obvious all along—about Moriarty's passion for control over everything at Holy Name, and for Church control over the vexing, unruly world abroad. Adrian's alarm subsided in a moment, when he realized no one in the community was about to mention the falling hem to Moriarty. As much as they might entertain discomfitting the poor man with a casual comment about it on the way out of chapel, that was only a thought, and would remain so. They were basically not a mean bunch.

At length Moriarty finished his comments, and Bob Holly stood to give the reading. It was from I Corinthians:

Stop passing judgment before the time of the Lord's return. He will bring to light what is hidden in darkness and manifest the intentions of hearts. At that time, everyone will receive his praise from God. [*]

Father Daimler read the intercessions, and then closed with a prayer.

---

[*]I Corinthians 4:5 *NAB*.

"All-powerful Father, we await the healing power of Christ your Son. Let us not be discouraged by our weaknesses as we prepare for his coming. Keep us steadfast in your love. We ask this through our Lord Jesus Christ, your Son, who lives and reigns with you and the Holy Spirit, one God, for ever and ever."

"Amen," said the seminarians.

Adrian was running late on Thursday morning, and was just buttoning his shirt as the bell rang for breakfast. He grabbed his tie and headed down the steps, tying it as he went. Striding down the first floor hallway, he spied a new piece of paper on the community bulletin board. Late though he was, he couldn't resist stopping to peek at it. It turned out to be the schedule for lectors in the new year. With one semester successfully behind them, the freshmen would now be allowed to take their turn at the lectern. The first freshman slated to read at Sunday Mass was Alan Hennessey. *Way to go, Alan,* Adrian thought. And then he chuckled; at himself or at Alan, he didn't know which.

Last weekend's storm had left a layer of snow atop a layer of ice at St. Francis Nursing Home. It streamed off the roof like heavy thatching. It rose in buttresses up the stone pillars of the portico, and lay in thick mounds along the sidewalks. Bitter cold had set in after the storm, and the packed snow crunched underfoot as Adrian trudged from his car up to the front entrance. Eileen was not waiting in the lobby, so Adrian went directly to "C" wing. There he found her, feeding applesauce to Trina Orzechowski.

"Hi!" he said.

"Oh, hello," said Eileen. "I didn't wait. I didn't know you'd be coming. I missed you last week."

"Didn't I tell you? Last week I had to present my thesis in Dr. Jenkins's Shakespeare class."

"No, you didn't."

"I hope I didn't worry you," he said. "I guess I forgot to tell you I'd be out."

"I guess you did," she said, dryly. "I was worried."

"I'm sorry," he said.

"You got two able hands, there?" said Angela, the head evening nurse.

"Yes, ma'am," said Adrian. He pulled a tray from the cart and sat down to feed one of the ladies.

"Pupa! Pupa! Pupa!" shouted Trina, through her applesauce. Eileen caught a fleck of it in her eye, and reached to wipe it out. Adrian scooped pureed peaches off Sara's plate and offered them to her.

"Open wide for me," he said.

As they finished with the trays, Eileen looked up the hallway toward Mrs. Haney's room.

"Shall we go pay a visit to Estelle?" she said. "She actually thought you'd flown the coop on us."

Adrian sighed, and wiped his hands on a wet washcloth.

"Next week, for sure, I will," he said. "Today I wanted the two of us to just get coffee, or something."

"I guess we can do that," Eileen said. She looked dejected.

"It'll be nice," he said. "We haven't been keeping up like we should."

At Bridgeman's the market for ice cream was pretty bust, so Adrian and Eileen had a waitress all to themselves. She promptly poured them coffee and brought an abundance of cream and sugar.

"How about some nice mincemeat pie with that?" she asked, hopefully.

"That sounds good," said Adrian. "How about you, Eileen?"

"Oh, why not," Eileen said.

The waitress had it on the table within seconds.

"Let me know if you need anything else, you hear?" She set to work sponging off a counter that already looked clean.

"I've decided to go back to law school," Adrian said.

"That's what Estelle thought," said Eileen. "I was hoping it wasn't true."

"Well, it's definitely the thing for me to do."

Eileen started to cry, and dabbed her face with her napkin.

"What's wrong?" he said. "It'll be okay."

"It's just not what I wanted—you know that. Estelle said she could tell by the way you acted that you weren't going to be at Holy Name much longer. She said that's why you'd been staying away. I started to worry that maybe you'd already left."

"I never would have done that. I wouldn't have left without saying goodbye."

"I didn't know for sure."

"Don't be silly, now."

"Well, you were so angry the last time we talked. I know I didn't want to hear it at the time. When I thought about it later...I wished I could have acknowledged it more."

"Eileen, I wasn't angry at you. I was pretty furious with Ratzinger and the pope, but what does that have to do with you?"

"Who am I, if not Ratzinger and the pope? Or everything they stand for? And if you leave the Church, it's sort of all the same, isn't it, whether you left because of them or because of me?"

"I don't understand that," he said. "Who's leaving the Church? I'm not going to be a priest. Does that change you and I being friends?"

"You think we could be friends?" she said. "I guess I don't see that happening."

"Of course we can," he said. "We will." He looked at her intently. "Why won't we? In fifteen years, I'll be a lawyer somewhere...in...Madison, let's say. And when you come to town for a conference or something, you'll call me up and we'll go out for coffee like this, at night. We'll talk about La Crosse—about Estelle, and that ground-up god-awful food we serve at St. Francis. We'll watch each other going grey, or bald and fat, or whatever it is we end up going."

"You really think so?" she said.

"Sure I do."

"You're really rushing me. You know that, don't you."

"Well, there isn't a lot of time," he said. "I'm leaving for Iowa right after finals. I can't just watch you vascillate about this."

"Will you still be alone then?" she asked.

"Well, with any luck...." He trailed off, and made nervous twists in his paper napkin. "I think you've probably figured this much out. I *hope* I'll be with another man."

"Adrian, that's the thing," she said, the words coming out rapidly. "I'm not sure that I approve."

"It's hardly about approval, Eileen. Is it?" After a second or two, he averted his eyes from her gaze. "I don't think your approval is what I've ever asked for."

She sighed deeply.

"How else do people get any handle on each other in life?" she said. "I ask that seriously. I haven't a clue. Who do you expect will ever stop and bother with you, care whether you're well or ill, if you live or die, if not the people who share a set of beliefs, who agree on certain rules? Who in the world do you connect to?"

"What's wrong with Catholicism, that we're brought up thinking that way? We have no intrinsic value, and are only worth something if we're free from sin?" said Adrian. "Aren't there ties of affection that don't have to be justified?"

After a moment Eileen met his gaze, painfully. "I went on this retreat last weekend," she said, "and in confession, the priest said to me, 'God is more loving than we are. He is less mindful of virtue and vice.' I guess Father Bob has something figured out that I haven't."

"Maybe you should make that retreat again next year," said Adrian.

She looked at him in exasperation. "You could be the death of me, you know that?" she admonished.

"I hardly think so," he said. "You've come through far worse, I'm sure."

She looked down. With the tines of her fork, she picked at the brown crust of pie on her plate. A moment passed.

"It's only lately I've been thinking about the future at all," she said.

"It's sort of surprising to hear you say that," said Adrian. "I imagine you staying on the reservation, although maybe closer to home. I could see you working with the Chippewa or the Menominee. And I'll do something not that different, with public policy, or the legislature."

"Your confidence about these things...," she said, shaking her head. "Maybe it's your age...and probably your disposition in general. It's just sunnier than mine. Even in my twenties I couldn't...." She didn't finish the sentence.

"I'll have to find myself a man who's less ornery than I am. I think that's what Doug has found in Ernie Jenkins. Then you and he can hit it off—you'll have more in common than you and I."

"Listen to you!" she said. "You really believe that's possible, don't you?"

"Of course I do," he replied. "Especially the part about you still being around."

Eileen welled into tears again.

"Why are you crying, now?" he asked.

"Because I'm a silly fool, that's why," she said. "I'd like to see a future with you in it, too. I would. I think I'm unclear about everything, but you say you'd like to be there, and I couldn't agree more."

"Well, what's the big deal, then," he said.

"You think it's going to be that simple?" she asked.

"Probably not," he said, "but what the hell. Just as long as you never tell me you've sent money to any of those television evangelists."

"Okay," she said.

"You promise you won't?"

"I promise I won't tell you if I do."

"Uh oh," he said. "That sounds like a crack *I'd* make."

The waitress refreshed their coffee cups, and took away their plates.

259

-20-

Choosing a Tint

Sitting in her car at the curb, Eileen reckoned she might have embarked on a risky journey. Not that the roads were still icy or the visibility was bad, but rather that she was unprepared for the role she was about to step into—like that moment in a nightmare when she was ready to walk onstage and had never studied her lines. Avoiding the last few steps up to Teresa's doorbell, Eileen dallied so long in the car the air went frigid, and she began to see her own breath over the steering wheel.

She'd sent a letter to Teresa, in a fit of optimism, after her conversation with Adrian at the restaurant. The parallel between Adrian and Teresa was so immediately clear that Eileen went home and wrote a response to Teresa straight off. An invitation from Teresa, to come for a visit between Christmas and New Years, was not what she had expected—never mind her own impulsive accession to making the trip. She didn't know whether to applaud or chastise herself for living so recklessly.

In the back seat was a box with presents for both of her hosts—a hanging bird feeder for Teresa and some gardening tools for her partner, Shirley. Eileen had consulted Sr. Bede for ideas, as if there were any logic to that. Eileen feared she was about to utterly leave her own element. How did a gay couple live? Would she ever say the right things in their presence? For an entire weekend?

"Look at you!" Teresa said, on the doorstep. "You haven't changed a bit!"

"Now, tell the truth," said Eileen. "Yourself—you look great. Older, but great. This must be Shirley...."

"Come on in. It's nice to meet you, finally," said the woman. Shirley was slight, with a thick head of hair and a broad smile. "We've got some coffee on."

Sitting at the kitchen table moments later with a steaming mug, Eileen studied Teresa's face. The lines forming beside Teresa's eyes and the swatch of gray in her bangs made her look more familiar, not less so; Eileen was struck by how much Teresa resembled Eileen's own mother in middle age. Age had amplified the similarities—the deep brown eyes, the severity of the brow, the high set of the cheekbones. Even Teresa's voice had deepened to a similar timbre.

"I wish someone had called me when your mother died," said Teresa. "I feel so bad I didn't even know about it. I went through a period, as you'd imagine, when I wasn't in touch very often with anyone back in the community."

"I hardly discussed her passing with any of the Bonaventures," said Eileen. "Other than Peggy, I'm not sure who even knew. There was something in the newsletter, months afterward, I know. By then, people probably thought you'd been told."

"Yes," said Teresa. "But still, they should have."

"Teresa tells me you were the only one to survive your mother," Shirley said. "That's how it was when my mother died. My parents had been divorced for years. It's an awful thing to go through alone."

"Well, you just put your head down and get through it, I guess," said Eileen.

"I think it's harder when you didn't get on that well when they were living," Teresa said. "It's hard to be relieved and grieving at the same time."

"You and your mother didn't get along?" asked Shirley.

"Well, not very...," Eileen said, fumbling for a response.

"Eileen's mother was basically difficult," Teresa said, authoritatively.

"Do you really think so?" said Eileen.

"No offense, dearie, but yes."

"Did you ever meet her?" asked Shirley.

"Yes, any number of times," said Teresa. "And I read a lot of her letters to Eileen. She was always negative about something, and expecting Eileen to do more about it than a person could do. Eileen was always sending her care packages and these really sweet greeting cards, and all she ever got back was criticism."

"I didn't realize you saw it that way," said Eileen. "That's strange."

"Well, it wasn't subtle, for heaven's sake," said Teresa. "Am I being too blunt?"

"I guess I'm reluctant to find fault with her," said Eileen. "I worry a lot of the time that I've become just like her. A disagreeable old woman, without friends."

"Don't be silly. How could you think that?"

"I seem to be worse since she died. I feel critical of everyone, the way she was."

"Meaning what?" said Teresa. "Have you swung to the right wing? Joined the Blue Army? The Legion of Decency? I thought it went out of existence."

"It has," said Eileen. "No, it's just that I find myself always angry and disappointed, the way she was."

"Maybe you're angry and disappointed with her. That would make sense," said Teresa, glibly. She sliced a loaf of banana bread and arranged it on a plate.

"Then why do I feel it toward everyone else?" said Eileen.

"It's hard to feel it toward them, you know," Shirley said. "I think that's the thing about grief and relief joined together."

As if some quip could illuminate anything of significance, Eileen thought, feeling annoyance with Shirley's comment. But there she was, being critical again, she scolded herself. Shirley was just trying to be helpful.

"I can't imagine you being like your mother," said Teresa. "You spent all your life bending over backward to be the opposite. You were always the most generous, accepting, tolerant person. Shirl was nervous when I said someone from the order was coming to stay with us, and I told her, 'Don't worry a bit about Eileen.'"

"But I wasn't any of those things," said Eileen. "I was pretty moralistic, in fact."

"I never saw it," said Teresa, shrugging her shoulders.

"It must have shown. It can't be entirely new."

"You still have to convince me that's what you've become," said Teresa.

"If you knew I was such a tolerant person, then why do you suppose we stopped writing?"

"I don't know. I was having my own guilt about coming out. I needed some time to adjust, myself. I didn't know, of course, what was going on with you. I never thought you'd have a problem with my being gay, or anything."

Eileen laughed.

"Do you?" Teresa asked, momentarily concerned.

"I don't know what I have a problem with," Eileen said. "I'm pretty sure my problem is with me, more than anything else."

"Poor girl," said Teresa. "You really have been alone too much. I'm sorry I've been such a rotten friend. Give us the weekend and we'll begin to make it up to you. You'll start to feel better. I promise."

The idea of Teresa and Shirley pampering her, in whatever way they had in mind, conjured a rush of specific memories—of afternoons she and Teresa spent in their dorm at college, with Teresa playing guitar and the two of them and a handful of other friends singing; of Teresa cooking oatmeal on a tiny hotplate in the morning by the sink; of a wool jumper Eileen stitched together for Teresa to wear to their Christmas convocation sophomore year.

"Remember that time we chaired the Christmas program together?" asked Eileen.

"Certainly!" said Teresa. "God, the mess we made in the kitchen making all those silly styrofoam centerpieces."

"I was thinking about me sewing you that plaid jumper the night before the party, and then panicking because I burned the

264

bodice with the iron trying to press it, and had to rip it out and sew in another piece."

"What I remember is your mother getting angry that you spent the money for it, and telling you that you were cut off from any spending money until after Lent."

"Oh, you remember all the worst parts."

"And you tend to forget them," Teresa protested. "I remember the good parts, too. It's just that in my mind, the good parts were all about you."

"Stop it, now. You'll embarrass me in front of Shirley," said Eileen.

"Shirley's already had to listen to me extol your virtues. Don't worry about her," said Teresa.

There was truth, Eileen supposed, in Teresa's version of things. Getting depressed was hardly her mother's sole failing. "But if we get started telling old stories," Eileen said, "we'll bore Shirley to death before the weekend is over."

"I hardly think so," said Shirley. "What are friends for, if not to tell old stories? I'm hoping you'll dish some good dirt about Teresa."

"Dirt about Teresa? Let's see what I can think of…," said Eileen.

"Careful with that one," said Teresa.

The women laughed, genially.

Back in La Crosse on Tuesday, Eileen took Elsie to the United Building Center to look for a replacement filter for her furnace. Eileen had gotten the number off the manifold, and could have simply bought the filter and had Elsie pay her back, but Elsie had insisted on coming along.

Even though she'd been a widow for eight years, Elsie was still a stranger to anything except the corner hardware store. She gazed in wonder at the products lining the aisles.

"You could build your own house, with everything they have in here," she said.

"Yes, I think you could," said Eileen.

Eileen was doing her best to make a bee-line for the air conditioning and heating section, but Elsie lagged behind, her eye fixing on various structural materials as if she were looking at the viscera of an animal for the first time. "Look," she said. "A door in a frame." She tested the hinges, and leaned her head across the threshold. A bit later, she said, "Look at this wash basin. It's cast iron." She read the sales promotion beside it. When they passed the lighting fixtures, Elsie flipped switches and tested pull-cords like a toddler.

"Elsie, come on," Eileen admonished.

Finally they were standing among the ducts and registers of the heating aisle.

"Here are the filters," Eileen said, with satisfaction. After scanning the labels for a few minutes, she found the right one for Elsie's furnace. She pulled it out and lodged it under her arm. "Okay," she said.

"Do you want me to carry it?" said Elsie.

"Don't be silly," said Eileen. They made their way back up the aisle.

At the checkout, the lines were long.

"Elsie, I was thinking, I'm going to do a lot of painting in the house when things settle down from the holidays. If you wanted me to freshen some rooms for you at the same time, I could do it. It could be a Christmas present to you."

"Christmas is past," Elsie said. "Besides, do you think they look dingy?"

"Not necessarily. But I know you said painting was more than you could manage. Maybe you'd just like a room or two brightened up."

"Well, that might be nice," said Elsie.

"While we're here, let's go over to the paint section and look at some color samples," said Eileen. "It will give this rush a chance to die down."

At the color display, Elsie hesitated, in contrast to her previous enthusiasm.

"Don't you love the names?" said Eileen. "*Kitten's paw.* Doesn't that sound nice?" She handed Elsie a chip bearing a delicate shade of mauve.

"I like my rooms the colors they are," said Elsie.

"Of course," said Eileen. "I was just looking at other colors for fun. We can find a close match for the colors you have. See, this blue looks close to the color in your hallway. Doesn't it?"

"Yes, I guess so," said Elsie. "I suppose I shouldn't be such a stick in the mud. A new color wouldn't hurt."

"No, you just know what you like."

They gathered a spectrum of blues for Elsie's hall, a palette of yellows for her living room, and a couple of shades of olive green to try in Eileen's stairwell.

"What do you think of this taupe?" said Eileen, handing Elsie a card.

"It's pretty, I guess. What room were you thinking to put it in?"

"Eventually, I have to paint mother's room, if I'm going to put the house on the market for anyone to buy. I'd sort of like to try something neutral. I want the downstairs hallway off-white, and I need something that will blend."

Elsie said nothing, but appeared a little stricken. She did not look at the color display at all, but gazed instead up the aisle toward the checkout.

"You're not in the mood to do this, are you?" said Eileen. "We can go home. I thought it might be fun."

"No, it's okay," said Elsie. "I knew you'd eventually have to sell. I guess I was hoping you might stay an extra year, and not be in a hurry to go back. I don't know why. Of course you need to return to North Dakota. The Church needs you where the Church needs you."

"But I can leave mother's room until the end. I don't have to be in a hurry to paint it."

Elsie wiped a tear off her face. "Don't be silly," she said. "You'll need to put the house on the market in the spring, if you want to be able to leave come summer. And if you're going to get ready to paint once after the holidays, you might as well do everything at the same time."

"I didn't know you had any feelings about mother's room," said Eileen. "I knew *I* did."

"I didn't know it either, until now," said Elsie. "That purple color was just so...*Brigid*."

"Purple? You think of it as purple?"

"Yes. What do you think it is?"

"I don't know. There's no red in it at all. It's briny. Like the deep sea."

"I've always thought it was purple, like...petunias," said Elsie.

"I don't know where you get that. Come have a look at it again."

"I'm not sure I want to. It's purple in my mind. I'll leave it that way," said Elsie.

"And what am I, in your mind?" asked Eileen.

"That's a silly question, now."

"No, it's not."

Elsie looked at her, anxiously. "I'm afraid to answer," she said. "I'll just get myself in trouble."

"It's not a trick question," said Eileen. "Really. But you don't have to answer. Let me just say this much: I don't want you to see me as my mother. I can't bring her back by staying here another year, or holding on to the house, or anything else I ever do."

"I know that," said Elsie, with a sniffle.

"*I'm* still here, though. Even when I go back to Fort Yates, *I'm* here, among the living. With you."

"Okay, okay," said Elsie. "I'll remember that. I will." She opened her purse, and tucked the paint samples in next to the coupons and the Kleenex. She took a tissue out and blew her nose.

Now Eileen was the one to look away, fighting off tears.

"I just miss her so much," said Elsie.

"I do, too, Elsie," Eileen said. She squeezed Elsie's free hand. "I do, too."

Elsie shut the clasp of her handbag, brushed off the front of her coat, and said, "I'm ready to go now. It's coming up on time to fix supper."

"Okay. We'll go," said Eileen. "We'll go."

Epilogue

"Are we taking two cars?" asked Anne, using one hand to keep her long blonde hair out of her sunglasses. The smell of Patchouli drifted off her skin in the breeze.

"I think with the picnic basket and the blankets, we won't all fit in one," said Eileen.

"Too many foreign car owners," said Terry, jumping into his Cabriolet convertible, parked in front of the convent.

"I'll ride with Eileen, then," said Anne. "We need to get to know each other."

"Do we all know where we're going?" Adrian asked.

"We'll head south," said Eileen. "Sitting Bull's grave is about fifty miles from here. I know a spot, just across the border into South Dakota, that would be great to stop for a picnic on the way. It's where one of the creeks enters Lake Oahe, and the lake is really wide there."

"We'll follow you, then," said Terry.

The place where Eileen pulled off the highway afforded an expansive view on each side of the road. Toward the river, grassland sloped into the shoreline of the lake, which filled nearly the entire vista. The far shore appeared as a tiny brown line in the distance. In the other direction, there were no signs of civilization in view—no electrical poles, no abandoned windmills, no farmsteads—only a sea of durum wheat writhing in the August breeze, filling the horizon with yellow waves.

"I feel like Laura Ingalls," said Anne, stepping from the car.

"This is gorgeous, Sister," said Terry. "Do we just leave the cars here, then?"

"Yes, we do," said Eileen. "There's a flat spot by the bank where we can spread the blankets."

"What's for lunch?" asked Terry.

"Adrian made it early this morning," said Eileen.

"Can you believe Sister Anastasia had fresh tarragon growing in the window box?" said Adrian. "I bought some chicken breast and walnuts, and made chicken salad. Anastasia sent a loaf of sourdough bread."

"Do we have wine?" asked Anne.

"We certainly do," said Terry.

"Great," said Anne.

They spread the blankets on the bank above the river and had a leisurely lunch. Afterward, they lay in the sun. Eileen took her veil off and rested her head on a bunched-up towel. Anne lay with hers on Terry's stomach, and read from her constitutional law book. There was silence, except for the singing of a meadowlark.

"Guys, look!" said Adrian, after a long while. A cloud on the horizon had grown into a tall thunderhead, and the sky grew dark in the distance. In the foreground, the sun still shone on the fields of wheat, so the world became a study of indigo sky and golden earth.

"How fabulous," said Terry.

"Don't you think we ought to be getting out of here and finding cover?" asked Anne.

"In a while," said Adrian. "The storm is ten or twenty miles away. We have time to watch it."

The anvil of the cloud grew mightier with the passing minutes.

"Do you think it might spawn a tornado?" said Eileen.

"It could," said Terry. "But it'll probably be just a thunderstorm."

"You'd better put your top up, then, if you want to be out of the rain," Eileen said.

"It only takes a minute," said Terry.

They all stood on the blankets now, eyes on the advancing storm. A bolt of lightning bridged the cloud and the earth, and a few seconds later, they heard the clap of thunder. The wind was picking up, licking the edges of the blankets. Adrian and Eileen packed the remains of their lunch into the basket. Terry hightailed it, finally, for his convertible.

"Yee-hah!" he shouted, leaping through the prairie grass.

Anne folded the blankets under her arm and handed Eileen her veil, which Eileen slipped onto her head.

"Is that everything?" Anne asked.

She and Eileen and Adrian hiked back toward the cars.

"Can you imagine this being more perfect?" said Adrian.

"I hardly can," said Eileen.

The first large drops of rain started to pelt the ground.

"Run!" said Anne, taking off. She held the blankets aloft like the spoils of a raid. Adrian and Eileen, lugging the basket between them, brought up the rear as best they could.

Printed in the United States
27884LVS00005B/82